MIKE KNOWLES

THE BUFFALO JOB

ECW PRESS

Printing: NORECOB 5 4 3 2 1
Printed and bound in Canada

Published by ECW Press
2120 Queen Street East, Suite 200
Toronto, Ontario, Canada M4E 1E2
416-694-3348 / info@ecwpress.com

LIBRARY AND ARCHIVES CANADA
CATALOGUING IN PUBLICATION

Knowles, Mike, author
The Buffalo job / Mike Knowles.

(A Wilson mystery)
Issued in print and electronic formats.
ISBN 978-1-77041-171-5 (PBK.)
Also issued as: 978-1-77090-509-2 (PDF),
978-1-77090-510-8 (EPUB)

I. Title. II. Series: Knowles, Mike.
Wilson mystery.

PS8621.N67B83 2014   C813'.6
C2014-900539-3   C2014-900540-7

Cover design: David Gee
Cover image: © Mohamad Itani/ Millennium Images
Text design: Ingrid Paulson
Interior image: blood spatter © itchySan/iStockphoto

The publication of The Buffalo Job has been generously supported by the Canada Council for the Arts which last year invested $157 million to bring the arts to Canadians throughout the country, and by the Ontario Arts Council (OAC), an agency of the Government of Ontario, which last year funded 1,681 individual artists and 1,125 organizations in 216 communities across Ontario for a total of $52.8 million. We also acknowledge the financial support of the Government of Canada through the Canada Book Fund for our publishing activities, and the contribution of the Government of Ontario through the Ontario Book Publishing Tax Credit and the Ontario Media Development Corporation.

Ontario
Ontario Media Development Corporation

ONTARIO ARTS COUNCIL
CONSEIL DES ARTS DE L'ONTARIO
50 YEARS OF ONTARIO GOVERNMENT SUPPORT OF THE ARTS
50 ANS DE SOUTIEN DU GOUVERNEMENT DE L'ONTARIO AUX ARTS

Canada Council for the Arts

Conseil des Arts du Canada

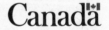

Canada

MIX
Paper from responsible sources
FSC
www.fsc.org   FSC® C103560

FOR ANDREA.
It could be for no one else.

CHAPTER ONE

The train left Union Station half full. It was early in the afternoon, two o'clock, and the lunch had left behind trash on the floor and stains on the seats. I was sitting in the rear corner of the car holding a day-old free copy of a Toronto daily newspaper in front of me. I looked over the paper with a practised false absorption. My eye movements were calculated and resembled reading when they were anything but. My toe tapped along to a beat that should have been coming into my brain from the earbuds I was wearing, but there was no sound coming from the iPhone in my pocket. The three I was shadowing were in the car ahead of me, separated by seventy-five feet and numerous layers of metal and glass. I had told them where and when to board and to sit together; so far, they had done as they were told. The men were going to run a security route so that I could look them over to make sure they were who they said they were and so that I could make sure that there was no one planning to crash the party. I had run afoul of a number of people over the past few years, bad enough men to force me to relocate to Toronto, and I wasn't looking to catch up.

The train lurched away from the station and I watched the men from the corner of my eye. They looked around at the other commuters on their car and tried to make eye contact with a few of the men who were sitting alone. No one returned their stares; several people got up and changed seats. One of the three men, a mid-twenties white kid with red hair and matching sparse stubble, checked the car I was riding in through the grimy window, but no one on the car gave him any reason to think he, or his friends, were being watched. I gave the trio a few minutes to get tired of looking around before I lifted my eyes from my paper and gave them a glance. When I looked down at the paper again, I tilted my head so that no one would notice that my eyes were closed. In my mind, I was recreating the scene I had taken in. The redhead was wearing a lightweight North Face jacket with a fur-trimmed hood. The man to his left wore a leather motorcycle jacket. The jacket was black and smooth enough to be less than a month old. I didn't see any patches sewn on, and the smooth baby face above the collar made the kid look more like a lesbian than a biker. He styled his hair with some kind of product that made it stand up high on his head like the plumage of an exotic bird. The third man had darker skin, not the even tone of an Italian or Greek, but something more washed out. His stubble went high up on his face and I guessed that he was the kind of guy who would have to shave at night before he went out if he wanted to look presentable. All three were under thirty, but only one of them held himself with the immaturity of a twenty-something. The redhead was nervous; the other two had the composure of men who had previously been checked out before a meeting. I went over each detail I could remember again to be sure, but the results were the same — I had never seen these three before.

The trio got off the train and stood on the platform waiting, as instructed, for another train. I kept my seat and watched the action outside the car. No one who got off with them waited around. I gave the faces on the platform equal attention and committed those who matched the age and appearance of the three men to memory. Half an hour later we were back on the same train again. I was already on board and I watched the three men get onto the train. None of the faces I had seen on the platform were hanging around. I watched the three men for two stops before getting my phone out of my pocket. I typed a short message and waited until the subway car briefly surfaced for air just after leaving Dundas West station to hit send. The short time above ground was long enough for my message to ricochet off some unseen satellite above the earth and fall back to a cell phone less than fifty feet away from me. I saw the man with the stubble react to his phone with a slight flinch before pulling it out. He read the text and then held his phone out so that the other two men could read it. The redhead took the cancellation of the meeting the hardest. I could read his lips, but the expletive he blurted out could have just as easily been decoded by the reaction of the civilians sitting around him. The three got off the train at the next stop; I did the same.

The train had let us off at Jane Street and I moved across the platform to the stairs while the three men that I had been watching spent a few seconds orienting themselves using a posted subway map. What they weren't doing was using their phones. If they had anyone shadowing them, they would have been placing a call by now. They weren't cops, and they weren't working for anyone who was trying to kill me. I had already typed in the next text when the train was pulling to a stop. I unlocked the phone and hit send as I started ascending the stairs to the street.

The air got colder as I got closer to street level. A massive thunderstorm a day earlier had taken the August heat with it and left only clouds and fifteen degrees for everyone else. After days of sunny thirty-degree temperatures, the sudden fluctuation felt aggressive rather than welcome. A brisk wind groped down the stairwell as the last few feet loomed ahead and I felt a chill work its way down my exposed neck. When I touched the sidewalk, I hooked left and began threading my way through the light midday foot traffic. I took advantage of an opening created by a bus stopping to cross to the other side of Jane Street. I took a spot at a bus stop and nestled into the herd. From my new vantage point, I could see the three men emerge from the subway. The same cold wind bit into the men and they fiddled with zippers as they looked left and right. The small huddle obstructed the exit and I watched several dirty looks fly from the busy men and women forcing their way around the men and onto the sidewalk. The one with the high stubble pointed in the direction I had just taken and his two partners followed him away from the stairs. No one was on a phone and no one was following in their wake — no one except for me.

I used my phone one more time before making my way back across the street. I matched the pace of the trio and followed twenty feet behind until the three men halted in front of a coffee shop with a closed sign posted in the window. The sudden pause in forward momentum shrank their lead from twenty to ten before the door to the coffee shop opened and a man in an apron that was now more beige than white ushered them inside. He was closing the door when he made eye contact with me; he gave the door a little shove and I shouldered it the rest of the way open. I stepped into the coffee shop a few steps behind the men I had been following.

The man in the apron quickly weaved through the bodies in his cramped establishment and stepped into the back room. The guy had run a coffee shop that was barely making ends meet for him before the Starbucks on the corner was erected. Now, with the caffeine juggernaut pumping out foaming lattes and other trendy drinks with the speed and efficiency of a middleweight boxer, he was going under. The offer of a couple hundred for the use of his front room during what would have been his now regularly scheduled afternoon lull was too good to pass up. He was so desperate for the cash that he didn't even question what I was going to be doing in his place. I'd given him some story about being a lawyer who had to do a deposition with a client who was planning to divorce his wife. She had put a private investigator on his heels and he had to meet in private places so that she wouldn't know what he was up to. The coffee shop owner accepted the story along with half of the cash; he would get the other half only if he stayed in back until I told him different.

I dressed the part. No one would ever take me for a high-priced lawyer, but the grey suit and trench coat I was wearing gave me enough of a professional look to pass for what I claimed to be. The only thing that gave away the deception was the revolver that I had pulled from inside the suit coat.

"Let's start with jackets and cell phones," I said. "If you have guns, they can go on the table with everything else."

The ginger was already on edge; seeing the gun gave him a hard shove that almost pushed him over it. "Whoa, man. Take it easy. We're on the same side here. We're the ones who called you."

The one with the stubble was already shrugging off the bomber jacket he was wearing. "Take it easy, Ray."

The jacket went on the table; the man's cell went next.

"Turn the phone off," I said.

Stubble dragged his phone off the tabletop and held down the power button until I saw the screen change. He turned the phone so that I could see that it was shutting down. After I nodded, he put the cell back with his coat.

The one with the styled hair took longer to get the form-fitting leather jacket off of his shoulders. The jacket was for fashion, not function. He put the coat down on top of his friends' and then bent and pulled a smartphone from the pocket. He fiddled with the phone and then turned the screen in my direction so that I could see it was powering down.

The redhead was still in his coat. He hadn't made a move to take it off, or to put his cell on the table. I could have used the gun to make him, but I had no interest in that. If he had trouble with the idea of taking off his jacket, I would just leave — no harm, no foul. If I got the sense that he was stalling me, or working an angle, there would be plenty of both.

The redhead looked at the gun, and then at the looks on the faces of his friends. It was the expressions they wore that did it. Finally, the ginger did as he was told. The redhead shrugged the hooded jacket off his shoulders and draped it over the pile of coats like a magician preparing a trick. The phone came next; he had a smartphone like his friends, but unlike the phone that had just come from the pocket of his partner's tight leather jacket, his was already off.

No one had put any iron on the table. "Guns," I said.

"We were told not to bring 'em," the one with the stubble said.

"Lift your shirts," I said.

"Why?" asked the redhead.

"Sometimes people are forgetful."

Each man pulled up his shirt and spun around. There was nothing on any of the men's lower backs but hair.

"Ankles," I said.

The one with the stubble laughed. "Ankles? What the hell do you think this is, a spy movie? You want to see if my watch is really a watch?"

I lifted the revolver in response.

Stubble sighed and bent to expose his shins; the other two followed suit. I gestured to a table far away from the jackets and phones and the three men went towards it without argument. When they were seated, I put the gun away. The pistol fit snugly into the holster under the jacket; I'd had a tailor alter the suit so that I could conceal a weapon without ruining its lines. I took a chair from a neighbouring table and turned it so that it gave me a clean line of sight on both entrances and the table next to me.

"We done jumping through hoops?" The one with the stubble was the most chatty — that made him the alpha.

I nodded after taking my seat.

"He said you would be a pain in the ass, but this — come on, man. This is not how you do business."

"Really?" I said. "How long have you been in business?"

The twenty-something smiled like he was laying down a flush. "Since before I could drive."

"And how many times you reach out for a fixer?"

The smile turned into teeth grinding. "This is the first time," he said through his clamped jaw.

"Money," I said.

Stubble got out of the chair and was about to take a step when he caught my eye. "The money is in my coat."

I nodded.

He crossed the room and pulled an envelope from an inner pocket of his jacket. I watched him closely, making sure that nothing else but money came out in his hand. He walked the envelope back and put it on my table as he passed. When he sat back down, he gestured to the envelope with his chin. "You going to count it?"

"Do I need to?"

"All five is there."

I nodded and left the envelope where it was. "Tell me about the job."

"We need you to steal a painting."

CHAPTER TWO

"We had everything planned out. We knew the camera hot spots, the guard rotation, the tour group times, everything. The only thing that we missed was —"

"The wire was a heavier gauge than you thought it would be," I said.

Stubble, whose name was really Ilir, looked at me in surprise for a second. "Yeah," he confirmed. "It was."

"I'm guessing you thought you could get it off the wall with something hand-held."

"We bought wire cutters special for the job," Ray said.

"That how they got you?"

The three men were quiet. I could tell that they were wondering if they had walked into some kind of sting.

"I was holding the painting out so Ray could get at the wire. Dante was on lookout. Next thing you know, some guard is rushing at us. He shouldn't have been there. There wasn't supposed to be anyone in that part of the gallery for another five minutes at least. He's coming at us and he already has his radio out. So Dante grabs onto him and they go down. They're rolling around on the floor, right, and everyone is starting to pay attention. People have phones out and if they ain't calling for help, they're taking pictures. I drop the painting and we go over to get Dante and get out, but the guard — he's on Dante like a fucking dog. He just won't let him go. I start hitting him to get his hands off Dante when Ray joins in."

Ilir looks at Ray, who is giving the table a blank stare. "I hit him with the wire cutters. I didn't realize they were upside down. I swear I didn't, guys. I didn't know."

"We know, Ray, we know. The wire cutters hurt the guy pretty bad."

"Hurt, or dead?" I asked.

"Hurt. The tip went through the skull and into his brain —"

"Oh, Jesus," Ray said.

Ilir looked at Ray and gave his shoulder a hard grip. "Easy, Ray, we got this. The guy is in a coma, but he isn't dead. We got the hell out of there, but in the car Ray realizes that he can't find the wire cutters. He dropped them somewhere on the way out."

"Everything was just happening so fast. I had no idea I dropped them."

Ilir cut Ray off. "Ray picked up the cutters the day before. He used his credit card to buy them. I guess some detective thought they looked new and did some checking. Ray got a call two days after the job went bad."

"Why try to go after the painting again?" I asked, even though I had an idea what the answer was going to be.

"I got a lawyer," Ilir said. "A good one."

"He's Jewish," Dante said.

"Mazel tov," I said.

"Fineberg figures if someone takes a second run at the painting and gets away with it, he can argue that there is a reasonable doubt that Ray wasn't using the snips he bought to try and steal the painting. It would just be a coincidence."

"'Cause what kind of idiot leaves behind a bloody weapon he bought with his own credit card a day before the job," I said.

Ray put his head in his hands.

"Exactly," Ilir said.

"There's a simpler way to handle this," I said.

All three men smiled and leaned in towards me. The look of relief on Ray's face looked almost orgasmic. It was premature.

"Kill Ray."

CHAPTER THREE

Ray jumped back from the table with his arms out. "What?"

"No fucking way, man," Ilir said.

"Nuh unh," Dante confirmed.

"Look at him," I said. "The kid was a nervous ball of energy on the subway. You really think he won't turn on you the second things get a little rough during the interrogation?"

"I'm no rat, Ilir. I'm not. I swear to God. You know you can trust me, man. You can." Ray's reaction told me that I wasn't the only one who had thought of this option.

"I know, Ray. I know. Sit down."

Ray slowly got back into his chair and pulled it back towards the table.

"You kill him and it doesn't matter if he bought the wire cutters for the job or not. No one will ever know who he was working with because I'm guessing if you're smart enough to get a meeting with someone like me, you're smart enough to not have left any other evidence behind."

Ilir looked at me and shook his head. "I grew up with Ray. I am not going to kill him. It's not an option."

"Then the lawyer's play is the smart one. Someone other than you walking off with the painting will weaken the case against you. If your lawyer is any good, he'll be able to use it to your advantage."

"We want you to do it," Ilir said.

I shook my head. "That's not how this works. That money," I said tilting my head towards the envelope on the table. "Buys you a plan. It doesn't rent me for a couple hours' work. I'm a consultant that deals in logistics, not heavy lifting."

"Logistics?" Ilir said.

"I manage the flow of resources to get you from Point A to Point B. The resources in this case being the necessary information, hardware, and people you would need to get the painting you are after."

"That is not a real thing," Ilir said.

"Way of the world, Ilir. There is plenty of stuff to steal out there, but it's getting harder and harder to walk away clean. I'm a product of the marketplace. Think of it like physics. You take science in high school?"

"I got high in high school," Ilir said.

I learned science out of garage sale books when I was in my twenties. The conscious hours of my teens were spent learning how to get into things people locked more than twice. "To every action there is always an equal and opposite reaction."

"I remember something like that," Ray said.

"Newton would be happy to know the headache from

that apple wasn't in vain," I said. "They created special-ized security consultants on their side. I am the equal, but opposite, reaction."

"Ilir, what the hell?" Dante said.

Ilir flashed a look at Dante that shut him up fast.

"I was told you were a fixer. That's what your man said. He said you fix things."

I nodded. "That's right. You need a painting that you can't get, I can fix things so that you can get it."

Ray threw his hands in the air. "Nice work, Ilir. We're fucked."

Ilir punched the redhead in the chest. The blow was like a nip from a bigger dog — just hard enough to remind everyone in the pack who the dominant mutt was.

I picked up the envelope and put it on the table next to mine. "You three seem to be in the wrong place. Wait sixty seconds before you walk out that door. Not fifty-nine — sixty. Understand?"

I tucked my chair in and walked to the rear door leading to the cramped storeroom I knew was behind it. I was one foot out the door when Ilir spoke.

"Wait."

My right hand snaked into the jacket and my finger wound around the trigger. There was enough give in the holster to let me tilt it upwards so that I could fire through the jacket without turning around. It would ruin the coat, but not my day. Ilir wouldn't be able to say the same. I turned my head just enough to see the three men.

Ilir was standing, but his hands were empty. "Five would get us a plan. How much would it cost to have you steal it?"

I turned and faced the younger man.

"You're acting as though you're asking me to pick up a pizza on my way home. This isn't a one-man job. It might have been once, but a botched theft and an attempted murder will have changed that. There will be more security and dealing with that takes time and manpower."

"We don't have time for that," Ilir said.

I nodded towards Ray. "There's always plan B."

Ilir looked at Ray, who had gone pale. He shook his head. "We're in a bind here. We need that painting and we need to stay out of jail. The only way we can get both is if someone steals it for us."

"How much are you getting for the painting?" I asked.

"Nothing."

My eyebrow raised half an inch.

"Seriously, it wasn't that kind of job. I can't explain it, but it's the truth."

"A lot of trouble for a job that doesn't pay."

All three men nodded.

I should have already been out of the coffee shop and on the street. I didn't need the work. I had come away in the black from a few jobs over the last year and a half, and the consulting criminal gig was just starting to pay off. Every crook has a job on ice in their head, something that would pay off big-time if they could just get everything to fall into place. It was a lot of work convincing society's most skeptical element to contract out something they held so close to the vest, but a few successes changed everything. Almost overnight, perceptions changed and word got out. At five grand a job, the money wasn't enough to live on, but it was good money. The only problem with contracting was that it was contracting. I would stand in places watching money move back and forth only to let someone else collect it. The job was low-risk easy money, but low-risk easy money went with a low-risk easy life. I was getting bored and the more boredom I felt, the more I wanted out of the consulting game. I wasn't desperate, or stupid, just itching to do more than write the plays so someone else could score a touchdown and fuck the homecoming queen. The three men and their missing painting didn't sound like much of a job, but it was a job and a chance to get off the sidelines.

"Sixty," I said. The number came out so fast that I realized it had been waiting in my head.

"Holy shit," Ray said. He looked paler than when I said they should just kill him. Being deep in the red for the ginger was scarier than being deep in the ground.

"That will cover everything. Manpower, expenses, whatever it takes."

Ilir ran a hand over the stubble on his chin. "We don't have that kind of money, man."

"I guess the free heist business isn't what it used to be."

I pulled my phone from my pocket and thumbed in the password. It took me less than half a minute to find the numbers I was looking for. I took a pen from behind the counter and found a pad of paper that was probably used for taking orders. I put both numbers on the paper and tore the sheet off the pad.

Ilir looked at the numbers. "What is this? A phone number?"

"The first number gets you in touch with a loan company. The company is run off a Native reserve in the States. Ask for Glen and tell him you want to take a loan. Tell him the loan is to pay a debt to James Moriarty. He'll ask for an account number to wire the money into. Give him the second number."

"You want us to take a loan to pay you?"

"Twenty each." I looked at Ray who just kept getting whiter. I gestured towards the cash-poor pale-faced attempted murderer with a nod and said, "Maybe twenty-five, twenty-five, ten. Whatever works."

"Sixty thousand," Ray said in quiet disbelief.

"Sixty-five," I said taking the envelope. "This is a deposit. Non-refundable."

The three men didn't balk. When you were already in for sixty Gs, what's five more?

"How long can you keep Ray away from the cops?" I asked. "I'll need some time to check the job over."

"About that," Ilir said. "Fineberg says the longer we put them off, the more they will think Ray is their guy. He scheduled a meeting with the cops tomorrow at five. They're going to meet Fineberg and Ray at his law office. Fineberg wants all of us there, y'know, as a statement of our innocence. We'll say Ray was with us, and the alibi will keep all of us safe so long as that painting gets lifted by someone other than us."

The side of my mouth twitched up into a grin. One day to pick up a painting that was almost stolen and the cause of an attempted murder just a handful of days before.

"Get the money transferred," I said.

"How do we know you won't just take our money and run?" Dante asked.

I looked at the feminine man; he crossed his arms and stood his ground. "We are not in a business that offers guarantees. If you have any doubts about this, don't transfer that money. All it will have cost you is a few hours riding a train and five grand split three ways."

"Thirty now," Ilir said. "Thirty when the job is done."

"Forty, twenty," I said.

Ilir looked at his partners, but I could tell from the looks on their faces that they were just waiting to follow his lead. "Done."

"Move the money," I said as I stepped into the back room.

CHAPTER FOUR

riday at four in the afternoon was bustling outside of the TAG. Tour groups passed me as they led tourists into the building. Native Torontonians brushed past me ignoring the cultural warehouse to their left. I nodded to the two men who were watching me with the focus of inebriated birds of prey. The two cleaned-up homeless men saw my signal and they immediately lifted their flyers into the air. Each held up fat pink stacks of paper that had all the markings of a genuine endeavour by the gallery. The barking that came from the two men was eerily similar to an old-timey carny trying to rope people in to see the bearded lady.

"Step right up, ladies and gentlemen. Step right up. In an effort to increase awareness about the arts, the Toronto Art Gallery is holding the first ever impressionist scavenger hunt."

Small groups of people disengaged from the herd to listen, but most kept walking.

"Inside the gallery, at this very moment, is ten thousand dollars. That's right, ten thousand dollars in cash."

The mention of money did what mere advertisement couldn't — everyone on the sidewalk who had been in earshot stopped where they were, changed course, and advanced on the two men and their colourful papers.

The two men that I had chosen saw the sudden influx of attention and turned their banter up another notch.

"That's right! Ten thousand dollars free to whoever finds it first. Just complete the scavenger hunt. What could be easier? Learn about art and have a chance to go home with some colourful paper of your own."

The flyers started moving fast. Each man had been supplied with two hundred sheets of paper; the thick stacks looked to be half of their original height when I passed by the two homeless men and quietly slipped each a fifty.

"Nice work, fellas."

"Thank you, sir."

"Yeah, thanks," the second man echoed.

I let the current of excited people pull me towards the bottlenecked entrance. The swollen line was gaining length and girth and I found myself jammed in behind three teenagers armed with flyers in one hand and smartphones in the other. They were all updating their Twitter accounts with information about the scavenger hunt.

I paid the entrance fee and walked with the crowd of scavengers towards the impressionist exhibition. All around me, I could hear people reading off the pages I had typed up with the help of information taken directly from the TAG website. There were five different sets of instructions in all — enough to keep the entire exhibit pregnant with a litter of uncultured reality TV disciples for at least a half an hour.

By my watch, it took less than a minute for the first security guard to break away from the established route he circled for the duration of his shift and show up in the wing housing the impressionist exhibition on loan from Philadelphia. It took another minute for the poor guy to realize that he was horribly outnumbered and overwhelmed by the throng and call for help. The night before, I had been in the gallery watching the space as it breathed. There was a rhythm in the space, as if the gallery were a hibernating beast. The guards — there had to be at least two more on duty than before the attempted murder — moved with the type of efficiency that only boredom-inspired autopilot could create. They circled their designated zones slowly and then started again. Every now and then they interacted with a patron, either to tell them to step back or to answer a question, but they always ended up back on their practised route. The same number of staff was working today and within a minute, the lone guard was joined by five others. One of them, a man in his late fifties with a flat nose and thinning hair, liberated a flyer from a young tween and began examining it. He brought his walkie-talkie to his mouth, but it was already too late.

"*Woman in the Water*! It's behind *Woman in the Water*!"

The young woman who screamed her solution to the final clue had meant to tell only her boyfriend beside her, but the herd picked up on the exclamation.

There was no painting in the gallery titled *Woman in the Water*, but there were three paintings on the wall with women near bodies of water. The crowds circled the three paintings like carrion birds. There was squawking from each huddle about the choice before the birds in each group began their slow timid approach. Fingers began tentatively reaching for the art, but the first shout started a frenzy.

The six security guards began yelling for order, but the crowd was too loud for anyone to hear them. Four of the guards plunged into the crowds while the other two brought radios to their lips. I saw more guards coming towards the impressionist exhibit as shouts turned to screams. People were being dragged to the floor as more and more bodies surged forward towards the paintings. Anyone who had been unaware of the scavenger hunt had backed away from the small riot, but they stayed in the periphery with their eyes glued to the chaos. The only exception, investigators would find when they checked the tapes, would be the man in the sunglasses and hat.

I kept my brim low as I passed through the gaze of the three cameras observing the European art collection. The room was deserted as I approached the two-by-three rectangle on the wall. The picture wasn't much to look at, surely nothing to shove wire cutters into a man's brain over, but art was subjective I guessed. The attempted robbery had resulted in an increase in warm body security, not in anything technical. I had toured the TAG the day before with a group. The guide was not enthusiastic about discussing the robbery, but she did remark with pride that the TAG's strict security measures had made sure that they did not lose a valuable piece of art on the sad day of the attempted robbery. She beamed with pride for just a second when she said, "The art never even made it off the wall."

It was just what I thought. The cable had done its job;

for the gallery, that would be a confirmation that they did everything right, and no one changes something that they got right.

I lifted the artwork and got it six inches from the wall before the wire went taut. I let the art down gently so that it was hanging against the wall. The frame had the wire affixed to its reinforced backing; the wire ran from the painting, through the wall, and into a mechanism behind the drywall. The wire was coated with a thick rubber that told me cutting it would immediately trigger an alarm. I took off my satchel and unzipped it. Inside the bag was a thick cloth that had been folded into a dense rectangle. I pulled out the cloth, unfolded it on the floor, and then unzipped the smaller rearmost compartment. I extracted the small electric handsaw and thumbed the power switch. The rotating blade would go through rebar — the thin security chain didn't even put up a fight.

The painting came down and within seconds I had it wrapped in the cloth and inside the shoulder bag; the tool went back into the small compartment and the bag was back on my shoulder in half the time. If there was an audible alarm, I couldn't hear it over the shouting and screaming still coming from the impressionist exhibit. I went down the stairs and rounded the base. There were cameras everywhere, but to the right of the stairs was a blind spot that covered four feet. I set down my bag and reversed my jacket. I pulled a different hat from the inner pocket and exchanged caps. The sunglasses changed next and then I pulled a flattened black duffel bag from an inner pocket of the satchel. I put the satchel into the duffel bag and left the blind spot. The main level was chaos as employees did double duty dealing with the small-scale riot upstairs and the excited onlookers downstairs. I walked out the front door, passing by two policemen on their way in. Who said art galleries were boring?

CHAPTER FIVE

"Tell me you didn't."

Ox had wanted to meet in person. I picked a spot on the waterfront overlooking Lake Ontario. The breeze coming in off the water did nothing to cool me off. With the humidity, the temperature was in the low forties. My skin was dewy with perspiration and it made everything I had on my body stick to me. I took a swig from the bottle of water I had bought just before I sat down beside the older man; it had already started to go warm.

"You know what? Don't even lie to me. I know it was you. I knew it was you before I really knew it was you. Who else would boost a piece of art in the middle of the day?" Ox pulled at the collar of his shirt as though he was letting off steam from somewhere down below. Not for the first time, I wondered how the neck of his shirt remained so tight after birthing Ox's head earlier that morning. Ox looked like a guy who should be named Ox. He had a huge bovine head accessorized by a sloped forehead more suited to early man. Supporting the massive skull was a body belonging to a smaller human. As Ox settled into the growing frailty of his sixties, his body began more and more to resemble abstract art.

The water felt as hot as the air in my mouth. I turned the bottle and let the remainder splash the pavement. The edges of the puddle had already begun to evaporate when Ox spoke again.

"Why the hell would you want to meet here? It's forty with the humidex. My goddamn junk is stuck to my thigh."

"You complaining? Usually it's stuck to your knee."

"Oh, he speaks, and he's funny." Ox lifted an arm and put it on the back of the bench. The sweat stain under his arm was making a break for his belt. "Make me laugh, funny man. Tell me the one about the guy who turned an easy bit of consulting into a robbery?"

I turned my head so that the broker could see my eyes. "This isn't a partnership, Ox. I don't run anything by you."

The big man showed more backbone than I was used to. He leaned in close enough for me to feel his breath on my face; the acrid exhalations were hotter than the air. "I know what this is, Wilson. I've been doing it longer than you've been alive, so cut the shit. I don't need you to run anything by me, but if I am setting up jobs for you, I need to know what kind of jobs my name gets attached to."

"You saw the papers," I said. "There are no leads and the cops are asking anyone with information to call Crime Stoppers. If the cops are asking for help, it means they have nothing. You're in the clear with the law and you got your cut. What is the problem?"

"What's the problem? What's the problem, he says. Let

me ask you this, what do you know about Albania?"

"I can spell it," I said.

"Anything else?"

I paused and gave it thought. "No."

"It's a tiny place in Europe. I think it borders Greece or something."

"Fascinating," I said in a tone that let Ox know that I found it anything but.

"Then, I'm guessing you don't know that the Albanian mob is going strong in your neck of the woods."

Ox meant the city, not the neighbourhood I lived in — he didn't have a clue where I bedded down. I had chosen the city because it would be a much bigger haystack for anyone looking to search through. I was harder to find than a needle — sharper too. I lived in a sparsely furnished apartment on Jane Street just down from Finch Avenue. The rent was cheap and the building reflected it: exposed pipes sweated all day long or, worse, dripped never-ending puddles into strategically placed buckets. The electricity was spotty and the heat non-existent in the winter time, but everybody kept to themselves. The building was full of immigrants who had the kind of suspicion and shyness that could only come with unstamped paperwork. I had been in the building almost a year and no one had bothered to so much as nod to me in the hallway.

"There's an Albanian mob?"

"There's an every kind of mob. Wipe that condescension out of your voice. The Albanians are a hard people and they are into some serious stuff."

"What kind of serious?"

"The mob here is connected to the other Albanian mobs across the border. The New York faction is the most powerful, but Toronto has serious clout with them."

"Why?"

"What do you mean why?"

"Exactly what I said. When has anyone been talking about New York organized crime and in the same breath said, 'You know who has clout in New York? Toronto.' By rights, it should be Chicago, L.A., or even Boston. Toronto makes no sense."

Ox laughed. "Always thinkin', ain't ya? It's simple. Toronto pushes a lot of stock across the border."

"Drugs," I said.

Ox nodded. "Among other things."

"Drugs," I said again.

"Yeah," Ox agreed. "Drugs."

"Why are we talking about this?"

"We are talking about this because you work for them now."

All of a sudden, I didn't feel the heat. "What are you talking about, Ox?"

"Nothing funny to say?"

The look on my face must have told the old man that he was pushing his luck. "That painting you stole for those guys. One of them is connected. The word *made* comes to mind, but who the fuck knows what Albanians call it. Anyway, the kid is made and the painting you stole was for him. *Ipso facto*, you worked for him, now you work for the guy he works for."

I felt my cheek twitch with a grin. "That a fact?"

"It is a definite fact. Right up there with water is wet. I got a call this morning. Early, like two in the morning. Guy on the other end tells me that he is looking for James Moriarty. I knew it was you he was talking about before he gave me the details of the job you did. Who the hell else would use a name like that?"

"What did you tell them?"

Ox turned his head and saw that I was looking at him. The stare spooked him. "Nothing. Nothing! What could I tell him? I told them what I tell everyone. I got a number. I told him I would pass on the message and if you were interested, you would get in touch yourself."

"How did that go over?"

"The guy wasn't mad, but he wasn't happy either. He mentioned something about knowing who I was and what I was about. He was trying to scare me without, y'know, scaring me."

"It work?"

"I'm here, ain't I? The guy said they had a job for you. Not wanted you for a job, or had a job in mind. They have a job for you."

"You give them the number?"

Ox shook his head.

I kept looking at him.

"Wilson, I didn't."

"Not yet you didn't. But meeting me here on this bench means you're planning to."

Ox didn't argue. "You said it yourself — this isn't a partnership. You didn't run anything by me. You went off the reservation, not me, and now we're both in the shit.

I'm supposed to just be a middleman. Trouble with the Albanian mob is nowhere near the middle — it's the goddamn eye of the hurricane."

"Things are calm in the eye, Ox," I said.

"Don't I look calm?"

The old man was lumpy and sweaty.

"Nope."

"That's 'cause I'm not. The goddamn Albanian mob called me this morning. They gave me twenty-four hours to get in touch with you and that is what I am doing. I'm not giving you up, but am sure as hell not standing in anyone's way."

"They give you a number?"

"No. Nothing. They said they would get in touch with me." Ox wiped at his forehead with the back of his arm. "Christ, it's hot. Can we get ice cream or something?"

I nodded and followed Ox's waddle to the ice cream vendor selling out of a cooler strapped to a mountain bike. The woman moved ice cream with the drive of a sled dog running from the lash. We took our spot in line with mothers and children and patiently waited for our turn. Ox gave the menu board a lot of attention while he shuffled towards the cooler in small increments. Every time the woman lifted the lid, Ox went up onto his tiptoes and tried to get a glimpse at what was left. When we got to the front of the line, I ordered a water and told the sweaty woman already holding the cooler handle in anticipation of an order that I would cover whatever Ox wanted.

Ox's nostrils flared when he heard me. "After that painting stunt you pulled, I'm getting two."

I paid for the two cones and the ice cream sandwich Ox added onto the order just before the woman closed the cooler lid, and we started back towards the bench. Our trip was cut short when we saw our previous spots occupied by a young mother and her baby carriage.

"There's shade over there," Ox said. He was moving towards the new spot before I could say anything. I followed Ox to a slim patch of grass protected by the foliage of a tree and took a spot leaning against the angled trunk. I watched as Ox unwrapped his first cone while holding the ice cream sandwich between his teeth with the same kind of care a tigress would show a newborn cub.

"God, that's good," he muttered as the wrapper of the cone finally came loose and freed up one of Ox's hands for the ice cream sandwich. Crooked teeth broke through the limp cookie layer in a barely contained frenzy and sent softened ice cream squirting out onto Ox's hand.

"What do you know about the Albanians?"

"I know to stay away from them." When Ox spoke bits of ice cream sandwich left his personal space like a rocket ship.

"You brought them to my doorstep. The least you can do is let me know who is knocking."

"I brought them? I brought them? Who stole the painting on a whim? 'Cause that sure as hell wasn't me."

I leaned in towards Ox and spoke through my teeth. "You sell yourself as a middleman. A guy who gets paid to make sure that one hand has no idea what the other is doing. But the second you get your hand caught in the cookie jar, you show up looking to lay blame and offload guilt."

Ox licked what was left of the ice cream sandwich off his hand and started in on the cone. "Alright, I'll cop to some of that. Yeah, I panicked when I got the call. But what do you want from me? You want me to go toe to toe with the Albanian mob on principle?"

"I just want to know what you know, Ox. That's it."

Ox put the remaining two-thirds of the ice cream cone into his mouth at once. When he finished chewing, he pointed at the mother walking away with her baby in tow. Ox hustled over to the vacated spot and took a seat. By the time I sat down, he had already gotten into the second cone. He let the wrapper fall to the ground and took a huge bite out of the chocolate-covered top of the frozen treat. I took a seat beside the broker and felt a slight breeze come in off the water. The view of the lake was spoiled by the sound of the smacking lips beside me. I had to wait until Ox was licking his fingers before he started to tell me about Pyrros Vogli.

The story started off the same way every other gangster story started out. Pyrros was an up-and-comer with an aptitude for making money by breaking the law. Blah, blah, blah, he puts in his time and makes all the right moves. Eventually, he fills a power vacuum caused by his predecessor's arrest and later deportation. The information wasn't linear; Ox would say something only to backtrack a few years to add some minor detail that didn't seem all that important. I gave Ox, and his story, just enough attention to retain what I had heard. The bulk of my concentration was focused on how I would deal with the new gangster in my life.

There was a small bit of my mind, a portion that had been shaped by years of repetition and physical reprimands, that ignored everything, the auditory input coming from Ox and the questions about the Albanians, and obsessed only with my physical surroundings. I had learned at a young age to never let my neck get comfortable. The way young drivers are taught to check their mirrors every quarter of a minute was the way my stationary life was also constructed. I checked around me and spotted three men twenty metres out. Their faces were as anonymous as any other in the park, but I noticed them because of how they stood out against the backdrop of the park. They didn't mesh with the family-friendly atmosphere around them. Two of the men wore T-shirts: one something sleek and designer; the other shirt was so big it could have doubled as a circus tent. The two men were a study in contradictions. One was clean-cut and handsome with a swimmer's build; the other looked like a rhinoceros trying to pass for a human. The two men were flanking the third like pack animals following the alpha. The big man was obviously uncomfortable in the heat; he wiped at his wide brow with the back of his hand and dragged the moisture across the pockets of his pants. If the one with the movie-star good looks minded the heat, it didn't show. The man leading the trio was short — just a few inches over five feet. He wore a short-sleeved button-down red Hawaiian print shirt without an undershirt. The yellow flowers on the shirt were accented with colourful birds fluttering near the stamen. His pants were a light-weight cotton; the ash-grey fabric hung like only designer clothes could. His grooming, or lack thereof, contrasted with the short man's impeccable clothes. Above his nose were eyebrows that meshed together to form an almost solid band of hair across his face. He could have passed for a regular middle-aged guy out for a walk in those clothes, but his eyes gave him away as anything but regular. Under the unibrow were two eyes that resembled the dark coal of a snowman's pupils.

The two men saw me looking in their direction. I saw the recognition in the shoulders of the much bigger man. There was a split-second build-up of tension that rolled up the steep slopes leading to the thick neck and then down again like a wave.

Ox didn't even bother to look. He knew what I had seen. The older man looked at his feet. "I'm sorry, Wilson. I had no choice."

"You had choices, Ox. But only one involved free ice cream."

The men were coming from the path that ran behind the bench, making the gun at my back inaccessible. If the three men saw me draw the gun, they would have a serious advantage standing behind me. I ignored the gun in favour of the knife in my pocket. I had the folding knife out at fifteen metres. I put the knife down on my thigh and let my palm rest on top of it. Ox was too busy feeling sorry for himself to notice what I had done. His preoccupation was a good thing. If he had seen the knife, he would have given it away with some nervous glance that one of the three men would have surely picked up on. I could feel the hard metal switch that would flick the four-inch blade free from the hilt, and I took a slow breath in through my nose as I prepared for what I might have to do.

The small man left the path and walked towards the bench with the other two men close behind. He stopped a few feet in front of us and put his hands into his pockets. The two larger bodyguards took up positions on opposite sides of the older man. "So you must be James," the man with the black eyes said.

"Only people I work with call me James," I said.

The small man smiled with everything but his jet-black eyes. "James it is then."

The man's voice was pleasant and contained the heavy stain of an accent I couldn't place. The bodyguards eyed the hands I had been sure to keep in the open. I spread my fingers slowly and kept them that way. I could see that the two men noticed the gesture, and that I showed no weapon. They kept their own hands empty, but they showed no sign of relaxing their vigilance. The park wasn't crowded, but there were enough people to make drawing guns a terrible idea. We were far enough from the parking lot to make escaping without someone getting a decent description a chore. Also, the number of people with cameras on their phones combined with the shift in public consciousness towards digital voyeurism made the idea of escaping without a video ending up on YouTube almost impossible.

"I don't know you," I said. I nodded at the two men flanking him. "Or them." The inclusion of the two bodyguards caused the big man to take a step towards me. The small man in the expensive pants stopped him with the raise of his right hand.

"You did not know that I was coming?" This was said to Ox more than to me.

"I, uh, I thought it best that you make the introduction, Mr. Vogli," Ox said.

"Did you?"

"If he knew that you were coming, he would have —"

"Not been here," I said.

The same soulless smile showed up again; this time it didn't pass the cheeks. "Maybe it is all for the best then."

Ox was sweating more than he had been a few minutes before. His right hand had crushed the wrapper that had been around the waffle cone of the second ice cream into a tight ball. Residual chocolate had oozed out of the crevices and stained his hand a sticky brown. If it came to it, Ox would have more oozing to do before this impromptu meeting was over. I looked at the man's fat sweaty neck and made a mental note of where I would put the blade. I could get the knife off my knee, open, and into his carotid artery in under a second. The knife would release a geyser of arterial blood on the way out that I would aim at the three men in front of me. The shock would buy me time to get over the bench and behind the hefty body of what would then be my former broker. After that, I would have time to draw the pistol from behind my back and thin the herd.

"May I sit?"

"You can have my seat," I said.

The small man snorted. "You are funny, James. A real joker — like me. Can I tell you a joke, James? I love jokes. I know so many. Can I tell you one?"

He was into the joke before I could say anything.

"A little boy is sitting in class and the teacher asks the students, 'Five birds are sitting on a wire. A farmer fires his

gun and four of the birds fly away. How many birds are left?'
The boy raises his hand and says, 'Zero. Four flew away and
the farmer killed the last one.' The teacher smiles at the boy
and says, 'The answer I was looking for was one, but I like
the way that you think.' Well, later that day the boy walks
up to the teacher and says, 'I have a question for you. There
are two women on a bench eating ice cream cones. One
lady is licking the cone while the other shoves the entire
cone into her mouth. Which lady is married?' The teacher
thinks about it and finally decides, 'I guess I would have
to say the one who shoved the whole thing in her mouth.'
The boy smiles at his teacher and says, 'I was looking for
the one wearing the wedding ring, but I like the way that
you think.'"

The short man jerked a hand to his stomach and barked
out a laugh. The two bodyguards, obviously used to being
the audience for the man's jokes, laughed hard and loud.

"You see, James, like the boy, I like the way you think.
That is why I wanted to meet you. I liked what you did for
my nephew and how you did it. You were able to think on
your feet — something that my nephew could not do. I have
need of a man who can think on his feet."

"I'm not looking for a job right now."

"No?"

"Nope."

"I think you are lying, James. Either to me, or to yourself.
From what I hear, your man Ox did not know that you took
on Ilir's job until after it was over. And from what Ilir told
me about his dealings with you, you took the job knowing
that you had only a day to steal something that had already

almost been stolen. That is dangerous work, and yet you took the job on. A man like that is reckless, and when I meet a reckless man I know that he is either reckless by nature, or bored. You are too old, and the job was too well orchestrated, for you to be reckless by nature. That leaves only boredom."

This Pyrros Vogli saw something in me and I didn't like it. I had not analyzed why I took the job. That in itself should have been a red flag, had I been looking for one. My whole life had been based on careful execution. I thought moves ahead and never let my gut overrule my head. Except, it seemed, when it came to Ilir and his two partners. I could have walked away. I should have walked away the second the consultation turned into a job offer. Instead, I stayed in that coffee shop. I sat there waiting for them to say anything that I could twist into a reason for doing the job. Reckless was a good word for it.

"How did you get Ox to give me up?"

Hearing his name caused the broker to slouch his shoulders even further. He was sharing the bench with me, but he wasn't the only visitor. The broker's discomfort seemed to occupy physical space on the bench as well. His shame hung around his body like bad cologne.

Pyrros' smile came back a little bigger than before. "Don't be mad at the man. Who he is and what he does is no great secret. Ox does not go to great extremes to hide his existence from those on our side of the law. I believe he spends more time worrying about the police being able to arrest him than the criminals trying to find a way to locate him. We have used Ox in the past. He came highly recommended, but I still had my people look into his business before we used his services. Information, like cockroaches, does not die. I had my people pay a visit to him yesterday to ask about you. He protested, but not for long."

If Ox objected to being spoken of as though he were not right next to Pyrros and me, he didn't say a word about it. His large head just retracted further into his shoulders like a turtle shrugging away from a predator.

"No money changed hands?"

Vogli laughed. "Why pay for what is obviously available for free?"

I nodded. Ox had given me up. I wasn't mad. For a year, the broker had acted as a middleman; he sat in the centre of a complicated web that connected everyone who worked the underground night shift. People reached out to Ox for information and connections, and he provided both — for a fee. He and I had worked well together and I liked the man; he liked me too. But like was for sixth graders, not criminals. Ox liked me; he loved his skin a whole lot more. The fault was all my own. I had let it become too easy for him to meet with me. I had made him able to jam me up. Again, reckless.

"I am sorry Ox did not inform you of my coming. He has disappointed us both, and I do not handle disappointment very well, I'm afraid." Pyrros glanced at Ox and the old man went a shade of white usually reserved for dairy. "But," he said looking me in the eye, "even though Ox has wronged us both, I am the one who is saying that he is sorry. Now may I sit?"

Ox didn't wait for a response. He scrambled off the bench, turning his back to the three men, and put his ass up in the air while he cleared the ice cream wrappers off the bench and picked up the sticks he had let fall to the ground. "Just a second. Just a second. There you go, sir." Ox even made a show of brushing off the slats of the bench with his hand.

The man Ox called Mr. Vogli sat down next to me. I noticed that only the toes of his shoes reached the ground. I shifted my body so that I could see both the man that Ox was terrified of and the two men that man paid to make sure the fear was justified.

The small man patted the hand concealing the knife as though he already knew what was there. "You have nothing to fear from me, James. I think I have proved that. Unless, it's making money that you are afraid of." He smiled again, but this time the smile was only formed by the mouth. The lips had pulled back enough to expose the whites in between. It looked more like a dog baring its teeth than a human smile. "Are you afraid of making money?"

"That depends on how it's made."

"How do you usually make your money, James? Is it only art that you steal?"

"Is that why you're here?"

"For art? No, that was something my nephew came up with on his own. He thought that he was doing a good thing, a smart thing, but it was a silly venture. His heart was in the right place, but his brain was not." Vogli slapped his knee. "Good one, eh?"

The three other men laughed heartily. I nodded. "So if the art wasn't something you needed, why are you making all this effort to find the guy who got it?"

"Because the real art was the job, not the painting. Anyone can make a painting. Once, my wife bought me a paint-by-numbers set to help with my stress. For a whole day, I sat in my office putting paint onto that canvas. And at the end of that day, I had something that looked just as good to me as what you took off the wall."

"You should have shared your opinions on art with your nephew," I said. "It would have saved him a lot of money."

Pyrros waved a hand. "That money taught him something about responsibility. It is a lesson we all must learn at some time. But the art wasn't for me. Ilir thought that it would make a good gift for someone, but that someone does not care about old European paintings. From what I hear, he likes the kind that don't look like what they are supposed to look like, but even then he only likes certain kinds. It's all — what's the word?"

"Subjective," I said.

"Bullshit," Vogli corrected. "Art is bullshit. What makes a painting of a cow that looks like a rectangle more valuable than the paint-by-numbers I did in my office?"

I didn't say anything. I had been around enough mobbed-up guys to recognize the rhetoricals a mile out.

"What separates them, James, is that someone is willing to buy the four-sided cow, while my art is only a treasure to me."

I looked at the man.

"It's good. It really is. I think I could have done it without the numbers. But what you did in that gallery, that I could not have done myself. That was pure art. The kind that I appreciate. The kind I would pay for."

"So what is your guy into, if it isn't the art Ilir had me boost?"

"You see?" the small man said to the two bodyguards. "He already understands what I am here for. It is so refreshing to not have to explain every little detail. This man does not want art; he has too much of it already. What he wants is music."

"Music?"

"A violin," Vogli said.

"You seem like a capable man —"

"Thank you."

"Why can't you get this violin yourself?"

"Have you ever been to Beverly Hills?"

I turned my head, surprised by the question, and looked at the gangster beside me. "No."

"I would have thought an art thief would be well travelled. They are in the movies and on TV."

"Mobsters are tall on TV," I countered.

There was no laughter from the man to my right. Judging from the looks on the faces of the two bodyguards, the topic was a sensitive one.

"Careful, art thief."

"Right back at you, gangster."

This got a laugh. "You are all balls, James. I'm surprised you don't roll away. So Beverly Hills has all these stores. Places like Gucci, Prada, Hermès. All the European fashion that the Americans wear and pretend is their own creation. These places, they have marble floors, millions in merchandise, and money. My God, they have money. You know what they don't have?"

I shook my head.

"Criminals charging them for protection. Now why do you think that is? Guys like us shake down titty bars, restaurants, and bars for nickels and dimes. Why would places that have enough money to put stone on their floors that most people can barely afford on their countertops go untouched?"

"Simple," I said. "They have money. Money doesn't suffer the way everybody else does."

"Correct, James. They would take one look at a gangster in the doorway and have some cop with bleached teeth inside the store before he made it to the register. That is my problem. I employ gangsters — criminals, thieves, smugglers, men who are good at threatening blue-collar workers and who are able to intimidate those people into giving them what they want. But what good are men like that in Beverly Hills?"

"The job is in Beverly Hills?"

"Close. Buffalo."

It was my turn to laugh, but all I gave Vogli was a grin. "The only thing close is the B," I said.

The gangster laughed loud enough to scare a woman wearing headphones who was walking her dog along the path running behind the bench. The bodyguards echoed the sound.

"Buffalo may not have a lot of movie stars and trophy wives, but it has what I want for a short time. This violin would not be out of place on Rodeo Drive. In fact, if it were there it would be the most expensive thing on the block."

"And you want me to get it for you."

"Correct, James."

"What is my cut?"

"I will pay you a flat fee of two hundred and fifty thousand dollars to get me my violin. If you need more people, it will come out of your end."

"Expenses?"

"Your end."

I stared out across the grass to the water of Lake Ontario. Out on the water, I could see a sailboat. The pregnant sail bound the wind inside and forced it to carry the ship along. Two specks that had to be people frantically moved back and forth on the deck trying to keep the craft going. I had spent a long time riding the wind. I had thought I was independent, but most of the time I was really just trying to channel something else's momentum to get where I wanted to go. I felt that same feeling on the bench; like I was being pushed and I didn't like it. The Albanian gangster had used the word *reckless* twice when he spoke to me. The word was bandied as though it was some kind of credential and not a liability. I doubted that he got to where he was by being reckless. Most who grab the reins have a bit of that in them, but those who hold them do it through discipline. I rolled the word over in my mind a few times until I saw the push for what it was.

I broke the silence. "How long?"

Vogli turned his head just enough so that his eyes could see mine. He spent a moment in thought before he said, "A week."

I shook my head. Maybe I was reckless, but I wasn't stupid.

Vogli replied as though it was the answer he had expected. "I understand, James. But before you say no, take a look at the job and tell me what you think. If you won't do it, then tell me how to do it and I will handle it. Ilir said your fee is ten percent. So, worst case scenario, you earn twenty-five thousand."

I didn't like how ready he was with a reply. He should have bristled at the refusal, not caved. There was another push there, this one more subtle.

"Fine," I said.

Vogli nodded. One of the bodyguards moved to reach into his pocket. I pressed my palm down on the knife instinctively. Vogli's artery would serve as a worthy replacement for Ox's.

"Easy," Vogli said. He was looking out at the water, but speaking to me. "It is just the information."

The bodyguard had paused at the word *easy*; another nod from Vogli set him in action again. The man produced a thumb drive from his pocket and passed it to me.

Pyrros got off the bench and took his place at the head of the pack. "Look it over. There is a number for one of my people on the drive. Contact him when you are done."

I nodded.

Pyrros started to lead the two men away before pausing to look at me. "But," he said, fixing his two coal-black eyes on me, "don't take too long."

CHAPTER SIX

"Look, Wilson, I —"

I got off the bench and Ox flinched. I didn't touch him; I didn't try to hide putting the knife away either.

"It's my fault, Ox. I got sloppy."

"I had no choice, Wilson. You gotta see that. Pyrros Vogli is not a man who fucks around."

"He's not the only one," I said.

Ox took a step back. I held out a hand to stop him. "It's like you said, Ox. You had no choice. It's my fault for making it so you had one to begin with."

"What are you going to do?"

I had a feeling he was asking more in the *what are you going to do to me* sense.

"Don't worry about what I am going to do. Worry instead about getting your end of the job done."

"My end?"

"I'm going to be calling you later for some talent. Reliable people who are able to work on short notice and can get across the border without any friction. That is the most important thing. If you even think they might have something the border cops would pick up on, I don't want them."

"What kind of guys are we talking?"

"Every kind," I said.

Ox furrowed his brow as though he was working out long division in his head. I made it easy on him. "I don't know a thing about this pricey violin Vogli wants. What I do know is that if I decide to do it, I'll need help, good help, and I don't have the time to do interviews."

Ox relaxed his brows; he'd gotten the answer — no remainder. "Okay, Wilson, sure. Whatever you want. I'm your guy."

I turned my back and left Ox standing by the bench. My guy — he couldn't have been any more wrong.

CHAPTER SEVEN

I spent ten hours on the contents of the drive Pyrros Vogli had passed to me in the park. He hadn't lied about the violin — the instrument was easily worth something in the high seven figures. It was hard to believe something made of wood could surpass most things made of diamond. The violin, and its relatives, followed the same principles as diamonds. They were rare commodities and that rarity made them expensive. A quick search told me that there were dozens of classical musicians lugging six- and even seven-figure instruments around with them. Google even turned up two stories of million-dollar violins being misplaced by their owners. One was left in a cab, the other on the subway. If it had been an iPad, no one would have ever seen it again. But iPads were easy to fence; violins were considerably harder to move. The instrument itself looked similar to every other violin I had ever seen. The one thing it didn't look like was something that was a few centuries old. The maple it was constructed out of was polished to a high shine, making the arced rings on the back stand out like stripes on the body of a bronzed zebra.

I knew that I would say yes to Pyrros after the first hour. If I was going to have reservations, or get cold feet, it would have happened way before the long hand on my watch circled the dial. The violin had the same potential benefit of the painting I had cut off the wall two weeks earlier. The violin, like the art, was worth a lot of money, but, unlike other high-value items, diamonds for example, the security was lax. People wanted diamonds. People often tried to steal diamonds. The same could not be said for violins. The reason for the disparity was the black market. It was easy to unload diamonds for cents on the dollar. It was much harder to move an instrument. There were few men who ran in the right wrong-kind of circles who could move such an item. And it wasn't like the kind of people who would spend millions on a violin were advertising that they would be interested in a stolen masterpiece. Pyrros having already agreed to buy the violin solved that problem.

The extra nine hours were spent on the internet researching the names and places that were on the drive. I coaxed Google into giving up everything it knew about the information I was given. It was just after two in the morning when I called the number Pyrros had left for me. One of the Albanian's people answered on the third ring.

"I'm in," I said.

"Alright." The voice was cool and if the time of morning bothered the man it belonged to, it didn't show. He gave me an address and told me to show up at nine the following night.

"There will be three of us," I said.

"Only three?"

"That's right."

"Are you sure that will be enough?"

"You think I should run it by you to make sure that it meets the high standards of the Albanian mafia?"

"I just want to be sure that you aren't trying to keep the numbers small so that the pieces of the pie stay big."

"Listen: the midget came to me, not the other way around. If he thought you had a clue, you would be doing more than waiting for me to call."

"Do me a favour, asshole, try out that midget shit when Pyrros is in the room."

"If I do, I'll make sure that someone gets you away from your secretary's desk to see it."

I hung up on the Albanian and entered the address he had given me into the GPS app on my phone. The place was somewhere out in Scarborough. Google Maps put the location in the middle of an industrial park. The out-of-season satellite imagery showed the snowy roof of the building. The long rectangle was similar to many other buildings positioned around it. I was due at a warehouse in nineteen hours.

My next call was to Ox. It took him longer than the Albanian to answer the phone.

"Hello?"

"I need two men," I said.

"Wilson? Jesus, what time is it?"

"Early for you, evening for me," I said.

I heard a click that was probably a lamp and then a snort followed by a phlegmy cough as the professional middle-man roused himself. "What is it?"

"I need two men."

"Just two? Are you sure?"

Everyone was an armchair quarterback these days. "I'm sure. I need a driver and a grifter."

"No problem."

"I'm not done. They need to have clean records. And the grifter needs to be a talker. Sell snow to Eskimos kind of thing."

Ox groaned and smacked his lips. "I know a guy. He's good."

"Not done," I said. "They can't have ever worked for Pyrros Vogli or any of his people before."

"I'll need to check into that, but it shouldn't be a problem. The Albanians do most of their stuff in house. Anything else?"

"I need them by four."

"Twelve hours? Wilson, that could be a problem. Guys like this aren't always the most reliable about calling me back."

"Ox, the only words out of your mouth after what you pulled today should be 'no problem.'"

"Hey, I'm just being realistic. But you're right, Wilson. You're right. I owe you."

It was the other way around, but I didn't say anything. Ox was unreliable and his lips were less than watertight, but he had a Rolodex of bad people in his head. If I spooked him, he might use that Rolodex to find a couple of hitters to meet me instead of the kind of people I needed.

"Tell them there's two hundred and fifty grand in it for them if they like what they hear and sign on."

A long pause stretched out into an uncomfortable silence. Ox broke his own interlude when he said, "That wasn't the number Pyrros told you."

"It's the number I'm telling him," I said.

"Wilson, this isn't the kind of guy you haggle with. If he sets a price on something, you do the smart thing and thank him twice before you knock a few dollars off."

"Name one business out there in the real world that lets the customer set the prices?" I asked.

"The kind that has clients who might decide to kill you for fucking around with them."

"The price is the price," I said. "If Pyrros doesn't like it, he can shop around. Hell, he can make it a DIY project if he wants to."

"You want my advice?"

"No," I said. "I want two men ready to meet at four, and two more waiting on standby."

"Two more?"

"Another driver and another grifter in case the first two you set me up with are flakes."

"Fine, fine. I'll get back to you when I know something."

"Nope," I said. "I'm changing phones. I'll call you in a couple of hours."

There was another pause. When Ox spoke again, he sounded sad. "You really think that's necessary?"

"Yes," I said.

"Wilson, I had no choice."

"I'm taking that ability to make a choice off your plate."

Ox sighed heavily. "Fine. I'll put some lines in the water and see who's biting."

"I'll be in touch in two hours."

Before I hung up, Ox spoke again. "Wilson, are we cool?"

"Get me those names and we will be," I lied.

Ox sounded hopeful. "Okay, okay, I'll get on it."

I hung up the phone and pulled out the SIM card. I replaced it with one of the clean cards I kept in a drawer in the apartment. The lie I had told to Ox tasted stale in my mouth. Without a number to call, Ox and I were as good as strangers. We weren't cool anymore — we weren't anything.

CHAPTER EIGHT

SUNDAY

I sat at a table with a naked stuffed bear in front of me. I never considered a teddy bear to be naked before I sat down today. Naked is a human concept — just ask Adam and Eve. Bears can never be truly naked; after all, they're covered in fur. But looking at this one, lying on the table in front of me, across from shelves of bear overalls, sundresses, ponchos, and even geisha wear, it occurred to me for the first time that bears could indeed be naked.

"We're all set for your party, Mr. Moriarty. You said you would be joined by two other gentlemen, but —" the woman consulted a clipboard. "No children." Nancy, the middle-aged Teddy Bear Toolbox store manager, couldn't hide her are-you-a-pedophile? stare behind her pleasant demeanour.

"That's right, two more," I said. "My brother and his wife just split. It was official yesterday and he moved the rest of his stuff out of the house this morning. Friday is his daughter's sixth birthday and he really wants to make her happy. After all, her world just came crashing down around her. So, I booked me and our cousin in. I figure between the three of us at least one bear will come out looking good."

"Oh," Nancy said. From the look on her face, I could see all of her previous misconceptions reshaping themselves. "That is so sweet."

"That little girl is the reason he stayed after his wife cheated on him again and again. But when she started drinking more and putting her hands on Dorothy — well, it had to be the end."

"My God," Nancy said. "That is terrible."

I nodded. "Listen," I said, leaning in a little to generate a conspiratorial closeness that was, in actuality, as real as aspartame. "If we totally screw up, are there bears we can buy? Ones that are different from the regular ones you can buy off the shelves?"

The manager smiled and put a warm hand on my forearm. "It's not that hard. And with all the love you have for that little girl, I'm sure that you will come up with something really special that she will just love."

"But if we don't —"

"I can help you," she said. "I have some things a little girl would absolutely love."

Nancy went on and on about the art of building bears from the heart; of course, she meant the heart with a little help from the wallet. I gave her just enough attention for her to think that I was listening. In fact, I was watching a man move through the store. He walked with the grace of a dancer straight out of old Hollywood. His looks were equal parts actor and fitness instructor. He looked like a young Gregory Peck — if the actor did yoga and could run a triathlon. He saw me through the glass and nodded a cautionary greeting. I gave a nod back and he started his approach.

Nancy caught my nod and turned to look out onto the sales floor. "Is that your brother?"

"It is," I said.

The middle-aged woman let an "oh my" slip from her lips before she unconsciously began smoothing her official Teddy Bear Toolbox smock.

The second member of my teddy bear party opened the door and paused in the threshold. He crossed one foot over the other and leaned against the door frame.

"Miles," I said.

"Hey, James."

"Hello, Miles," Nancy said.

He beamed a smile at the woman that caused her to immediately run a hand through her hair. The hand stopped primping when I cleared my throat. "I'll let you talk while you wait for the third member of your party to get here. When he arrives, we can get started."

"Actually," I said. "If it's not too much trouble, we'd like to work on our own. I've done some research and I think we can handle things."

Nancy looked at Miles even though I had been the one who was talking. "That's not how we usually operate," she said.

"I know and I'm sorry. We just have some things to talk about. Private things that might be a little hard to say in front of someone we don't know."

"Oh," she said, remembering the sob story I had spun for her. "I completely understand."

"Maybe I can stay after and you can check over my work," Miles said. "You probably have tricks up your sleeve that would put what's out there to shame."

Nancy blushed. "Tricks, no. I just have a lot of practice. That's all it takes."

"Maybe that's just what I need," Miles said.

"Let's see what we can get done on our own before you try and get the teacher to help you with your homework."

Miles looked at me and saw that I was reining him in. The manager didn't notice. She was back to playing with her hair. Miles moved the door open with his hand and she happily ducked under his arm to leave.

"Do a good job, or I'll give you a detention," she said.

Miles leaned in a little and said, "I'll stop by on the way out to see if there is a way I can get some extra credit."

Nancy put a hand on Miles' arm as she laughed. "You are so bad."

When the horny store manager had finally left us alone, I said, "You're supposed to be newly divorced and making a bear for your daughter."

"With all that flirting, I guess we know whose fault it was. And all the poor kid gets is a bear? I'm not much of a father or husband, I guess."

"It was my idea."

"Shitty uncle then." Miles looked around the room at the shelves of bears and bear accessories. "Nice place for a meet. I was getting so tired of flower shop after flower shop."

"Sit down, Miles."

"How did you know I was Miles? We've never met and I remember you telling me on the phone that there were two people coming."

"You don't walk like a car guy. Your posture is too good for a guy who has spent his life under a hood. You're also too handsome to be a grease monkey. If I'm wrong, and the con man is another looker, I'll consider finding someone else to drive to avoid any unwanted attention."

"You're not so bad yourself, handsome," Miles said.

"I didn't have Nancy all over me." I didn't mention that the manager might have been better able to keep it in her pants if Miles had just toned it down a little. It wasn't the time for that, but I did wonder if the grifter was able to be subtle if he had to. A man who didn't have an off switch could be a liability. "Add it all up," I said. "You're the con man, not the driver."

"Con man." From his tone, I could tell that Miles didn't like the term.

"You're not?"

"The term implies that all I have up my sleeve is confidence. Idiots are confident, drunks are confident — hell, small dogs are confident. To lump what I do in with them is offensive. Like calling a flight attendant a stewardess. Not to mention the title says nothing about my sex appeal."

"Confidence does seem a little far-fetched for a guy like you."

Miles took a seat to my right so that he could see the front of the store. A good sign. "Short notice," he said.

"It's a thing with these guys," I said.

"Who are we talking about?" he said. I couldn't pick up

any hint of a bluff. Miles seemed to be in the dark about the job, meaning Ox hadn't told him anything, or given him an opportunity to earn a bloody bonus. Another good sign.

"Let's wait for Carl. No point doing this twice."

"So what, we just sit here and shoot the breeze?"

"Build one of those bears for your kid," I said.

"What's her name?"

"Dorothy."

"I named her Dorothy and I'm leaving her mom? We should have done this meeting at a car dealership."

Within minutes, the handsome grifter had a bear started that looked to be the equal of anything on display. It even earned a knock on the glass followed by an enthusiastic thumbs up from Nancy, who had been pacing back and forth outside the door like a hungry tiger the entire time we had been in the room.

"Dorothy is going to absolutely love this," Miles said.

"Hope she likes her new mommy," I said.

Miles followed my eyes and saw the manager giving him a lingering stare out of the corner of her eye while she pretended to straighten an already uniform row of bears.

"She works at the teddy bear factory. What's not to like?"

I saw a man angling through the tightly packed aisles with ease. He wasn't graceful like Miles; he was just skinny — not diet skinny, but rather the kind that would make Ethiopian kids slide something off their plate to help him out. The bones in the man's face were prominent and the veins on his neck climbed like blue vines towards the base of his chin. The manager was too fixated on Miles to notice the third man until he was inside the room.

"Carl," I said.

The man didn't have Miles' posture. He had his hands in his pockets and his head jutted out from his body like a pelican's. He looked at me, then at Miles. Under the thin man's nose was a thick heavy moustache — the kind usually reserved for brooms. The thatch of hair was the only thick thing about him.

"You James?"

"Only to my Albanian friends," I said.

Miles looked up from the rhinestones he was carefully gluing into place on the bear's jacket. "Albanians?"

"This is Miles," I said.

Miles nodded to Carl. "Pull up a bear," he said.

Carl looked at the table skeptically, then shrugged and took a seat. He sat down across from Miles and began examining the bear left out for him.

Miles glued another rhinestone down and then looked up from the bear at me. "If it isn't James, what is it?"

"Wilson."

If either man had heard the name before, it didn't show on their faces.

Carl pushed the bear forward on the tabletop. "I was told on the phone that there was money to be made."

Miles took another rhinestone with the tips of his tweezers and dipped it into the adhesive. As he applied what looked like his hundredth stone, he said, "I was told there was a shitload of money to be made."

"I like his version better," Carl said.

"What does eight million dollars look like?" I said.

"Depends on the denomination," Carl said. "In small

bills you're looking at a couple of hockey bags at least."

"A million is twenty or so pounds in hundreds, so eight is around one-sixty. You go down to twenties, it's just simple math. Multiply by five and you end up with just over eight hundred pounds," Miles said as he placed a final rhinestone down on the bear's jacket. He held the stuffed animal out at arm's length and examined his work. "You think a cowboy hat would be too much?"

"Less," I said.

"I thought I was going overboard too, but without the hat the bear will just look unfinished."

"He means less weight," Carl said. "That means what? Thousands? That is damn hard to move. Even a little at a time would be a bitch. And if we outsource the job of laundering it, we're looking at cents on the dollar."

"What if I said eight million dollars weighed under three pounds," I said, "and was small enough to fit into a backpack."

"Not money," Carl said. "We talking stones here?"

"Do either of you like Mozart?" I asked.

CHAPTER NINE

Three hours later, the three of us were sitting inside a warehouse in Scarborough. The parking lot had been mostly empty save for a handful of vehicles parked close to the main entrance. In the spot closest to the door was a Humvee. Not the scaled-down soccer mom type, but the kind Schwarzenegger used to roll around in when he still did sit-ups. The Humvee was parked down the centre of two spaces. I imagined what the little Albanian gangster looked like getting in and out of the military transport; Miles vocalized it.

"Do you think one of his guys is the designated boost? If not, how do you determine who does it? They got to have a plan, because who wants to make the boss have to come out and say it?"

I regretted telling him about Pyrros' height being an issue. "Get it out now," I said. "He won't take that shit to his face. Not in front of his people."

"*Short*-tempered, is he?"

This got a laugh out of Carl. His moustache shook like

a wet dog while we rounded the corner.

The door to the warehouse was open and when we stepped inside we were met with a wave of humidity. The thick air shoved its way past me looking for a way out of the building. The large rectangular space was made for inventory; what it got instead was a wrestling ring. Rows and rows of folding chairs stretched back from each side of the raised square in the centre of the floor. A short fire hydrant of a man was in the middle of the ring along with a pack of steroid users, some abusers, all running on the spot around him. Every thirty seconds or so, the fire hydrant would blow a whistle and the spandex-clad men around him would drop to the mat into push-up position and then scramble back to their feet as fast as they could so that they could resume running. Pyrros was ringside in another Hawaiian shirt — this one green with white surfers riding blue waves. Pyrros yelled criticisms over the loud voice of the man in the middle of the ring. Each wrestler kept his eyes on the man with the whistle, but they nodded every time Pyrros finished a sentence. The only man immune to the critiques was the big man I had seen flanking Pyrros the day before. The big man wore a black wrestling singlet with two crossed swords crested onto the back. He absolutely dwarfed every other object between the ropes.

Miles, Carl, and I worked our way down the aisle to the front row as the man leading the practice blew two sharp notes with his whistle. The men took up positions against the ropes on opposing sides and then began taking turns running from one side of the ring to the other. The man running the drill called out names one by one, and each person called moved to the middle of the ring. The running wrestlers leapfrogged the man in the centre before ricocheting off the opposite ropes and coming back. The man in the centre would then drop to the mat so that the runner could step over him. When it came time for the man I met in the park to run, he covered the distance with a speed few would have thought possible for a man his size. He glided over the body in the centre of the ring like a thoroughbred jumping a fence and then took his spot back in the lineup.

We took three of the seats in the front row and watched as the exercise ended and the ring cleared out. Pyrros' big bodyguard stayed in, and so did a man who would have seemed seriously imposing were he not standing next to the man in the black wrestling gear. The big Albanian towered over the other wrestler, and — from the look on the man's face — he knew it. The fireplug yelled for the men to begin and the two wrestlers locked arms in a violent embrace. Pyrros' man won the contest of strength and pulled the smaller man into a headlock. The hold lasted a few seconds, but it was enough to produce a loud yelp from the man inside the muscle-and-bone vice. The Albanian shoved his opponent towards the ropes and the taut cables sent him back at the bigger man with a little extra shove. I doubted that he was grateful for the help because the Albanian used the momentum to hoist his opponent up and into the air. The man came down face first on the mat; the impact generated a loud bang and then a groan from the squeaky springs underneath. The match that followed was one-sided; it felt wrong acknowledging that another side even existed at all. When the smaller man pushed the Albanian, he went nowhere. Conversely, the bigger man manipulated his opponent with ease, and every hold and move was synced to a loud yell of agony by the much smaller practice dummy. A violent slam that put the obvious loser down on his head seemed to signal an end to the un-fake beating, but I was wrong. The big Albanian made eye contact with me before starting up the buckles joining the corner of the ring. The big man stood on the top rope with surprising balance and kept eye contact with me. He lifted a thumb and then looked to Pyrros. Pyrros held out his own fist, but his thumb was turned down.

"Do it," he yelled.

The big man took to the air like a World War Two bomber. His bulk shouldn't have been able to fly, but it soared through the air with the same mystifying aerodynamics as the Enola Gay. Only the Albanian didn't keep soaring; gravity pulled him down head first towards the man lying out of breath on the mat. I saw the bodies of everyone around the ring tense as the huge steroid-infused Icarus crashed into the human sacrifice on the mat. The sudden commotion told me that something had gone terribly wrong, or right, depending on your perspective. Blood soaked into the canvas as the instructor screamed for help while simultaneously using his hands to hold the cracked skull in front of him together. Pyrros slid under the ropes, walked across the ring, and took his bodyguard by the straps the way a man takes his dog's leash. Pyrros pulled his man's head down and spoke into his ear for just under a minute. The hushed conversation was intense and there were a lot of hand gestures coming from the Albanian gangster, but the talk ended with a loud slap on the ass. The bodyguard took the top rope in his hands and used it to leap over the cables and down to the floor. He walked up to the guardrail, never once taking his eyes off me.

"Come," he said.

We got up from the chairs and followed the sweaty hulk to the aisle. Ahead of us Pyrros Vogli, Albanian gangster and apparently wrestling promoter, walked towards an office door. When we entered the office, Pyrros was on a couch smiling like a cat who woke up to find that someone left the birdcage open.

"Impressive, eh?"

Miles wasted no time. "Oh, sure. Especially when he totalled the other kid's face."

The big wrestler snorted. "His fault. He moved."

"No doubt," Miles agreed. "Maybe next time he'll think before you jump on him."

The wrestler looked at me. "Not so fake, eh?"

"Bit much for a practice," I said.

"I hear they sacrifice a virgin at the live shows," Miles said. This got a snort from Carl.

The laugh got under the wrestler's skin. I doubted he was used to being made fun of. "You want to see how real it is?"

I stepped in front of Miles. My hand was on the small of my back. "If you show me yours, big man, I'll show you mine."

Pyrros lifted a hand and said, "Attila." The single word shut the big man down like a power cord being pulled from the wall.

"Always the hard man, James. That hardness might get

you in trouble one day when you find that you don't have the upper hand you think you do."

The wrestler nodded emphatically.

"He's going to jump on you," Miles said in a whisper loud enough for everyone to hear. "I hear the trick is not to move."

Attila looked confused. I could tell from the look on his face and the darting of his eyes that he was new to being picked on and he didn't like it. He was trying to come up with a response, but the door opened before he got the chance to get out whatever lump of coal his heavy brain was trying to forge into a verbal diamond.

The trainer ran into the room out of breath. His sweats were stained with blood. "Mr. Vogli, we can't wait for an ambulance. We need to get Elvin to a hospital now."

"Attila will help."

"That's okay, sir, I have things handled."

"Attila will help," Pyrros repeated. This time there was no counter.

Attila shouldered past the man and angled his massive shoulders out the door. "Come," he said to the trainer.

"Attila," Pyrros called. "Tell Len to come in."

I heard the big man bellow the name loud enough to produce an echo off the warehouse walls.

"Attila?" I said.

Pyrros shrugged. "He gave himself the name, but I think it suits him. He is a barbarian, plain and simple."

A man knocked on the open office door and waited just outside. Pyrros sighed and said, "Just come in, Len. It's your office."

A well-dressed man stepped inside. He was the second half of the pair I had met the day before. Dressed in a linen suit and small gold-rimmed glasses, he looked like what Attila might evolve into in a few thousand years. "I did not want to interrupt anything."

Of the two men working for Pyrros, Len was clearly the brains. He looked like a banker at the end of a long day. He wore the suit without a tie and the stubble on his face was a few hours past five o'clock and just starting to sprout an inch below the eyes. Pyrros had the same thing, only his stubble was already in full bloom. I pegged them as kinsmen. Len took a seat behind the desk and opened a Mac laptop.

"This is your crew?" Pyrros asked.

I nodded.

"Kind of small, don't you think?"

"Depends," I said.

"Depends on what?"

"Depends on how you do the job."

"Like Newfies and light bulbs," Pyrros said slapping his knee.

"Was that Albanian?" Miles whispered.

"He likes jokes," I said.

Pyrros immediately looked to Len, giving me the impression that the spiffy underling was no stranger to being a one-man audience. Len was already in the process of closing his laptop in order to give his boss his full attention.

"How many Newfies does it take to screw in a light bulb?"

Len shrugged.

"Three. One to hold the bulb, two to spin the ladder."

Len barked out a laugh that was louder than the one that came from Pyrros a second later.

"Seriously?" Miles said.

"That was one of the first jokes I learned when I came to this country," Pyrros said.

Len guffawed for a few more seconds until a tense quiet filled the room.

"I am surprised that you brought them here, James," Pyrros said.

"Uh hunh," I said.

"Did you not feel safe coming alone?"

"It's a job — they're part of it, so they're here."

"Like I said, I am surprised. Do you think I bring Attila everywhere with me?"

"Don't you?"

"He accompanies me when I need someone to stand beside me and look scary, but not to listen to business."

"Like you said, he's a barbarian, plain and simple."

"And you are —"

"Not plain, not simple," I finished.

Pyrros smiled to himself. It wasn't a smile that came from thinking happy thoughts. "So are you both up to speed, as they say?"

Miles and Carl nodded.

"So we are all classical music lovers in this room, eh?"

"No one likes classical music," Miles said.

"You are right there. No one likes classical music, but people pretend to. People pay to look like they do. And that is what matters — that people pay. People use the music as a tool, a ladder, to show that they are above the rest of us. Am I right, Len?"

Len had opened the computer again and was busy connecting a wireless mouse. He stopped everything when he was addressed and again closed the laptop. "Pyrros is correct. While not mainstream, classical music does have the appearance of respectability. Old money is an established benefactor of the classical arts, and new money contributes almost double in an effort to prove that they are themselves no less than their peers."

Pyrros nodded sagely. "Like I said, it takes money to be above the rest of us; that's why the penthouse is so expensive."

"Here I thought it was because they showed more skin than *Playboy*," Miles said.

Len looked nervous, but Pyrros barked out a laugh. Len came in a second later. "I like this one, James. He is funny."

"He thinks so," I said.

"I think so. Len thinks so. Right, Len?"

"Yes, Pyrros. He is very funny."

"Funny doesn't pay the bills," I said.

Pyrros nodded. "That is true. I do."

"Two-fifty is too low," I said.

Pyrros looked at me. "Another joke."

Len started to laugh, but he quickly stopped when he realized Pyrros hadn't started.

"I went through the drive Len gave me," I said. "It isn't some fiddle you want — it's a Stradivarius. There are only about 600 violins made by Antonio Stradivari in existence today. Two years back, a Stradivarius sold for just under sixteen million. One lost in a cab in New York back in oh-eight was worth four million. Now, Len didn't put a price tag on the violin on that drive he gave me, but the age of the instrument was listed. This particular Stradivarius is 288 years old. Older than the one that sold for four, but younger than the one that went for sixteen. That time period puts it right at the end of Antonio Stradivari's golden period. Best estimate, I figure the violin is worth eight million."

"And what do you want?"

"Ten percent," I said.

Pyrros laughed. Len didn't even try to join in because it was clear that it wasn't that kind of chuckle. "Eight million dollars is only eight million when you can find someone to pay it. This isn't like fencing diamonds or gold. There aren't people on every block looking to buy old violins."

"What is your buyer offering you?"

Pyrros looked at Len. It was a quick look, nothing but eye movement, but I caught it. "Not your business."

"Close," I said. "Not my problem. What is my problem is crossing the border, stealing the violin, and getting back here to get paid. Doing all of those things within a week adds up to ten percent."

Pyrros looked at Miles and Carl. "He speak for all of you, funny man?"

Miles shrugged. "Depends on what he is saying. In this case he wants to pay me two hundred sixty-six thousand whereas you want to pay me eighty-three. So, yep, in this case he talks for me."

Carl spoke without being asked for his opinion. "A lot of hassle for eighty K."

Pyrros dug around in between the couch cushions until he came out with a small orange basketball that paired with the small plastic net above the door. Pyrros didn't go for a shot; he just squeezed the ball hard enough to make the rubber bulge between his fingers. He crushed the ball with enough force to push the veins on his forearms to the surface. He squeezed, then relaxed his hand before ratcheting up the pressure all over again. He said something to Len in Albanian. The words were harsh sounding and seemed to be packed with the danger of machine-gunfire. Len spoke back in the same language, but his words didn't seem as volatile as his boss's. Whatever the well-dressed man said, it pissed Pyrros off. He raised his voice and barked something back that shut Len up.

Pyrros looked back at me. "No," he said.

I nodded and went for the door. Miles and Carl followed me out.

When the door closed behind us, Miles said, "Waste of a day, Wilson."

"Five each," I said. "For the trouble."

"Cool," Miles said.

"I won't fight you on it," Carl said.

"If," I said.

"If what?" Miles asked.

"If this job falls through."

"What do you mean if, Wilson? The man said no."

"Miles, that violin has a shorter shelf life than day-old bread. In a week, he won't be getting at it. I don't speak

Albanian, but I would guess Len was trying to make his boss see that. They don't have the time to find someone else to do this job for what Pyrros wants to pay."

"Unless he does the job with his own people," Carl said.

"If this guy thought that his own people could handle the work, he would have never found me."

"So we wait," Carl said.

I nodded. "If we don't hear any accented English after a day, I pay you out and you can go back to your day jobs."

"Job?" Miles said. "If I wanted to have a job, I wouldn't be a guy who steals for a living."

CHAPTER TEN

We never even made it out of the parking lot.

Len came running out the door, to find the three of us still talking.

"So you got him to come around," I said.

"And then you got sent to run around," Miles chirped. He looked at Carl. When he said nothing, Miles leaned over and whispered, "Your turn. It has to work in the word 'around.'"

We all ignored Miles.

"Pyrros says ten percent."

"Half up front," I said.

Len put his hands on his hips. "You have got to be fucking kidding me!"

CHAPTER ELEVEN

We were all back in the office. Len at the desk, Pyrros on the couch, the three of us standing by the door. Pyrros hadn't handled the half up front demand very well. After giving Len an earful, he turned his dwindling rage on me.

"You want me to give you four hundred thousand dollars for doing nothing!"

"Down payment," I said.

"And how do I know you will get me my violin, James? How do I know you won't just run off with my money?"

"How do I know you'll pay me when I get it?"

"Carl, you feel left out?"

Both Carl and I spoke at the same time. "Shut up, Miles."

I continued, "Half now keeps everybody honest, Pyrros."

The Albanian gangster ran a hand through his hair. He looked at Len and spoke more Albanian. This time the words weren't as sharp, but I bet they could still hurt if Pyrros wanted them to.

Len typed at the computer with hard keystrokes. After a minute, he looked up from the screen and spoke to

Pyrros in Albanian.

"Done," Pyrros said.

"Tomorrow morning at nine, have Len meet us with the money at the poker tables inside Fallsview Casino. The money will be in one bag. Bound stacks of twenties. Nothing larger, nothing smaller."

"Why all the way out there?"

"We need to cross the border tomorrow to check things out in person," I said. "The casino is a good spot to meet." A good public spot to meet is what I meant. A place where it would be hard for Attila to jump on me without a lot of cameras picking it up.

Pyrros nodded. "I will tell Ilir."

"What the hell is an Ilir?" Miles asked.

"He is your fourth man," Pyrros said.

"When did that happen?" Carl asked.

"When you asked for half the money up front," Pyrros said. "I am not handing over that kind of money without someone to be there to make sure I get what I paid for."

I expected as much. There was no way I could say no to this. If I showed any kind of friction, Pyrros would take it to mean that I had some kind of scam in mind. It was a good play, but it was a pawn I was ready to give up. "He's on your payroll, not ours."

"Agreed," Pyrros said.

"Tomorrow, Len," I said.

Len looked to Pyrros before he nodded to me.

I was in the doorway when Pyrros spoke to my back.

"Did you ever hear the one about the thief who robbed the gangster?"

I turned and looked at the gangster. He wasn't squeezing the ball anymore — he was passing it back and forth in his hands sort of like a cat playing with a ball of yarn. I shook my head.

"No? It's a good one, a classic. These three thieves rob a card game. They come in wearing masks, guns out, screaming all kinds of typical stick-up talk. You know how it goes. 'Freeze,' 'Nobody move,' 'Fuck this,' and 'Fuck that.' Well, at the card table are a bunch of men who used to be the kind of guys who yelled, 'Fuck this' and 'Fuck that.' But now, these guys are respectable — sort of. So these three masked men start taking money off the table. They start with the pot and then start taking what each of the card players has in front of them. When they get to last man, he looks at the one who seems to be the leader and says, 'Do you know who you are fucking with?' The thief says, 'No,' because he really doesn't. The older criminal says, 'We were pulling stick-ups before you were born, you little shit. We were all full of piss and vinegar. We were young and stupid. We were you.' The thief hits the man with his gun like this —"

Pyrros lifted the ball in his hand and slammed it into his fist.

"The thief says, 'If you were me then you should have seen that coming.'"

Miles chuckled, but he was the only one; not even Len laughed. Miles looked at everyone and said, "What? It was a good line."

Pyrros holds up a hand. "I'm getting to the best part. So he hits the older man with the gun. He says his clever line. Then the three men run with the money. The next day the five old men meet back at the same table. Only this time, there are eight players. The five from the night before are there and so are the three thieves. The old men brought more money, and the thieves had the money they stole. The game went on all night. The thieves were playing like shit. Mostly, they complained that the rope around their ankles and chest hurt, but they had a lot of money and the game went on. When the first thief ran out of money, they made him bet his clothes. The same happened to the second man. When they ran out of clothes, they bet body parts. Teeth first, then fingers, toes, cock, balls, arms, finally legs. When they ran out of body parts they went out the back door still tied to their chairs to settle up. The last thief left was the one with the clever line. The five old men took his money bit by bit, then his teeth, then his fingers and toes. It was the one he hit who took the rest. He won the cock with two pair, the balls with a flush, and the arms and legs with a full house. And as they were dragging the last thief out, the older man said —"

Pyrros waved a hand in the air.

"What did I say, Len?"

Len looked as sober as a kid on the first day of school. "You said to the thief, 'I meant what I said. You are just like me when I was your age. The problem with being a young me is that I didn't learn how to cheat at poker until I was in my forties.'"

"Tell them the best part, Len. Tell them what happened next."

Len paused for a second, not for effect. There was a look of strain on his face as though the memory was something heavy and hard to move. "You dragged the table into the back room and you made me, let me, play poker with you while they took the thief apart. It lasted hours."

Pyrros looked at me, the stress ball loose in his hand. "And that is the one about the thief who robbed the gangster."

No one laughed. No one said a word.

"Get it?"

CHAPTER TWELVE

MONDAY

Nine a.m. in a casino is an interesting time of day. It's too early for casual gamblers and the all-nighters have usually crashed just after breakfast. What's left is a leper colony of the lonely and the addicted. I sat at the table with Miles and Carl playing my fifth hand of poker. I had been watching Miles and Carl more than my cards. Carl was playing it conservative while Miles aggressively pushed the pace and the bets. The seat I chose was against the wall and it gave me a clear 180-degree view of the floor. I had already looked over the staff and the sparse crowd of gamblers before I sat down. None of them gave me any notice; they were all focused on the slots or the cards.

I had just folded my sixth hand when I saw Len and Ilir. Len had opted for a blue lightweight suit and another open-collar shirt. The black bag over his shoulder looked like an unorthodox piece of luggage. Ilir wore jeans and a tight black T-shirt that showed off a well-defined chest and thick arms.

Miles caught sight of Len and Ilir a few seconds later. "Our guys are here," he said.

I nodded.

Carl turned his head and looked at the two men approaching our table. He gave them a few seconds of thought and then went back to looking at his cards. He pushed five ten-dollar chips towards the centre of the table and said, "Raise fifty."

Miles' head snapped back to the table. He didn't look at his cards; he looked at Carl. After a second he pushed fifty into the pot. I folded.

Len took the vacant seat next to me; he put the bag down between us and nodded to me when our eyes met. Ilir took the empty chair next to Carl. We all watched the dealer turn the last card over in the river. Neither of the men holding cards said a thing. Carl just gave his cards another look. Miles, his head cocked slightly like a bird perched on a power line watching a field for mice, kept his eyes on Carl.

Carl raised again, and Miles followed. When it was time to turn the cards, Carl said, "Shit."

Miles took the pot with a pair of deuces.

"You have enough for the buy-in, Len?" I asked.

"I can cover it," Len said.

Len played two hands poorly before excusing himself. He left without the bag, and without Ilir. We went a few more hands; Carl tried another bluff, but Miles saw it coming and folded. The next hand Carl baited Miles until the pot was fat. Then he went all in and Miles followed suit. Carl took the pot with a flush.

"Shit," Miles said as he examined his diminished stacks of chips. "How much did I just give up?"

"Most of it," Carl said. The driver smiled; the expression made his moustache look even wider while he collected the chips. I stood and shouldered the bag. The money was heavy and it dug into my shoulder. I slid back the zipper and peeked inside at the bound stacks of cash in the bag while everyone else got up from the table and collected what they had left on the felt.

"We're good," I said. "Let's go cash out."

CHAPTER THIRTEEN

Ilir was surprised when we passed the exit; he didn't say anything, but his head starting moving more than it had when we left the poker table. When we walked into the buffet dining room, he spoke up, "What are we doing here?"

"Breakfast," I said taking the seat with the best view of the entrance.

"Most important meal of the day," Miles said as he took a chair opposite me.

Carl sat beside me and Ilir took the last seat. He craned his head around to take in the buffet, but it might have been to sneak a look at the entrance for a friend. I watched the entrance. Breakfast had been going all morning, so the initial rush of hungry gamblers was over. Now stragglers came in to fuel for the day or to feed the hangover dragging its nails down the chalkboard behind their eyes. No one came in alone, and none of the pairs stopped short when they suddenly spotted Ilir and his three new companions. I rested a foot on the bag at my feet and thought about the money. Coming up with four hundred thousand in cash is no small feat when the window is so short. That put a number of people in the know beyond Pyrros, Len, and Ilir. That kind of money in cash, in a bag, makes people greedy. Done right, a snatch could be the perfect crime. Pyrros wouldn't be offended because the money wasn't technically stolen from him — once it changed hands it was our responsibility. We wouldn't be in a position to go after the robbers either because we had such a cramped time frame to get the job done in. The more I considered the bag at my feet, the more I thought there could have been a chance that Pyrros would send someone after the money himself. He was livid when the price of the job changed and even angrier about being forced to pay half up front. Taking fifty percent of the money back would make the job a much easier pill to swallow for the Albanian gangster.

A waitress came by the table and I told her that all four of us would be taking the buffet.

"Great choice, guys. Can I get you something to drink?"

Everyone ordered a coffee except Ilir; he wanted iced tea.

"Seriously?" Ilir said. "We're eating."

"Best breakfast for an hour in any direction," I lied. "Miles, show him."

Miles got up and Ilir followed suit. I listened to the con man's loud voice as he walked the kid to the egg station. "So how do you spell 'Ilir'? One 'e,' or two. None? Get the hell out of here."

Our coffee showed up and I let the waitress pour and make chit chat before I bent over to give the contents of the bag a closer examination. I brought out a banded stack of twenties and held it in my lap while I went through the bills with my thumb.

"Everything cool?" Carl asked.

"Money is all here," I said.

Carl took a sip of the black coffee. "We here to see if anyone else is?"

I nodded.

"I can think of a few reasons why someone might be tagging along behind us."

"I can think of four hundred thousand reasons," I said.

Carl chuckled and took another drink of coffee. "Better odds than the slots," he said.

Miles and Ilir came back. "Guess who's never been to a breakfast buffet before?"

I looked at the pyramid of cinnamon rolls on Ilir's plate. He saw me look and defended his choice. "They're free, man. Totally free. It's awesome."

"Amateur," Miles said. "You'll learn, kid."

"I'm not a kid," Ilir shot back through a mouth full of sugar and pastry.

"Says the kid who scraped the icing sugar off the side of the container," Miles said back.

"You said there was no rule against that."

Miles laughed as he popped a piece of bacon into his mouth. Carl went up a minute later and came back with eggs, bacon, and toast.

"Live it up, Carl," Miles said.

Carl gave the con man the finger and started in on the food like a kid cramming for a test — head down, no talking.

"You not eating?" Ilir asked.

I shook my head.

Ilir wiped at his mouth with a napkin and drained the rest of his iced tea. "I'm going again."

When the Albanian was away from the table, Miles said, "I like him."

Ilir put down three more plates of food before I was satisfied we didn't have any chaperones. I paid the cheque and walked with the three men to the parking garage. No one followed us. We took the elevator to the second-lowest level. When the doors opened, I stepped out first and gave the garage a once-over. When I was sure it was clear, I nodded to the men in the elevator and then walked down the ramp to the lowest level. In the corner was a black Ford Explorer. The suv was dirty and the tires looked a little bald, but so did the driver. I smacked the hood twice, heard the locks release, and then opened the rear door. I put the bag in the trunk, slammed the door, and stepped out of the way. The suv revved to life and then backed out of the spot. The Ford reversed just enough to clear the cars on either side and then accelerated towards the exit. As the suv hit the ramp, I caught site of Ox in profile and then he was gone.

"What was that?" Ilir asked.

"Can't take a bag full of money across the border," I said as I walked to the vehicle that had been parked next to the Ford. Carl opened the doors with a set of keys and got behind the wheel of the dark green Jeep. Miles got in behind him and I took the other rear seat. Ilir took the only seat left.

"So who was that guy?" Ilir asked.

"Safe deposit box on wheels," I said.

"A lot of money to trust a guy with."

"There's not enough in there to make running the rest of your life worth it," I said.

"People have done more for less," Ilir said.

"Not to me."

By now, Ox was halfway to a storage space parking lot where he would check the bag for anything that wasn't cash. After he was sure that the money was clean, he would take it back to his place where he would lock it up in a safe hidden under the floorboards. After we crossed back over the border in a few hours, Ox would meet us in the city to hand the bag back over.

The Jeep started with a smooth purr that should have been foreign to a vehicle so old and so American, but Carl was a driver, and like all drivers he was a gear-head. He had worked on the Jeep and turned it into something special that no one would notice unless they sat inside the cab. Carl wound the Jeep through the garage with the precision of a shark gliding through water. We paid at the gate and rolled onto Fallsview Boulevard without feeling the bump of the curb.

"You handle the car well, Carl," I said.

"Better than I do most things. I drive semis cross-country most of the time. This other stuff just supplements."

"Supplements what?" Ilir asked. It was a rude question, like asking someone how much they made, but the kid wouldn't know that.

Carl's face didn't flash any sign of annoyance in the rear-view. He inhaled deeply through his nose and let it out slowly as he changed lanes. "My kid is sick and we need to travel out of the country for the kind of treatment he needs. I do alright hauling things back and forth across the country, but alright doesn't mean the same thing when you apply it to a stack of medical bills. Being a wheelman is the only way I can keep all the plates spinning, y'know?"

"So you're pretty good?" Ilir said.

It was another question people didn't ask. Carl was good because he was on the job; no one takes on someone they can't count on, not anyone good anyway. Ilir not knowing that instantly brought everyone in the car up to speed about the young Albanian.

Carl hooked around a senior citizen taking his Caddy out for a drive. "If I was, you would never know. A good driver gets people away clean. If they get away clean, there aren't any headlines. No headlines means no reputation."

"That a yes or a no?"

"I'm good, kid."

"I'm no kid, old man."

"No?" Carl asked.

"Young man fancies himself a grown-up," Miles said.

"I am a grown-up," Ilir said in a tone that came out whinier than he probably wanted it to. "I'm a fucking gangster."

Carl and Miles made eye contact in the mirror and started laughing.

"What's so funny?"

"Nothing, kid," I said. "The word gangster just doesn't command the kind of respect it used to."

"Not in this car at least," Miles said.

"If my uncle were here, you wouldn't say that."

"He might say it for us," I said. "After all, he's neck-deep in gangsters and yet he went looking for an outside crew to do this job."

Carl laughed as he hooked around a red Pontiac and got onto the Queen Elizabeth Expressway.

"That's 'cause we're working in Buffalo," Ilir said.

"What does that mean?"

"Nothing," Ilir said, but the speed with which he said the word meant the opposite.

"Sounds like somebody's got a secret," Miles said. "Care to share with the rest of the class, Ilir? What's in Buffalo? Other than overpriced instruments of course."

"Forget it."

Outside the Jeep, I could see that traffic on the expressway was moving smoothly. The swarm of cars was like a herd of aerodynamic animals. "Pull over," I said.

Carl was good. He didn't argue, and he didn't ask what I meant. He slipped into the middle lane and eased off the gas. The second the car riding in the Jeep's blind spot moved ahead, Carl drifted through the opening and onto the side of the road. The driver's movements were so smooth and precise, there was not one car that had to adjust for the Jeep; the herd just kept on pushing forward at a hundred twenty kilometres per hour.

"This is just like when Dad used to pull over on vacations because me and my brother wouldn't stop fighting," Miles said.

"I doubt it," I said as I went up and over the seat. My right arm snaked around Ilir's head and held him firm against the headrest while my left hand unlocked the seat belt. With the belt off, I used both hands around the gangster's neck to pull him over the front seat and into the back with me and Miles. Ilir bucked and kicked the roof as his hands clawed at his closed windpipe, but he couldn't do a thing to keep his body up front. I clamped down hard on Ilir's neck with my left arm and used my right to pull the door handle. The door opened a crack and bright daylight put a line across the Albanian's forehead.

"What the hell is this?"

I used the Albanian's head to push the door open another inch. Through the rear window I could see a green Toyota Corolla riding the line about a kilometre back — Ilir saw it at eye level. I gave him time to watch the car approaching; then, at the last second, I gave him a shove. His head and shoulders left the vehicle as though he were being birthed by the Jeep. The driver of the Toyota had no time to react or swerve, and all Ilir could do was watch the automotive guillotine slice the air six inches above his head instead of his neck. He screamed, but the sounds of traffic drowned him out. When I pulled him in, he was pale, not like he'd seen a ghost pale — like he was a ghost pale.

"I'm going to ask you again, Ilir. What is in Buffalo?"

I could see Ilir's face reflected in the side window. He was using his two bulging eyes to look to Carl for help. None was coming.

"Last chance, Ilir. What is in Buffalo?"

"My uncle —"

"Should know better than to keep us out of the loop. What is in Buffalo?"

Ilir said nothing.

"A Ford is coming up," Miles said. "Good news, it's red. The blood won't show. Well, good news for them anyway."

I pushed Ilir back to the door. The second his forehead began to crown into the daylight, he broke.

"The Albanians in Buffalo," he screamed.

I pulled him into the car and closed the door. "Go," I said.

Carl let his foot off the brake. The creases in the concrete lane-divider to our left began to click by faster and faster. Carl let the red Toyota pass us and then we were on the highway again. The Jeep thanked its master for the chance to run with a mechanical purr from under the hood.

"Buffalo Albanians? I thought they only had chicken wings," Miles said.

"They hate us!" Ilir was screaming like he was outside instead of on my lap.

I righted the gangster and forced him into the small spot between Miles and myself. "Spill it," I said.

Ilir put his head in his hands. The adrenalin was still pumping hard and his lungs were struggling to keep up with the beating of his heart. "Jesus Christ."

"Deep breaths," I said.

"Shut the fuck up, James."

"That's not my name."

"What?"

"My name isn't James. It's Wilson. Now you know something about me. Return the favour, Ilir."

"My favourite colour is blue," Miles contributed.

"Like that," I said, "but better."

"The crew in Buffalo have hated our side for generations.

It all goes back to the mother country. We work with each other on certain things, but there are rules. There are rules on top of rules. They don't let us operate on their turf and we don't let them onto ours. If they found out we crossed the border for a job, they would want a cut. *If* they knew about this. What we're after — they would kill us."

"Why would they care about a violin?"

"It's not the violin, it's who is going to get it."

"Who's the buyer?"

"No one is buying it," Ilir said. "It's going to be a gift."

The road signs let me know that the border was coming up. "Buy us some time, Carl."

"Got it," Carl said from up front. The Jeep slid through traffic like breeze through an open window. We pulled into a carpool parking lot and stopped. Carl left the engine idling.

"Give me a name."

"You won't know him," Ilir said.

"A name, Ilir."

"Arben Malota."

"Never heard of him," Carl said.

"I bet Arben Malota is probably like John Smith over there," Miles said.

"There is only one that matters," Ilir said.

"Why is Pyrros giving a violin to this guy, and why would it matter to the Albanians on the other side if no money is changing hands?" I said.

"Because Arben is going to retire soon and he has not named a successor. Both families, ours and Buffalo, have stakes in the outcome. We both have family back home who are next in line."

"So the violin is meant to tip the scales in your favour," I said.

Ilir nodded. "Now, you know everything."

I got out of the car. "Out," I said.

Ilir was slow to move, so Miles gave him a shove. He tentatively got out of the Jeep, keeping his eyes on me the whole time.

"Why are you involved?" I said. "If Pyrros wants to keep this quiet, why involve you? Len was already in the loop, so why add someone else lower on the food chain?"

Ilir didn't answer.

Miles leaned out the open door. "Do you really want to play Whac-A-Mole on the highway again, kid?"

"He wants me to watch you to make sure that you don't decide to sell the violin to another buyer."

"Why you?"

Ilir sighed, "I am his nephew. He trusts me. This whole thing, going outside our crew, was my idea."

"Smart kid," Carl said.

"I'm not a kid," Ilir said.

"He's a gangster," Miles said. "An important one, from the sounds of it. A gang star."

"Ilir, here, went outside for help once," I said. "It worked then, so he thought, 'Why wouldn't it work again?'"

Ilir looked at me. It was a pretty good hard stare. I was sure it could have scared some portion of the civilian population to cross to the other side of the street, but out here, a few clicks from the border in front of a car full of men who had stopped being intimidated by looks long ago, it was a waste of time. "That's right," he said.

"Is getting this violin important to you?" I asked.

"Yeah."

"'Yeah' is how you answer when someone asks you if you want to supersize your meal. It doesn't belong in this conversation. Is this job important to you?"

Ilir nodded. "It is."

"Pyrros held out on us, and you went along with it. If this little outing is going to work, you need to be up front about everything."

"You didn't need to know who the violin was for, only that you would be paid for it."

I took Ilir by the throat so fast his hard stare was still there when he landed on his ass. The scary look disappeared when I put the Albanian's head in the corner of the open door. I took a grip just under the window and closed the door on his head. The door stopped all at once, but I kept pushing. "You don't get to tell us what we need to know and what we don't."

Ilir screamed, but no one who heard him cared.

"I want you to listen close, gangster. Pop quiz, Miles and Carl. Ilir doesn't mention who the violin is intended for. How could this affect us?"

Ilir's eyes bulged in his head as the door closed another half of an inch.

Miles leaned over and looked at Ilir. "I got this," he said.

"We could end up bumping into another crew going after the same thing as us," Carl said.

"I was going to say that," Miles said as he slumped back into his spot in a mock snit.

"Correct, Carl, you get a gold star."

"You ever think about that, Ilir?"

The gangster didn't respond.

"Speak!"

"No."

I let the pressure off the kid's head and he slid onto the pavement cradling his skull.

I looked into the interior of the Jeep. "This change anything for either of you?"

Miles shook his head; Carl gave it some thought. Eventually, the driver shook his head too.

"If this job is important to you, then it's important enough to get over being shoved around. You can get back in the car, or you can walk up the road to whatever is over that hill. But if you get in, *you get in*. Understand?"

Ilir only stared.

"You're a gangster," I said. "Problem is we don't need a gangster — we need a heist man. Can you be that?"

"I told you I'm a gangster, not some punk."

"I said heist man, not gangster."

"What's the difference?"

Miles laughed from inside the Jeep. Ilir turned his head and then gave up on the idea and grabbed at his newly sore neck.

"Gangsters are all about telling the world how tough they are and bullshit fights over turf. That's why Pyrros wants the violin; for turf and rep. A heist man is about the job. He does it for money, not pride, or vanity."

Ilir looked unsure about what to say.

"I'm asking you if you want to be a gangster on this job or a heist man. A gangster would want revenge for his pride being bruised. A heist man would understand that secrets are dangerous to the job and get over it. A gangster would worry about his rep. A heist man would get back to work."

I stepped over the kid and got into the back seat. In a minute, Ilir got off the ground and made his choice. He got back into the Jeep. "Let's go," he said.

CHAPTER FOURTEEN

The line at the Peace Bridge was moving at a steady pace; unfortunately, it was the pace of a paraplegic learning to walk again. A posted sign told us to have our passports and identification ready. I pulled the document with the name Adam Worth printed on the inside next to my picture and waited. Adam Worth didn't live or breathe, not anymore, but digitally he was an active, upstanding citizen. When I uprooted myself and moved to Toronto, the name I had been using died. On my way out of the city, I stopped at a mailbox I kept and retrieved a package I had hidden inside in a false back. The package contained all of Adam Worth's ID and papers, and all of it was one hundred percent legit. My uncle was a man who lived his life with his eye on the door — always ready to move and never look back. Growing up he had taught me to always think moves ahead, and as I got better at the game I began to think moves ahead of the moves ahead.

"How far can you run if it all goes south?" he once asked me while we were sitting in a four-door sedan watching for a bookie to leave a bar.

I looked over at my uncle and saw that he had not taken his eyes off the street to ask me. I went back to staring at the bar. "I have enough to get by for a year, maybe more."

"What if it was more?"

"I could stretch it."

"This year or more include the price you would have to pay for new ID?"

I shook my head. My uncle didn't look at me, but he knew that I shook it.

"I could lay low," I said.

"For a year, but what if you need a year and a half? What if you need two?"

"There are ways to make money," I said.

"But then you ain't laying low." My uncle went quiet after that. He was somehow able to create a silence so heavy that it made his presence almost impossible to notice even when he was right next to me. In that silence, I watched the street and thought about what my uncle had said. There was a lesson in his words — there was always a lesson.

"How long can you run?" I asked.

My uncle's cheek twitched as a familiar grin formed on his face. A grin that was cold like the chill that finds its way down the back of your neck — a mean cold grin. "You would run because you'd have no choice — me, I would disappear. There would be no trail to follow because like that —" The snap of his calloused fingers sounded like a hammer being cocked. "I would cease to exist."

My uncle turned to look at me for the first time in a long time. Something he read on my face didn't sit well.

"You dream?"

"When I was little, not anymore," I said.

"But you remember it, right? The dreams."

I nodded. "Some of them."

"You ever have a nightmare? Not a bad dream, but a real nightmare. The kind where you wake up and start running because you're sure whatever was after you ain't done yet."

I remembered something like that. It was after my parents had died and I had moved in with my uncle. I had outgrown monsters under my bed and bad dreams — at least I thought I had. The nightmare was something I never forgot. It was as though the bad dream had been written into my memory in permanent marker. I had been fifteen then, and I hadn't thought about it for years, but the simple mention of it there in that car brought every detail back as though I was still that young boy under the covers on that strange bed inside that foreign house. I remembered the nightmare as well as I remembered my own name, but I said nothing to my uncle.

He read the silence right. "Yeah, you know the kind I mean. There's a moment when you're running. This one instant where you realize that there is nothing behind you. That whatever had been chasing you is gone, but gone isn't the right word because it didn't really exist in the first place. At least, not the way other things exist."

I stared at the street and tried not to let my memories show on my face.

"When things go bad, because they will one day, as

things always do, I will cease to exist like that thing that chased you out of your bed. I will vanish into nothing because I never really existed like everyone else to begin with. That is the difference between me and you. But it doesn't have to be."

I didn't answer my uncle, and that was fine with him. He wasn't lying; he never did. He would disappear, but it wouldn't be like my nightmare. The monster that had chased me in my nightmare hadn't faded away. It hadn't stopped existing when I turned around. The monster that followed me out of bed in those moments between sleep and waking that night wasn't some dark shadow, or fanged demon. It was the man sitting in the seat beside me. The monster became my world until eventually I became it.

Learning the difference between running and vanishing took years. The final step began on the streets. I spent nights on the streets moving from steam grates to alleys to shelters until on the third day I found what I needed. Six-two, brown hair, late twenties. Samuel Bennett came to the city to go to university. He had a good thing going until the dormant schizophrenia broke the surface like a malfunctioning periscope. It took the mental illness two years to undo twenty years of eating vegetables, listening to Mom and Dad, studying hard, and playing fair. Just over five years later, Samuel was a junkie fresh out of a fifth discharge from the psych ward. He had a vial of dwindling prescription medication in his pocket and hepatitis. I pulled Samuel off the streets and put him up in a clean place. I paid for it, furnished it, and kept it stocked with food. I didn't need Samuel to stay in it; he just needed to be there long enough for a few things to happen. I convinced him, with enough cash for a generous fix, to clean up. I cut his hair and deloused him but left his shaggy beard in place. A few days later, the promise of another handful of bills bought me his company for the afternoon. We visited four government offices and applied for all of the pieces of ID that Samuel had let lapse. The next day, I changed the locks. Samuel dropped back off the grid, while I waited for the new ID to show up in the mail.

If Samuel Bennett had a personal motto, it would have been: life starts at twenty-eight. On paper, Samuel suddenly bloomed into existence after a long hibernation. A few months later Samuel Bennett vanished again when he legally changed his name to Adam Worth. His face was close enough to mine that no one questioned the ID. The absence of a beard was such a huge difference that it eclipsed any other small discrepancies between my face and Samuel's. The government clerk completing my application took one look at the bearded man in the photo, made a joke about how my chin must have felt cold all of a sudden, and processed the application. The new name obscured the medical history from casual searches, and soon after I was in possession of a clean identity.

Identities, like living things, require attention to stay alive. Adam Worth paid taxes, had an income, had credit cards, got parking tickets. He shopped online and he even travelled domestically. Within a year of the name change, Adam was as real as anyone else. After a decade, he was more respectable than a large percentage of the population.

I wasn't worried about the ID holding up. I had tested it at the border a couple of times. It had been a risk, but necessary. The papers on Adam Worth were for when the wheels came off. When that happened, crossing the border would be a logical first step. On the run was no time to take my stolen identity out for a test drive. I crossed over at peak hours and got nothing more than a glance into the back seat. On the way back, I got less than that. My papers were solid.

I watched the cars in the lanes beside me first on the left and then on the right. No one had four men inside. There were families, couples, and single drivers. The car was going to stick out. I looked from man to man — no one was fidgeting or looking nervous, not even Ilir.

A new window opening to our immediate right shot us to second in line. The car in front of us had barely stopped before it was waved through. Carl said, "Looks like we got a good lane," before he stepped on the gas.

"Keep your answers short," I said out loud, but really just to Ilir. "Any questions are for Carl unless the guy asks you directly."

The Jeep stopped next to the window and the border cop said, "Passports please." The woman who collected the four documents was short, maybe five-two, with red hair and a deep tan — the lifelong kind that would eventually erode wrinkles deep into her face. She already had plenty around her mouth and eyes — too many for a woman in her forties. Pretty was long gone; now, she was fighting against ugly with all her might. The border cop checked the passports and then went to the computer to run the vehicle. When she finished typing, she craned her neck to look inside the car. The tinted windows gave her some trouble and earned the back seat extra attention.

"Purpose of visit?"

Carl shifted in his seat a little and said, "We're all going to an information session at Samaritan College."

"What kind of information session?" The woman asked the question with no sign of personal interest.

"It's on adult education," Carl said.

The cop's eyes narrowed on Ilir. "All of you?"

Miles leaned through the gap between the two front seats. "We all got laid off a month or so back. We're going to this session to figure out if we meet the criteria for a second career in a different field."

Miles' good looks were like a whirlpool that pulled in attention instead of water. The border cop forgot about Carl and focused on the con man. "What field?" She wasn't flirting, but she wasn't ignoring him either.

Miles smiled a genuine-looking smile — the kind the Grinch smiled when his heart grew two sizes too big. "Don't laugh, but we're looking into nursing."

The border agent didn't laugh, she didn't crack more than a thin smile, but that was okay — the fractional smile was all the opening Miles needed. "The company we worked for shipped off the whole operation to Mexico. The whole factory is being outsourced. Manufacturing is dying back home. The only thing growing is health care." Miles put a hand on Carl's shoulder. "That's 'cause guys like this mug over here are keeping them in business. He's had a heart attack, and kidney stones twice. They say it's the salt that does it. It was the last bout that gave us the idea of coming here. We were in visiting our sick friend here when the nurse comes in to check his vitals. After she left, I said, 'Hell, the kid,'" Miles gave Ilir's shoulder a playful shake. "'He could do that.' Then, it dawned on me. We could all do that. Good money, good pension, good —"

The border agent cut him off by extending her arm and the four passports. "Have a good day, sir."

Miles looked as though he was suddenly embarrassed for talking too much. "You too, ma'am. And thanks for not laughing."

Carl eased on the gas and rolled away from the window. He was careful to leave the window down until we were fifty metres from the cop sheds. "That was good, Miles," Carl said. "Real good."

Carl was wrong; it was better than good. The talking was on point, personal but without any real details, and — most importantly — he never used names. Carl was his "sick friend" and Ilir was "kid." Miles saw that Carl's mechanic responses were drawing more attention than they were meant to, and he must have realized that questions for each of us were coming. Four people meant a high probability of a mistake and a mistake at the border would have meant an end to the job.

"Thanks, Carl, but it was easy. The way she was check-ing you out, I could have said anything and she would have waved us through. She was captivated by you, buddy. I think it's the moustache. You and me should hit a few bars when this is over. I could be your wingman. Or we could both grow moustaches. Think of the trouble we could cause then. Ilir, can you grow a moustache?"

Carl turned the radio up loud enough to drown out Miles.

CHAPTER FIFTEEN

At ten minutes to curtain, the concert hadn't sold out. From the look of the last-minute turnout, there was little chance it would. The show was in its fourth and final week and everyone who had wanted to see blown-up mascot-sized versions of their child's favourite television characters had already shown up and done their time in kiddie gen-pop. The final concert was the only show at the Samuel Hall for the next three days. We had no choice but to stop there first.

We got an odd look from the teenager working the ticket booth. There was no way around it, really. If we bought tickets alone, or in pairs, it still would have seemed odd. Four men buying twelve tickets at once was the best option. It said we were each with two other people, and most people's brains would automatically assume a wife and child. We each pitched in fifty bucks and I slid the money through the small opening in the Plexiglas divider separating the teenager from the customers.

The change came back with a few small bills, some coins, and a suspicious glance.

"We're not into kids," Miles said.

The teenager looked surprised, but unconvinced.

"Seriously, it's the puppets we're into. It's a fetish. I don't know if it's the life-sized thing, or the softness, but —"

I cut in. "Quit being an asshole and go find the kids before they all have to pee again."

Carl pulled Miles away. I watched the con man go for a split second and realized that what I was looking at was a natural talker. He had probably been a con man when he was five. He had a gift, the same kind of thing Gretzky or Jordan had when they were kids. The difference was Gretzky and Jordan had a system they had to work their way through before they became pros. Con men don't have a farm team before they get to the big leagues. Miles had probably gotten by on talent his whole life. But he would need more than just talent if he ever wanted to do more than get by.

I leaned in to the voice box installed in the Plexiglas. "Sorry, kid, he's just pissed he had to come today. We had to listen to the music on the way in, discuss the best characters on the way from the car. Tommy just wants to get in enough trouble to get his butt sent to the car. That way he can sit there and listen to a game on the radio instead of the 'Banana Song' for the hundredth time."

The kid laughed. "I get it, man. I get it. I've been listening to this stuff for weeks. I'm about ready to kill myself."

I left the ticket booth and found Miles standing with Carl and Ilir a few feet from the stairs leading up to the theatre floor. The three men turned when I caught up and then started walking. I tilted my head towards Miles and spoke just loud enough for him to hear. "You're good with your mouth, better than most I've met. But you need to learn when to open your mouth and when to keep it shut. We need to spend some time here looking around, and that won't be easy if some kid at the ticket booth thinks we're into kids and lets every usher know where we are. And nothing sets off someone's radar like a person denying something. You say you're not into kids, he automatically thinks you are. And once someone forms a thought about you, it's next to impossible to change it."

Miles looked at me; the glibness was gone. Underneath the smiles and jokes he wore like armour was something else. Something I had not seen before.

"Kid touchers are shy," I said. "Did you know that? They try their damndest to go unnoticed, but their size on the playground always gives them away. The one thing they never do on their own is engage with people. The second they engage, they open themselves up to questions they can't answer."

I stopped talking long enough to hand my ticket to an elderly usher. She gestured towards the rear of the theatre and we set off.

"Why would four men of varying ages go see a children's concert?"

"I have no idea," Miles said.

"Exactly. No one does. The burden isn't on you to invent a reason. If you put an idea into someone's head, their brain pulls at it like it's a loose thread hanging from a sweater. But if you let them come up with the idea on their own, they leave it be. Short eyes want to go unnoticed, right?"

Miles nodded.

"So get noticed. Let the teller notice you doing something that they wouldn't do. Something like showing up in a group and buying a bunch of tickets. The kid behind the glass gave us a look, but that's all it was — a look. He wasn't concerned, or angry — just momentarily interested. His brain was writing a script and he would have bought his own fiction until he forgot about us. Except you —"

"Put a word into his head."

I nodded. "You would have been better off to talk about something that is considered safe to the masses. Something in the opposite spectrum of deviancy."

"Like sports," Miles said.

"Like sports," I said. "Sports are based on teamwork, fair play, family. Sports don't occupy the same space as child molestation in the public's perception. People don't really know child molesters, you can count on that, but they are well versed in what they saw on *Law & Order*. That kind of knowledge has a rigid structure — things are black or white. If you know that, you can bypass all of the triggers and they will automatically file you into some other category."

Miles nodded again. "Most jobs don't have heart-to-hearts like these."

I ignored the con man as we approached another usher checking tickets and helping people find their seats. I spoke first. "I swear to God, if they don't lose Jeter, I'm going to become a Red Sox fan."

Miles picked up where I left off. "You're crazy. It's not Jeter's fault. They got no defence."

The usher took my ticket and I caught his eye. "Tell my brother he's crazy."

The usher was another senior citizen. The old man was likely a pensioner supplementing a meagre income with some work that required little movement. "I like Jeter," he said. "I like those girls he brings to the game, too." The old man laughed and everyone joined in. Everyone except me.

"That's the fucking problem," I said. "He's too focused on the girls instead of the game."

The language sobered the usher and he glanced around to make sure none of the kids had heard the word I had used. He pulled out of the conversation all together and went for a gesture instead. He pointed out our seats and waved us on. We stopped at our row of seats and turned to survey the chaos. Kids were everywhere — running in the aisles, eating out of reusable containers, crying, and pulling their parents towards the washroom. Floating in the sea of chaos were vested ushers doing their best to keep everyone sitting down.

"Miles, Carl," I said. "You need to use the washroom. On the way, see if you can get backstage passes."

"Got it," Carl said understanding my meaning.

When they left, Ilir said, "So you're in charge, hunh."

"Miles can get pensioners to sign over everything they worked their whole lives to earn. Getting backstage at a children's concert should be boring for him. We'll be lucky if he doesn't get antsy and decide to pick someone's pocket."

"So what are we doing?"

"I need to get upstairs and into those offices," I said.

"What about me?"

"You stay here and get the lay of the land. I want to know how this place operates. Where do the ushers stand? Where do the performers enter and leave from? Are there places in and out that we don't know about?"

"Alright, no problem," Ilir said. He wasn't giving me his full attention. The ass of the young mother two rows up from us was siphoning about seventy-five percent. "No problem."

Free of my partner, I walked out into the aisle. I scanned the crowd and saw Miles and Carl speaking with one of the ushers. Miles took something from his pocket and showed it to the usher. A few seconds later, the usher was guiding Miles backstage with a helping hand on his back. I grinned at the con man and then started back for the lobby. There was what looked like a last surge of people flooding in before the curtain was set to rise. Everywhere employees were busy working or answering questions. I flagged down the most exasperated-looking person wearing a name tag I could find. The woman was in her mid-forties and not wearing a red vest like the other old ushers. The woman had brown hair streaked heavily with blonde and too much mascara. She had a walkie-talkie in her hand and frowned at my interruption. "I'm with the show. Tom needs to speak with the person in charge ASAP."

The woman looked up at me and was unable to mask her confusion.

"Tom?"

"He manages the show, and he is not happy with the way things are going backstage. It's like no one even read the rider. He wants to speak with whoever is in charge."

"What seems to be the trouble?" the woman, already going into damage control, said.

"I don't know all of the details. I just know that Tom is freaking out and he is demanding to see whoever is in charge."

"Okay, okay," she said running a hand through her hair. "I can radio Mr. Dickens and he can call your boss right now."

I shook my head. "Nuh unh. It won't be enough, not for Tom anyway. He wants a face-to-face." I lowered my voice and leaned in a little bit. "I shouldn't tell you this, but Tom has a habit of suing venues. The suits are bullshit, but the places always pay up. Don't give him a reason to scream B.O.C."

"B.O.C.?"

"Breach of contract."

"Oh, I see."

She didn't, but she looked worried. "I'll go get Mr. Dickens now."

The woman turned and hustled past the entrances to the floor seats. She finally stopped in front of a door that required a keycard to open it. The woman scanned the card and pulled the door open just enough for her shoulders to slip inside. I had followed her, keeping twenty feet behind, like a lazy bloodhound, and took a spot against the wall. My right hand found the plastic egg inside my pocket and lazily spun it around.

A few minutes later, the door opened, revealing a set of steps just inside. An older man in a finely tailored suit came out ahead of the woman who had gone looking for him. The well-dressed man had a head of snow-white hair that stood out against his dark tanned complexion.

My hand closed around the egg and forced the plastic to quietly pop open. The Silly Putty that had been incubating inside oozed between my fingers. When my hand came out of my pocket, no one noticed the flesh-coloured putty hitching a ride on my palm. I caught the side of the door and politely held it open for the woman with the walkie-talkie while I mashed the putty into the lock. I let the door go after the woman passed me and extended my suddenly empty right hand towards her boss. "Mr. Dickens, nice to meet you. I am with the production and there are some concerns that my manager would like to speak with you about."

"Certainly. I'm sure it's nothing we can't work out."

I gestured for the two employees to lead the way and kept pace. I followed the pair to the theatre entrance, but stopped short when I suddenly had to take a call. It was Dickens who noticed my lag and he turned an exasperated expression in my direction. I held the phone up and shrugged my shoulders as if to say, "What can you do?" Dickens narrowed his eyes and then he turned his back on me and started for backstage.

CHAPTER SIXTEEN

Dickens had not given any sign that he wanted the woman to follow him. She waited, watching him march away from her, until she felt it was clear he wasn't going to ask her to join him. Free of her boss, the woman with the streaked hair pulled the walkie-talkie from her belt and resumed looking frazzled. I, phone to one ear, open palm to the other, weaved through the screaming children in search of a quiet place to take a call. I found my way back to the door Dickens had exited and pulled the handle. The putty had done its job keeping the mechanism from engaging again. I pulled the Silly Putty out of the lock and moved up the stairs two at a time to the second floor.

The second floor had a medium-sized conference room and a number of offices. I could hear people muffled by walls, but still audible because of open doors. I let the stairwell door close and moved up to the third floor. The third floor was the final level and the stairwell door exited onto a long hallway that overlooked the floor of the auditorium. The silence told me that the glass was soundproof. There were two large offices at the end of the hall. The first, locked and dark inside, had the wrong name posted on the door. The second had its door ajar, lights on, a computer still logged in, and a name plate on the door for John Dickens. I gave Dickens another few minutes to realize he had been duped and another couple for him to make his way back to his office — more if he stopped to yell at the woman who got him involved in the trick.

I walked the perimeter of the room and tried the file cabinets only to find them locked. There was a door in the corner of the room that could have either been a private toilet or a closet. It was a closet. It being summer, there was nothing hanging on the rod. Above, on a shallow shelf, was an umbrella with an expensive-looking handle. I closed the closet, took a seat at the desk, and began pulling drawers. There was nothing in the files about the charity event or the violin. I went to the computer next and began a dated search for documents modified in the last seven days. I got multiple hits — most were files related to the operating system, but there were several document files with the word *benefit* or the date of the concert in the title.

I opened the first file in the list and found an updated VIP guest list. The first name on the list was no surprise — Alison Randall, now known in the press as recent widow Alison Randall. Telecommunications magnate and philanthropist Allan Randall had died last week. Part of his estate was left to the ailing Samuel Hall. Samuel Hall was home to the Buffalo Metropolitan Symphony Orchestra and, according to newspapers, one of the last bastions of true classical music in the city. Samuel Hall had been built in the fifties on the waterfront of Lake Erie. The concert hall was built, and survived, on patronage and Allan Randall had been a major benefactor to the hall. He had been personally responsible for rebuilding the stage after a fire had gutted it ten years ago. In death, he was no less generous. Included among the assets left to the organization was the violin — an extremely rare Stradivarius made in 1720. The estate bequeathed the violin with instructions to sell it in order to fund the hall and the orchestra for years to come. The donation ended up occupying a short paragraph in an article about Randall. The short paragraph fathered numerous follow-up stories on the Stradivarius as offer after offer came in. After two days, the Buffalo Met released a statement that the violin had been sold. The buyer was not named, but there was unverified speculation that the Stradivarius had been sold to a buyer representing a Chinese billionaire. The violin had yet to change hands — the Board of Directors of Samuel Hall had made plans to honour Allan Randall and his generosity with a benefit concert. They had secured the world-renowned David Lind to play the famed violin on stage on the night of the benefit. The Stradivarius would change hands after the concert and where it went from there was anyone's guess.

Currently, the violin was still in a vault inside the Randall family home. Allan Randall had built a hermetically sealed vault to house his instruments while he had still been alive to appreciate them. The vault was visible in a fifteen-year-old profile done by a classical music magazine that I had come across online during my research on the contents of the drive given to me by Pyrros in the park. The piece was done before Randall acquired the Stradivarius and featured him standing, arms crossed, in front of a glass case displaying several brass instruments. The writer went on and on about the fact that the vault controlled humidity and dust, thereby keeping the instruments in the ideal conditions. I could tell by looking at the portion of the door that was visible that breaking into the vault would be difficult — impossible if we didn't add a jugger who could tackle something like that to the crew. There was the option of moving on the violin on the day of the concert when it preceded the widow to the show, but moving something like that Stradavarius wouldn't be a toss-in-the-trunk kind of operation. There would be security, likely an armoured truck, involved. The insurance company representing the new owner would demand guarantees of safe transfer; so, probably, would the buyer. Thinking about the layers of security surrounding the violin made me think more and more about the venue. A vault was a single, meant to be impregnable, space, whereas a charity event, planned with just over a week's notice, would be porous and full of mistakes and missteps that could be taken advantage of. I was still going to look at the house and the vault, but I wasn't putting much faith in it.

Below the widow's name were two open spots. There was no indication who was meant to occupy the second and third most important places on the list. I guessed the spots were left open in case the rumoured Chinese buyer and a date decided to show. I gave the list a quick read through before minimizing the window and moving to the next file. It took thirty seconds to find everything else related to the event. I pulled a USB drive from my pocket and went under the desk to insert it. I heard the computer respond with a chime and dragged the files onto the drive. While the computer copied and pasted the documents, I went to the window and looked down at the concert floor. I saw Dickens right away because he was one of the few bodies moving in the wrong direction. The curtain was about to rise and everyone was moving towards their seats. The older man was moving out of sight as he neared the curtained entrance to the seating area. At the pace he was moving, I had maybe a minute tops before he was in his office. I pulled the drive from the CPU and restored the screen to the way I had found it. I got out of the chair, making sure to slide the wheels of the chair back into the grooves indented into the carpet, and then crossed the room and got into the closet.

It took longer than a minute for Dickens to come back — maybe he was out of shape and the stairs presented more of a challenge than I gave him credit for. From the sound of his footsteps, he had barged into his own office. If he had expected to find someone, he must have felt silly seeing the room empty because he didn't look around. I heard the chair groan in a way it hadn't for me when it caught his weight and then angry key strikes that sounded like the peck of a diligent woodpecker. I checked my phone and saw that the show was going to go for an hour and a half. How long Dickens would stick around after that was anyone's guess. I quietly pulled my phone out of my pocket and sent a text to Carl.

Be a little while. Go grab something to eat. I'll let you know when I'm done.

A minute later, I got a silent reply. Carl didn't ask any questions; he just sent back one word:

Sure

I took a slow breath in and let it out. I kept dragging the air slowly into my lungs until it only had to happen twice a minute. Doing the job at the concert hall had potential, and that meant I had to keep from being noticed by the boss. I watched the thoughts form in my mind and efficiently disassembled them. Eventually the thoughts waned, leaving emptiness behind. I set up camp in the emptiness and waited. I could wait for days like that and had before. Although I saw potential in taking the violin from the concert hall, I wasn't yet sold on it — I had to hear what Carl and Miles had seen backstage, and I had to go over the information John Dickens had on his hard drive before I would even consider committing to the location. But the hall did have a major benefit that had to be taken into account: there was no vault.

It ended up being three hours before Dickens got out of the chair. The squeak that came with the release of pressure sounded like a sigh of relief. I heard heavy footsteps as John Dickens moved around the room shuffling papers and opening drawers before shutting them hard. Eventually the sliver of light that had been stabbing into the closet from underneath the door receded, leaving me in total darkness. I stayed exactly where I was and waited another thirty minutes. I had no idea if Dickens was the kind of boss who stopped to talk to the people who worked for him before he left for the day — it was best to wait and reduce my chances of a second face to face with the boss.

I left the closet and walked out of the office, being careful to quietly close the door behind me. Below the balcony windows, I could see that the concert floor was dark. I paused at the top of the stairwell and listened — nothing. I took the steps at a brisk pace, not a run, just the walk of a busy man. If I bumped into anyone on the stairs, I would greet them like I belonged there and keep moving. No one came out of the second floor stairwell door to meet me on my way down. On the ground floor, I looked through the slim rectangular window to the foyer. There wasn't anyone around. I opened the door and walked straight for the closest door. A janitor was down the hall mopping the floor with the bent posture of a man who had done the job ten thousand times before. The man had headphones on and he didn't lift his head to acknowledge my wave. I hit the push bar and stepped into the heat.

CHAPTER SEVENTEEN

"Where are you?"

"At a bar," Carl said. "Not far from where you are. You out?"

"Yeah."

"Give me five minutes."

"I'm not standing out front. I'll start walking towards the city centre on Erie."

"On my way," Carl said.

I heard Miles yell shotgun before the call ended.

Carl rolled up to the curb at close to exactly five minutes from when I started walking. Ilir was up front with him.

"I thought you called shotgun," I said.

"Ilir said you could only call it when you can see the car. Carl agreed with him."

Miles saw the look on my face and spread his hands apologetically. "He was tricky about it. He called shotgun when he saw the car and then told me about the rule. But two guys said it was a rule, so there you go. You have to play by the rules."

"Rules? You're a con man," Ilir said.

"The important rules, kid."

"Any luck?" Carl asked.

"I pulled enough to get us started. I got my hands on a guest list, complete with addresses for the VIPs. I got an itinerary for the night, too."

"Ilir got a number," Miles said. "Hey, kid, is she a VIP?"

Ilir smiled. "She will be."

"Turns out our boy here is a stud."

"Shut up, Miles," Carl said. "What's our play, boss?"

"It's boss now?" Ilir said.

I ignored Ilir. "We need to find a motel room. Somewhere that doesn't ask questions and takes cash."

"I don't know the area," Carl said.

"Go back towards the border," I said. "There's shopping there. Where there is shopping there will be motels."

"Got it."

"What? We're staying the night?" Ilir asked.

No one said anything.

"Shouldn't we have a vote or something?"

This got a laugh out of Miles. "Is that how gangsters do it? Democratically?"

"So he says we stay, and that's how it goes?"

"I just need Carl to agree," I said. "He has the car. You want to get out and take the bus home, be my guest."

Ilir crossed his arms and shut his mouth.

CHAPTER EIGHTEEN

Dinner was beer, roasted chicken, and fries from a Tops grocery store. Carl and Ilir had gone for the food while I was down the street using the free wifi in a Kinko's where I printed what I took off the USB. I almost considered the food as a bit of a payback from Ilir for the way I handled him on the highway, but that idea ended when I saw the smile on his face. He lifted the plastic dome-shaped lid from the chicken container that he had repurposed as a bowl, and showed me the bounty inside with the excitement of a kid seeing his first swimsuit issue. I ate the chicken and ignored the rest, knowing I could find something else later.

The room would have been cramped with one person in it — with four it was claustrophobic. Carl sat on the bed, propped up by the pillows, watching SportsCentre. Ilir, not wanting to lie beside Carl, took part in his own television vigil on the smallest corner of the bed that could still be considered on the bed. Miles walked a circuit from the bathroom, around the bed to the chair I sat in by the door, and back again.

"So we here all night or not?" Ilir said when Sports-Centre went to baseball coverage.

"Depends," I said.

"On what?"

"On what we learn tonight."

"What the hell does that mean?"

"We need to learn everything we can about the hall, the violin, where it's being kept, and the major players."

"We're just taking a stupid violin," Ilir said.

"Do you have a plan?" I asked.

"We wait on the widow to move it out of the vault, and then we take it on the way to the concert."

I flipped through the pages in my hand until I found the right one. I passed it to Miles as he neared me and he delivered it to Ilir on his way back to the bathroom. "Read it."

Ilir's lips moved as he went over the itinerary for the night of the charity gala. When he finished, he looked at me and said, "So what?"

"So, there's a scheduled delivery of the violin at four in the afternoon."

"If they're expecting delivery," Carl said from his spot on the bed. "That means that someone is delivering it. Has to be some kind of security company."

"Why?"

"Ooh, let me," Miles said from inside the bathroom. "It's a publicized event. Everyone knows that a priceless violin that is going to save the concert hall will be handed over. Everyone knows famed violinist David Lind will be playing there before the violin is officially considered sold.

The Buffalo Met has no choice but to provide security. It will be in a contract somewhere."

"It is," I said holding the document up.

"So, we hold up a bunch of rental cops," Ilir said. "There's four of us."

"A downtown hold-up is tricky," I said. "Trickier still when the thing you are after is on a timetable."

"But it could be done," Ilir said.

I pulled off another page from the stack and held it out. Miles picked it up on his way by and gave it to Ilir.

"Pass it to Carl," I said.

"Why?"

Carl took it off Ilir before I had to answer. We all watched Carl look at the map — everyone but Miles, who just kept pacing.

"This is where she lives, hunh?"

"First impressions," I said.

"Hitting an armoured car is already hard," Carl said. "The trick is getting the damned thing stopped so you can get in. Usually, people stick up the driver or get at 'em when they open the doors. You see these lines here and that square?" he said holding the paper out to Ilir. Ilir glanced at it and nodded. "If I had to guess, those lines are fences around the community and the square is some kind of guard shack. Expensive, but judging from the size of the houses on this map, they can afford it."

"So? It's probably just some fat retired cop," Ilir said.

Miles spoke as he passed. "Some fat retired cop with a phone."

"Exactly," Carl said. "One call gets out and the guys

loading the truck close the doors and start moving, or shove the violin back into the vault."

"So we get it coming out, or on the road."

"On the road is impossible. It's not making stops. We don't have the time or the manpower to set something up to stop an armoured truck. That leaves coming out of the gated community. They might have to stop at the guard booth, but maybe not. I'd have to see it."

"See," Ilir said with a smug smirk on his face. "It can be done."

"He's not done, gangster," I said.

Ilir looked at Carl, who was concentrating on the TV. Carl broke away after a few seconds. "Sorry, I just never get to watch this at home."

"I got it," Miles said. "Say it slows down. Hell, say it stops. What then? How are we getting into that truck? We have what —"

"Five days," I said.

"Five days to get the right kind of gear to open up an armoured truck. And it has to be the right stuff because all of those guards will be sitting inside calling for help on their radios while you stand outside jimmying the lock."

"My uncle can get us what we need."

"Not this stuff," Miles said. "It's not like getting a gun. You need serious gear for this and serious gear means you need time to get it from places that don't want you touching it."

"Can't be done," Carl said without taking his eyes off the screen.

"Maybe not."

"Maybe?" Ilir said. "So you agree with me?"

"No," I said. "But I'm not ruling anything out, not until I see it. And we can't see it until tonight. We need time to see all of the angles and we can't do that in broad daylight, not if there is a guard shack there to stare back at us."

CHAPTER NINETEEN

"**H**oly shit!" Miles said.

We all nodded. *House* was the wrong word for what was a hundred metres up the road. *Mansion* didn't seem to cut it either. *Compound* was closer. *Palace* was better.

"Get out," I said.

Miles and Ilir got out of the back seat and walked off the road into Delaware Park. The park had enough trees near the side of the road to conceal the two men from anyone driving by. Carl drove up Nottingham Terrace to the gate and paused next to the shack fronting the private drive. I got out and walked over to the window. Inside, a guy in his sixties was sitting on a stool. The sports page was open on the desk next to him and I could hear a base-ball game playing on a radio somewhere inside tuned to an AM station.

"You in charge?" I asked.

"Can I help you?" The question was asked with an air of authority. The small blue eyes hiding under the snowy brows squinted at me with the hard stare of a man who had seen it all and liked none of it — he had cop written all over him.

"Don Ames," I said. "Flushing Insurance. Our company insures Samuel Hall. Five days from now, a violin will be moving to Samuel Hall prior to its sale. The instrument in question is worth a lot of money and Flushing has been hired to provide extra security until the violin changes hands. I just wanted to let you know that you may be seeing us," I gestured to the Jeep and Carl nodded. "Driving by throughout the night."

The security guard leaned out the window and took a look at the Jeep. I watched his eyes narrow on the plate we'd boosted from another Jeep in an outlet mall parking lot before we came.

"You have any ID?"

I went into my pocket and came out with a business card I had gone back to Kinko's to have made. The card had all of the same information I had just communicated, but somehow seeing it on cardstock always made things more believable.

"The first number is mine," I said. "The second will get you my supervisor day or night."

The cop gave the card a long look before putting it down on the desk next to the newspaper.

"I can't let you in," he said. "And any harassment of our residents will be reported to the police."

"Sounds good," I said. I turned to leave, but came back after five steps. The guard was still staring at me. "Listen, if we go on a coffee run later — do you want anything?"

The cop dropped the stare and smiled. "Large black."

"Done," I said.

I got back in the Jeep and we drove away. When we picked up Miles and Ilir I said, "He call yet?"

"Yeah. Seems like a fun guy."

"What did you tell him?"

"I let Ilir talk to him."

I turned in my seat and looked at Miles.

"Jesus, Wilson, I told him everything we talked about. It was fine."

"Why is letting me talk a bad thing?" Ilir said.

No one answered.

"Seriously, what is wrong with how I talk?"

CHAPTER TWENTY

We rolled past the guard shack on fifteen-minute intervals. The huge black fence sprouting from either side of the small building that stood sentry at the mouth of the private road labelled Sherwood Avenue surrounded seven properties and hundreds of acres. The Randall place was the crown jewel of the bunch. The huge estate stood out amidst the other mansions like the Taj Mahal with its manicured lawn and architectural opulence. By our fifth circle, the guard didn't even look up from his newspaper. On the seventh, we parked down the street in a spot that gave us a sightline on the property.

"Anyone still think working here is a good idea?" Miles said. "Bad enough they own their own watchdog that can walk on two legs. You know they are running top-of-the-line security systems in those places. I'm guessing the response time is under five minutes."

"That's if the alarm goes off. If it doesn't, there is no response time," Ilir said.

"Anybody in here up to date on the latest alarm

technology?" Miles asked. "No?"

"We'd need another man," I said.

Carl nodded. "Do we have the time to pick up another body? Figure we'd waste a day getting word out, another sifting through the names we got. That would leave three days for this guy to get down here, source out the security system, and find a way around it. And then there's the vault to deal with."

I didn't say anything. Instead, I stared at the house. Minutes went by and they slowly stretched into hours. I ruled out the idea of bringing someone else in. If we did it right, we could bypass the house altogether. The violin had to leave the front door to get into the back door of the van. There would be a thirty-second window when the expensive alarm wouldn't mean a thing — we just had to be in exactly the right place. I grinned when a thought came to me. There would be a time when the guard in the small shack would let us through — four o'clock on the day of the event. With the right vehicle, uniforms, and paperwork, the guard would wave us up to the house towards a woman waiting to hand over her violin to a uniformed security guard. The idea had legs, but it also had a long list of gets that I would have to secure in under a week.

"He looked at us again," Carl said.

I took my eyes off the house and looked at the guard shack. The former cop had put his newspaper down and was now looking at the Jeep.

"Don't move yet," I said. "If he thinks he spooked us, his wheels will start spinning. Better to stay put for a few more minutes.

I rolled down my window and felt the hot humid air rush into the car. I held up a hand and gave a slow wave. A few seconds later, I got a similar motion back. Then the older man resumed reading his paper. "There's a Dunkin' Donuts five minutes south of us. Let's get him that coffee we mentioned. If he brings up anything about us being parked on the shoulder, we'll just say we were on the phone with the office."

Carl eased away from the curb and started down the road. We drove to the end of Nottingham Terrace and took a left onto Loxley Drive. The turn would take us along the side of the fence protecting the huge homes from the other millionaires in the neighbourhood. As we turned the corner, I noticed something. There was a dark blue panel van parked against the curb under the wooden fingers of a branch extending from a large tree. The windows were tinted and no one could be seen inside save for the driver, who was smoking a cigarette behind the wheel. Out of the corner of my eye, I saw the small burning circle of tobacco glow orange as we rode past. I turned my head as soon as we cleared the driver side door and took a look at the back of the van. The rear windows and doors had no markings of any kind, and someone had done a poor self-tint job on the glass. Bubbles along the edges of both windows had crept inward leaving pockmarks on the glass. I looked down from the dark glass to the rear wheels. The shocks on the van were compressed under a heavy load. Something was in the back of the van.

CHAPTER TWENTY-ONE

"**F**orget the coffee," I said. "Do another loop."

"What's going on?" Ilir asked. Carl and Miles didn't ask anything. Carl glanced at the rear-view and Miles craned his head to look behind us.

"Got it," Carl said when he had gotten a good enough look at what was behind us.

Carl eased the Jeep around the crooked circle we had been driving all night another time. When we turned the corner towards the van, he clicked on the high-beams before the Jeep completed the turn. We passed the van again; this time the driver was illuminated by the head-lights. He was white, middle aged, and dark haired; so was one of the men behind him in the rear of the van.

"How many heads did you count?" Miles asked.

"Three for sure," I said.

"I got four," Carl said.

"Four sounds right. Three wouldn't be enough."

"What the hell are we talking about? That van?" Ilir said finally catching on.

"Whose name is the Jeep under?" I asked.

"Mine," Carl said. "Why?"

"If the four guys in that van manage to get the violin out of that house, we need to get it out of that van. We don't have any guns, and I doubt harsh language is going to do the job, so all we have left is two tons of Jeep to throw at them."

Carl sighed. "It's in my name, Wilson. If it gets totalled over here, so do I."

I nodded. "Ilir, your uncle has connections over here."

"Yeah."

"If we needed to see someone about some bodywork tonight could he make it happen?"

"Probably."

I nodded again. "Find out. Carl, put us somewhere where we can see the driveway, but the guard can't see us."

"Alright."

We listened to Ilir talk to Len while Carl put the Jeep down the road from the guard shack. We were positioned on the side of the road with the engine off. I passed the map to Carl and told him to get familiar with the roads. He nodded and lifted the paper to try to catch some of the light coming off of the streetlights. Carl had done too good a job obscuring the Jeep from view. The pocket of darkness we were in made seeing the Jeep difficult but reading in the Jeep impossible. Carl had to settle for using the light from his cell phone display to see the map that I printed.

An hour and a half later, the van made its way around the corner. Miles had been the one who spotted it. He leaned forward in his seat and squinted at the darkness.

"There," he said.

It took the rest of us a few seconds to catch up. The driver had turned off the headlights, making the blue van barely a shadow in the night. We all sat motionless as we watched the dark van move over the pavement with the silence and menace of a crocodile. The driver didn't signal when he made the turn onto Sherwood; the van just lazily rounded the corner. The vehicle finally broke its camou- flaged approach when the driver applied the brakes. The rear lights gleamed like monsters' eyes as the van stopped next to the guard shack.

CHAPTER TWENTY-TWO

I could have closed my eyes and called everything that happened like the Amazing Kreskin on his best day. The van pulled up next to the shack. The driver parked real close. Close enough to speak to the guard without yelling — close enough to block the guard's view of the rear doors opening.

"You see that?" Ilir said. His voice was loud in the confined space of the car. We all saw it, but none of us outside the young gangster were surprised.

What happened next was quiet. The three men who had slipped out of the back of the van had knives or something bigger and duller that would do the job just as quickly, but a lot messier. Less than a minute later, two of the three men moved across the light cast from the guard shack and got back into the rear of the van. The last man came out after the motorized gate had been activated. The man rounded the front of the van and got in the passenger seat just as the van sped up the hill towards the Randall house.

"Carl," I said. "I need to get in that guard shack."

Carl nodded and the Jeep's engine revved. He left the

lights off as he followed the path the van had taken. When we got to the shack, I got out of the car and entered through the rear door. The old man was slumped in his chair. The light blue uniform that was meant to look official was a dark red down the front. I was right the first time. It had been a knife — something big and sharp. I looked around the surfaces surrounding the body for the piece of paper that had the dimensions I was looking for. I found the card I had passed the man under his newspaper. The corner of the card had been bent. The crease was likely an absentminded gesture made by the guard's thumb while he checked my story with Miles. I carefully picked up the card and put it in my pocket. I crouched by the guard and ignored the shirt in favour of the belt. On his hip, the cop carried a small-calibre revolver. The gun was a black Smith and Wesson with a walnut grip — likely something supplied with the shirt and pants by the wealthy people on the hill. I removed the gun from the holster and checked the load; all six cylinders were full. I put the gun in my pocket and backed out of the shack without touching anything else. I got back into the Jeep and Carl reversed without a word.

The Jeep turned sharply in the street and everyone was thrown to the left. Carl, who had anticipated his own turn, corrected himself as he threw the Jeep into drive and started back down the road.

"Why not just wait here?" Ilir said. "They gotta come down the hill. We can cut them off there."

Carl didn't answer right away. He was already slowing the Jeep down as he cut the wheel to the left and rounded his way back into the spot he had just been occupying a few minutes before. He pulled to a stop, put the Jeep in neutral, and engaged the emergency brake; he left his hand on the lever. "If that guard hit an alarm before they got to him, the cops are already en route. Out front next to a body is a bad place to be. Better to wait here out of sight."

The van was not visible from where we were parked. The driver had put it somewhere out of the reach of the huge decorative lights that lit up the grounds around the mansion as though it was midday and not closer to the opposite. I looked at the pockets of shadow and chose the dark patch that covered ten feet against the side of the garage. It was the place I would have chosen. I divided my time checking the clock, the house, and the roads. Either the van would emerge from its cave and start down the road, or the cruiser lights of the first responders would add a new colour to the night sky as their sirens broke the kind of silence that could only exist on a weekday after the late-night newscast.

In the end, it was the van that won out, but only by a hair. I saw four specks run across the porch to the side of the house. A second later, the van came out of the pocket it had been stored in like an ugly machine being birthed into the world. The van took the hill without using the brakes; the driver moved through the space in the gate that had been left open when the crew had entered the compound and swerved in our direction.

The hill had given the old van a good push and the tires squealed as it tried to handle the unnatural speed combined with the sharp change in direction.

Carl put his hand on the stick shift. His arm tensed as

the van tore past us and within a second the brake was disengaged and the Jeep was in gear.

"No, wait!" Miles said.

We were all thrown forward when Carl hit the brakes.

We all looked at Miles until he pointed up the road. "That house is getting pinker."

We saw the lights before we heard the sirens. Two cruisers came into view just as the van passed us.

"They turn up the driveway," I said, "you floor it after them."

Carl's hand wrung the wheel and it made a sound like a tree bending beyond its limits in the wind. He nodded.

The cruisers picked up speed as they passed the guard shack.

"Down," Miles yelled as the cars screamed past us.

"Go!" I said when we were left alone on the road.

Carl shoved the stick into drive and slammed his foot down on the pedal. The Jeep's tires squealed and kicked up stones until the tires got the traction they wanted; the Jeep U-turned and the momentum that followed propelled us back hard into the seats.

The van was nowhere in sight, but we could see the lights of the police cruisers as they gave chase up ahead. The direction of the van put it on a collision course with the Scajaquada Expressway. The van already had a head start down Nottingham. That put the getaway car well on its way to being out of the nest of near-million-dollar homes that slummed it next to the gated compound the Randall property occupied. There was just over five hundred metres before the sleepy two-lane would offer a turn-off onto the expressway.

"They're going for the highway," I said.

Carl nodded as we came onto a stretch of straight road. He fed the engine more gas and the Jeep responded with a roar. "Only way to go in this direction."

"Shit," Miles said.

"What?" Ilir wanted to know.

"We know that the highway is where they're going and we just looked at a map a few times. Local cops know these streets better than the people who planned them. They'll know about the highway and they'll have radioed ahead."

We ran a red light at Delaware and narrowly missed a car driving through the intersection. The teenagers in the blue Chevy came close enough to hitting the Jeep for me to identify the teams on their hats. Carl was cool behind the wheel; he was sure of himself and the Jeep, and he gave the narrow escape no attention.

"Up ahead," he said in a voice so low and even it was almost monotone.

The entrance to the expressway was lined with cones and the road behind it was crowded with road workers and equipment.

"They kept going," Miles said, motioning to a set of tire marks arcing away from the cones.

"I see it," Carl said. The wheelman fed the engine more gas and I felt another pull towards the back of the seat. Nottingham Drive ran along Delaware Park and the late hour had turned the road into a vacant straightaway for the cops and robbers. The van and the two cruisers had thirty seconds on us, but on a stretch of empty blacktop thirty seconds was a lot of distance. The only sign that we were even on the right track was the distant flickering lights of the rearmost cruiser.

"Is there another on-ramp?" Miles asked.

I used my phone to check the map. Half a click ahead was another access point. From the turn-off, it was only one hundred metres to the expressway.

"Can't be more than a click, and they're already a good chunk into that."

The Jeep left the ground for a split second as it skipped over the first in a series of small potholes. Suddenly, sooner than expected, the artery came into view; so did the van. What was left of it anyway.

"Slow down," I said as I rolled down the window. I wiped the gun I had taken off the security guard with my shirt and tossed it out of the Jeep. The revolver was loaded, but not only with bullets; it was loaded with years — a life sentence. Taking the gun had been a necessary risk, but it wasn't necessary anymore. The van hadn't made the turn. A pickup truck had turned for the highway at about the same time as the van. For a brief second, the same small space must have been home to both a van and a truck. Then, a briefer second later, it was all sorted out. Both van and truck were obliterated.

Carl managed to slow down without causing the tires to skid and we rubbernecked the scene. Through the broken windshield of the van we could see the two men up front had their chests crushed against the dashboard. At least that was what we had thought before we passed by. Ahead of the wreck, sprawled across the side of the road, were two mangled bodies — the men in the driver and passenger seats. They had been in such a hurry that they neglected to buckle up before they fled the scene of the crime. The men crushed by the dash had to have been thrown forward from the rear compartment — no one had used a seat belt.

The two cruisers that had been following the van were on the side of the road behind the wreck. Up ahead were two cruisers that had already been in place to intercept the van before it made it to the highway — a dead end before the men knew it.

CHAPTER TWENTY-THREE

We rode the Jeep back to the motel and mimicked sleep in the cramped room. The next morning we found a dive diner with free refills of bad coffee and read every newspaper article related to the murder and robbery at the Randall mansion. Only one paper used the word *attempted* in the headline — all of the others liked the sensational word *robbery* much better. Every story had the same basic facts. Four men entered through the front gate after murdering a decorated retired BPD officer who had left the job only eighteen months ago. After killing the guard, the perpetrators then entered the house by smashing in a window next to the front door. The men did not find the widow at home, but there were two maids in the kitchen. The burglars learned of the violin's whereabouts and executed the two maids. The vault that housed the instrument, along with other instruments that skirted the title of priceless, was unopened. It seems the four burglars were unprepared for a vault on a timer. After several attempts at opening the vault with gunfire, the robbers fled the crime scene. A police chase ensued and three of the four thieves were killed in the pursuit. The fourth unidentified man was, at that moment, brain-dead according to all of the papers.

"That rules out hitting the house," Miles said when we all put down our papers.

"It rules out everything," Carl said.

"Whoa, whoa, whoa," Ilir said. "You were hired to do a job. You were given half of the money up front. You can't back out. No one backs out from my uncle."

Carl laughed. The show of emotion looked strange on the serious driver's face. It was like watching a robot programmed to laugh. "He can have his money back."

"He wants that violin," Ilir said.

"Tell him to come and get it himself then. This job is dead."

I shrugged.

"Wilson," Carl said, "you can't be serious. That thing will be under guard twenty-four seven until the show."

I nodded. "You're right," I said. "That thing will be under guard twenty-four seven. Until the show."

CHAPTER TWENTY-FOUR

WEDNESDAY

It was a big day for Andrew Dickens; that fact didn't get him out of bed any earlier, but it was still a big day. Samuel Hall was about to get a donation that would amount to a six-and-a-half-million-dollar cash infusion when the violin changed hands after the benefit concert.

I had learned a lot in the two days I had been shadowing the director of Samuel Hall. The first day was spent in meetings. I had been in the parking lot for four hours when Dickens angled his car into his reserved space at nine-thirty and strolled his way into the building. He paused at the door and stifled a yawn while he went into his jacket pocket for his keycard. The card went into a slot next to the door and the tired director went inside the building. He got about ten minutes to himself before another car showed up. This one was an expensive white sedan with two men in expensive suits riding inside. The two men waited in their car until a second vehicle arrived. The second car was a large pickup truck with a black finish as dark and shiny as obsidian. The man who exited the car shouldered a bag and met with the other two. There was a short conversation before they were greeted at the entrance by Andrew Dickens. When all four men had been inside for a few minutes, I left the car, a Chevy I had boosted earlier in the morning from a car-pool parking lot, and did a quick walk around their white Infiniti. I took shots of the sedan's plates with my phone and checked the doors just in case someone had been careless — no one had. Through the passenger window I saw a cup in the cup holder. A stainless steel mug with the emblem of Coleridge Insurance on the side. I went to the pickup and took a shot of the vanity plate. The licence read *SECUUR*. The metallic grey logo on the side of the truck identified it as a company vehicle. I guessed it belonged to the owner of Taylor Security.

I walked back across the lot to the Chevy. The car was parked at the edge of a cluster of other vehicles that belonged to employees of Samuel Hall. There must have been a rule about parking away from the entrance because everyone who had shown up for work that morning had put their car in the same general area. Back behind the wheel, I Googled Taylor Security. It was a private firm with offices in New York and California. The site was expertly made and had the vague details that only a service that catered to the wealthy could get away with. The dots connected in my mind. After what had gone down at the Randall place, Coleridge had demanded an increase in security and Taylor was the answer.

The meeting ran an hour and ten minutes; the next

meeting started twenty after that. The second meeting was with two more people in expensive suits. These men were Asian and I guessed they were associated with the buyer. The attempt on the violin must have scared a few people with a lot of money. The knee-jerk response would have been to cancel the event and just proceed with the sale of the instrument. But the donation, and the concert, were big news, the kind of press the Buffalo Metropolitan Symphony Orchestra wasn't used to but sorely needed. Dickens would want the concert to proceed, and to do that he needed all of the parties involved to stay on board.

At one o'clock, the fourth meeting had just ended, and my first began. Carl pulled up to the Chevy and rolled down the passenger window. Miles passed me a bag from the passenger side window.

"Everything you asked for is there."

I nodded. "Did you —"

"Charge it and hook everything up? Yes, Mother."

"Thanks," I said.

"You good?" Carl asked.

I nodded. "Where is the kid?"

"Making the calls you told him to make."

"He talk to the uncle?"

"Yeah," Carl said. "Pyrros doesn't know anything about the robbery that we don't know, but he said he would look into things."

Violins don't get stolen every day. The idea that two people were going after the same instrument in the same week meant that more than one person was thinking the same thing, or about the same person. There was bad blood between the Albanians on both sides of the border. The American Albanians could have just as easily hatched their own plan to steal the violin so that they could bribe the godfather back home. There was a second option, though. Someone in Vogli's organization could be after the violin themselves. It wouldn't be the first time some power hungry lieutenant went after the boss's job. Pyrros had hired outside of his own mob to keep this thing under wraps. Hiring outsiders meant the insiders were a problem. It also meant Ilir couldn't be trusted — not completely anyway.

"Keep an eye on the kid," I said.

"You don't think he's in on this, do you?"

I shrugged. "I've seen his work before. He's a smash-and-grab guy."

"Maybe," Carl said. "You said he failed to impress his uncle once. This could have been his chance at fixing things. Using outside guys would have been smart. If the job failed, there wouldn't be any blowback."

"Can't be smash-and-grab and crafty at the same time," Miles said.

"Nope," I said. "But we might not see all of the angles." Criminal organizations were more complicated than anthills. There were lots and lots of workers, but unlike single-minded worker ants, mobsters all had aspirations of running the crew one day. Ilir was a gangster and gangsters wanted the throne. Pyrros' opinion of his nephew was clear, making succession unlikely. If Ilir couldn't climb into Pyrros' chair, maybe he thought he could tip it over by tipping off the Americans. Helping the competition acquire the violin would greatly improve their odds of overseas succession, and a power shift like that in Europe might then lead to another shift back home. With new, more grateful, hands on the reins of power, Pyrros would likely find himself out, and Ilir in, north of the border.

Another car was turning into the lot. Carl saw it. "We'll watch him."

The Jeep pulled away, leaving me alone with my thoughts.

CHAPTER TWENTY-FIVE

The new visitors were cops. There were no direct markings, but the signs were all there. The clothes, the nondescript black sedan, the haircuts, and the durable shoes. Every promotion got a cop farther and farther away from a uniform, but their shoes never went far from beat cop. Sure, the shoes were nicer, but they always had the kind of comfortable soles a man who was on his feet all day would prefer.

The cops had been in for half an hour when Alison Randall arrived. The widow showed up in a green Bentley. The car was one of the newer models that ran in the six figures. The blonde who got out of the car was closer to pin-up girl than debutante. She wore the debutante clothes, a sensible dress that covered her in all of the proper ways, but the body underneath had a way of making everything look sexual. The high neckline, the low hemline, all of it somehow screamed sex when it moved on Alison Randall. She didn't wear clothes; the clothes seemed to ride her. She walked to the door and pulled. When the door didn't open, she called someone on her cell phone. A few minutes later,

Andrew Dickens was holding the door for the woman. She stepped into the building and then the two cops walked out. Both men were watching the woman that had passed them and the two cops collided when they didn't realize that they were moving at different speeds.

I waited for the cops to leave before I got out of the Chevy. I took the duffel bag Miles had passed me to the white BMW parked in the spot reserved for the director and stopped next to the driver's side door. I bent as though tying my shoe and snaked my hand into the open bag. I brought a small metal box out of my pocket and held it under the car. The powerful magnet took over and the box adhered to the underside of the BMW with a loud *thunk*. The box was a GPS unit that Miles and Carl had crossed state lines to pick up. The box was something paranoid husbands and private detectives used. The unit had a lithium battery and was motion activated, so it would stay running for a month before I had to recharge it. That was twenty-six days longer than I needed. I went back to the Chevy and pulled the laptop from the duffel. The laptop had a full charge, a wireless card, and the GPS software was already installed. I checked that everything was working and then closed the screen.

Alison Randall walked out of the building forty-five minutes later, rolling her hips like a big-screen seductress. The walk must have been natural, or meticulously practised, because there was no one other than me watching. She got in the Bentley and drove out of the lot. The widow drove the Bentley fast, like someone who had enough money to buy another after lunch if necessary.

The widow was the last appointment. Dickens didn't

leave right after her, though. He spent another hour inside before walking out into the sunshine at three thirty. Dickens left the lot with much more care for his vehicle than the widow had shown. He drove to a nearby gym and pulled a bag from the trunk before walking inside. A few minutes passed before I saw Dickens again. He walked in front of the large window facing the parking lot on his way to the free weights. He had changed the professional clothes for a pair of shorts and a sleeveless Under Armour shirt. He was a tall man with more weight around the middle than his expensive suit let on. In the tight workout gear, his skinny arms and round gut had nowhere to hide. I watched Dickens work out and then disappear for a few minutes before coming out into the parking lot with wet hair.

After the gym, Dickens went home. The pay for running the Buffalo Met must have been good because home was inside a luxury high-rise condo downtown. Andrew pulled to a stop in front of a metal garage door and waited for it to lift. The BMW drove into the parking lot and the garage closed behind it. I found a parking spot a few blocks over and walked by the building. The front doors opened to a small interior room containing a wall of buzzers. Beyond the interior room was a security guard stationed at a desk. The guard was looking down, but he wasn't sleeping. The small head movements told me that he was watching a monitor of some kind. I noted the address of the building and went back to the Chevy. Twenty minutes later, I was back at the motel.

CHAPTER TWENTY-SIX

THURSDAY

I didn't watch the director leave his place the next morning. At least, not in person. I sat in a diner next to Miles waiting to order. Carl and Ilir sat opposite us. Ilir's foot bounced under the table and caused the salt shaker to slowly vibrate its way across the scarred tabletop.

"He's going," I said when the laptop received an update from the tracking program about the device being activated.

Miles looked at the clock above the diner counter. "Eight forty-five again. Poor Andrew is not an early riser." He shrugged. "Must be one of the perks of being the boss."

A waitress, who already looked exhausted, sauntered up to the table and went for her pen and pad. "What can I get you?"

I ordered oatmeal. Miles and Carl asked for eggs and bacon. Ilir got a waffle with whipped cream, strawberries, and chocolate sauce.

"What?" he said when he caught us looking at him. "It's good."

"Do all gangsters eat this way or is it just the Albanians?" Miles asked.

"Shut up," Ilir said.

"You want me to ask the waitress if they have crayons and those paper placemats with a maze on the back? I don't want you to get bored while the grown-ups are talking."

Ilir gave Miles the finger.

We all drank coffee while we waited for our food. After the waitress dropped everything off, I put three cell phones on the table next to a hard cardstock FedEx envelope.

"Your own phones go in the envelope. The burners go in your pockets," I said.

The three men shot each other looks. The envelope was something we had never talked about. The three men at the table were all criminals, and all criminals share one thing in common: they hate being told what to do. Telling them to put their phones in the envelope automatically raised everyone's backs. The demand was also a statement about the pecking order. They would think I was marking my territory — I wanted it that way. Marking territory was something they understood, and if they thought they understood my actions, they wouldn't question them.

"There are three numbers programmed in each of them. No names — the numbers are assigned alphabetically," I said.

"So Carl, me, Miles, and you," Ilir said.

"Good job, sport, now eat your waffle," Miles said.

"Shut up, man. I'm just making sure is all. Where does

the envelope go?"

"To Ox. He will give everything back when we're home."

"That really necessary?"

"There's a reason they're not called dumbphones, kid. A good tech guy can pull all kinds of incriminating things off a phone. It's best to have it out of the picture."

I picked up the envelope and pointed it at Carl and Ilir. Both men put in their phones without complaint. Miles kept his hands on the table. I shook the envelope in his direction and he rolled his eyes. "I know it sounds cheesy, but it's a business phone. I got contacts in this thing." I shook the envelope again. Miles looked at Carl and Ilir, but he found no help — they had already put their phones inside. Miles looked at the envelope. I watched his eyes narrow as something in his mind raced around looking for an escape. He noticed me watching him, and his face, still reflecting his racing mind, decelerated into something jovial. Finally, he fished into his pocket and pulled out a white cell phone.

"I'm on level 78 of Angry Birds. I swear to God if anything happens to that phone, or my save, I'm going lose it."

"Angry Birds," Ilir said. "What are you, twelve?"

"You have whipped cream on your nose, gangster."

Ilir swiped at his face and then licked the dab of cream from the edge of his palm. We all stared at him.

"What?"

Miles put the phone in the envelope and immediately went for a swig of his coffee. He brought the cup up to his face, but it never got high enough to block his view of the envelope.

"You get anywhere on the men who tried to rip off the widow at her place?" Carl asked.

Ilir nodded as he sliced an edge off of his waffle. "They were Albanians."

"That wasn't in the papers," Carl said.

"And it won't be, but my uncle has connections to the Albanian community over here. They are mourning four dead. Do the math."

"He have any idea how they got wind of the violin?"

Ilir shovelled the last quarter of a waffle into his mouth and chewed. The high pile of whipped cream that had been sitting on top pushed through the Albanian's pursed lips while he tried to get everything down.

"It's not like the violin was a secret."

"So coincidence," I said.

Ilir licked his lips with a tongue that was white from pushing around heavy cream. "Looks like."

I ate some of the oatmeal in front of me and thought about how many times a claim of coincidence had turned out to be just that. On the job the score was still zero. Coincidences didn't happen — people just said they did.

"You think they'll take another run at the violin?" Miles asked.

I shrugged. "What did the almighty Albanian eight-ball say?"

Ilir spoke with his mouth full, but each word made it less so. "He doesn't know the four guys personally. He just knows they're Albanian. But something like this has to come from the top."

"So is that a yes?"

"I don't know, Miles."

"There'll be a lot of heat when the cops figure out the names of the guys who murdered that old cop —"

"He was retired," Ilir said.

"Try telling them that," Carl said.

"Going after the same thing again would be a bad idea," Ilir countered.

"Are you saying this is a bad idea?" Miles asked with a smirk on his face.

"People will see it that way," I said. "That will give us a blind spot we can manipulate. The question is, will the Albanians see it the same way?"

We all looked at Ilir. He was scraping his plate with his fork and licking the syrup off the tines. He stopped when he saw us looking. "You asking me?" He put the fork down on top of the plate and took a drink of coffee. "Those men were soldiers. There are plenty who can replace those four. If their boss wants it bad enough, they'll try again."

"The fun never stops," Miles said.

Ilir craned his neck left and right until he saw the waitress. He raised a hand and she came over to the table. "Could I get some more waffles?"

The waitress walked off leaving four empty plates and three pairs of eyes staring at the young Albanian. "What? They're good."

"I guess we're staying a little while longer," Miles said.

The we didn't include me — I had other plans. None of us had slept more than a couple of hours. We had been over everything we had learned and spent the end of the afternoon into the early hours of the morning polishing the plan into something sleek and efficient. We all had our roles to play and mine didn't include watching the young Albanian challenge his metabolism to a game of tug-of-war. I got up from the table. "Don't let the kid get too hopped up on sugar. He needs to spend most of the day sitting still."

Ilir spoke through the mouthful. "Quit talking about me like I'm a child."

"He gets like that when he's tired. Maybe we can get him down for a nap later," Miles said.

"I am not a kid. I keep telling you that. I am a gangster, damn it."

"Kids today," Miles said as he tousled Ilir's hair.

"You're lucky this waffle is so good, asshole, or I would come across this table."

I leaned over the table and took the envelope. "Be ready for when I call."

"Why don't you let me mail it?" Miles said. The words came quickly out of his mouth.

"You don't trust me, Miles?"

"It's not that, Wilson. You just seem like you're in a rush to get out of here is all. I'm just trying to lighten the load."

"You just get your part done," I said. "Now if you'll excuse me, I have to see a man about a bicycle."

CHAPTER TWENTY-SEVEN

The part about the bicycle wasn't a lie. I did need to see a guy about getting a bicycle. The stop that I needed to make before I met with that guy wasn't a lie either — technically, it was an omission.

I pulled into the parking lot of another diner, this one a Denny's. I walked inside, sat down, and ordered a glass of iced tea. From the look I got from the waitress, the tea was just barely enough to hold the table. I wasn't thirsty, and I wasn't getting addicted to sitting in diners — the Denny's was where I had been told to go, and the iced tea was what I was told to order. The tea came and the condensation had not even dripped onto the paper napkin before a man peeled away from a table of four and approached my booth.

"Mr. Wilson?" The voice was higher pitched than the heavy jowls would have suggested. The British accent clashed with the Steelers golf shirt he was wearing, too.

"Mr. Menace," I said.

"Call me Dennis," the British man said as he worked to suppress a chuckle over his choice of names.

"Dennis," I said. The tone of my voice told the larger man that he was the only one who was amused.

"Yes, well," he said regaining his composure. "I believe you have something for me, mate."

I handed him the envelope. "There are three phones in there. I want everything you can get off them. Specifically numbers called in the last five days and any numbers belonging to phones in the States."

"It will take a little while," he said.

I nodded. "You have three hours."

Dennis shook his head. "Won't be enough time. Not for three."

"Start with the black Samsung," I said. The phone belonged to Ilir. With the four men in police custody coming up as Albanian, he was the best place to start.

"Alright." Dennis passed me a card. There was a number written in pen on the back. The pen had been leaking and there were blots wherever Dennis had started or stopped writing.

I put the card in my pocket and brought back a wad of bills. Dennis was smart enough not to count it at the table.

"I'll get right on it," he said.

"Make sure that the envelope gets dropped in the mailbox when you're done."

Dennis nodded, got up, and then weaved his way back to his table. When I crossed the dining room, I saw the Brit shovelling the remnants of a plate of eggs, sausage, and toast into his mouth. If he felt any pressure to get the job done, it didn't show. I sighed and shoved open the door. I had no choice but to rely on the chubby Brit to do what Ox promised he could do in the time he promised he could do it in. I had used Ox to find me someone to work with because the job didn't give me any time to shop around for someone else who could hack into a cell phone. After what had gone down in the park with the Albanians, Ox was eager to help me any way he could. I took the help, not because I trusted Ox anymore, but because the job was for Pyrros Vogli. If the Albanians were scary enough to make Ox turn on me, then they would be scary enough to keep him in line.

CHAPTER TWENTY-EIGHT

FRIDAY

Saturday was going to be one of the biggest days in Andrew Dickens' professional life, but you would never know that on Friday. I sat around the corner from the Buffalo Metropolitan Symphony Orchestra director's home, this time in a stolen Volkswagen, watching a blip on a computer screen. The blip was the white BMW that belonged to Dickens. He had gotten behind the wheel at three thirty, the same time as yesterday, and driven out of the parking lot of Samuel Hall. There had been no stop at the dry cleaner today, no stop at the gym either. Instead, Dickens stopped at a mall. The blip on the screen stayed put for half an hour in the mall parking lot before it began its route home. When the dot stopped at a light three minutes away, I got out of the car and took the bicycle out of the trunk. I was dressed in blue coveralls and a blue baseball cap. I walked quickly with the bicycle beside me, a white drop cloth tucked under my arm. A paint can hung from the handlebars, making steering awkward.

I walked down the incline to the garage door Andrew Dickens had used the day before and leaned the bike against the wall. The wall was made of painted white brick that had been stained beige by city stink. I opened the drop cloth and pulled out the spray paint and brush that had been set between the folds. I popped the cap and sprayed a squiggle on the beige wall. I set the can down and draped the cloth over the bike. I jimmied the lid of the paint can and began immediately painting over my tag. I dipped the brush and streaked it across the centre of the still-damp graffiti in one smooth confident motion. The wet spray paint mixed with the topcoat and created a dull grey splotch that would be noticeable if anyone chose to stop and stare. I dipped the brush again, but the touch-up was short-lived. A white BMW pulled into the ramp and the garage door began to rise. Andrew Dickens didn't even make eye contact as he passed. The snub was fine by me — he didn't notice me pulling the bicycle from under the cloth, or me jogging under the ramp with it.

I rode the bike behind the BMW down two ramps to a parking space marked 826. I kept the bike close enough to the cars parked on the opposing side to feel their bumpers graze my pant leg. Riding to the far right didn't make me invisible in the rear-view, but it would make it tough for a cursory glance to pick up. In the end, it didn't matter — Dickens was comfortable in his underground garage, so he didn't look behind him once. When he pulled into the empty spot, I overshot the BMW by two spaces. I leaned the bicycle against a Land Rover that barely fit into the cramped parking spot provided by the building and walked back the way I had come. Andrew Dickens had only managed to get a single foot on the pavement; he had parked so close to the car next to him that he was unable to step out of the car under his own momentum. He had put a hand on the door and was using it to support himself as he struggled to get out of his seat. His peripheral vision picked up movement and he turned his head to confirm what he thought he saw. His head never made it all the way around to look at me. My fist connected with the base of his jaw, just under his ear. There was a loud cracking sound followed by the even louder sound of the door dinging the neighbouring car. The Buffalo Met director's head moved diagonally up between the door and roof of the car. He crested six inches above the door and then began a quick descent back into the crevice created by his partially open door. The downward momentum buckled his knees and sent his unconscious body backwards onto his car seat.

I unlocked the doors of the BMW using the button on the door armrest and lifted Dickens' feet into the car. Before I closed the door, I popped the trunk. I retrieved the bicycle and began the quick disassemble that was its best-selling feature. The bike went easily into the slim trunk and I closed the lid. I opened the passenger side door and pulled Dickens across the middle console and into the seat. I quickly zip-tied his hands behind his back before using two larger ties to bind his ankles and legs above the knee; after that, I buckled him in.

It only took three slaps to rouse him. As soon as he got out his first "What the hell?" I slipped the largest tie around his neck. The thick plastic band was meant for securing large trees, so it fit a human neck with no problem. I pulled the ends back hard enough to bounce Dickens' head off of the pad. He struggled, but stopped when he heard the plastic teeth begin to click. I had fastened the tie behind the headrest and eliminated some of the slack.

"Stay still," I said. "Or I make it tighter."

Dickens stopped moving and turned his head to look at me. I pulled the tie closed another few inches.

"I didn't move."

"I know," I said. "I just told you that so you'd hold still."

"What do you want?"

"For you to stay put," I said as I got out of the back seat.

I got behind the wheel of the BMW and reversed out of the spot. I drove back through the garage and used Dickens' automatic door opener to raise the door. I pulled out of the garage and pulled the emergency brake. I got out and collected the paint can I had left behind along with the can of spray paint. I got into the car again and tucked the paint behind the passenger seat. Dickens looked at me with panic set so deep in his eyes that it might have taken a lease there.

"What do you want?"

"Same thing, Andrew."

"How do you know my name?"

I grinned without taking my eyes off the road.

"You don't have to do this. You can have the car. Take it. Take the keys, my wallet, my computer. I won't report it."

The grin on my face stretched a little wider. Someone might mistakenly call it a smile, but not if they really looked. If they looked close, they would see that the grin was something else. I had inherited it from my uncle. His grin always came at times when a grin was the last thing you expected to see. But that was just it — the grin showed up and it spoke scary volumes. It told people that things weren't what they seemed. I had inherited the grin, but not genetically. As a youth, I had practised the look in mirrors, in car windows, anywhere I found myself alone. Eventually, the grin came to feel natural — that was when I knew that it was mine. Andrew saw my mouth pull wider and it took something from him.

"What do you want?"

"I'm not stealing the car, or your wallet, Andrew," I said. "I'm stealing you."

At that moment, the fear that had leased space in his eyes opted to buy.

CHAPTER TWENTY-NINE

I didn't drive the BMW back to the motel. We had taken up residence in a new place for the job. Miles had spent the previous day with a realtor checking out properties around the city. To hear Miles tell it, the woman was more than happy to spend the day showing him as many places as he wanted to see. According to the con man, the last place on her list was a two-bedroom apartment in the city. The property was hers — it wasn't on the market, but the bed was available for a short lease. Miles wasn't interested in square footages, costs, or the woman — it was the details he wanted. The realtor had no idea that some of the small talk that took place between the flirting and touring was the real business being conducted.

It was the third place out of nine that turned out to be the one. The house had been on the market for over a year after the bank had foreclosed and found an old woman dead under decades of hoarded trash. The garbage and the body were cleaned out easily enough — the mould was another story. The asbestos was a lengthy afterword. The house was good for nothing other than a teardown, but all of that effort would eliminate any chance of earning a profit — no amount of granite and hardwood would change the neighbourhood the house was in. What set the house apart from all of the others Miles looked at in the eight hours he spent with the realtor was the garage. It had one, and it was attached to the house. It was this very garage that I drove the BMW into. Miles had been waiting since my call and he slid the door up seconds after the tires touched the driveway; he slid it back down a few seconds after that.

We cut the ties holding Dickens to the seat and carried him into the house. We put the concert hall director in the kitchen. There was nothing about the room that said kitchen other than the proximity to a battered sink. There was nothing homey or functional in the space. The room was bare save for four folding chairs we had picked up at a pawn shop and a scarred card table that had been left in the attic. Not even the walls had escaped the decay. Someone had stripped away drywall leaving old insulation, studs, and pre-war wiring exposed for any visitor to see.

We let Dickens fall into one of the chairs and watched as the older man fought to keep it upright using only his bound legs. Miles stayed with Dickens while I went back out to the garage to get everything that belonged to the director. I put his laptop and workbag on the floor, and then I fished his phone out of his suit jacket. The expensive dress shirt was soaked through with sweat. The abandoned home was hot in the late summer month but Dickens' perspiration came from something other than the heat — it was fear that was making him sweat.

"If it's money you want, I can get you money."

I looked at the man and lifted my index finger to my lips. I shhh'ed gently. Andrew's eyes locked onto mine and he saw something in them. Something that made him close his mouth.

Ten quiet minutes later, Carl and Ilir showed up with food. They walked in with a bucket of chicken and a bag of sides and each took a seat at the card table. Carl put a second bag on the table and shoved it towards one of the empty seats. I sat in front of the bag and looked inside. There was a salad in a hard plastic container. On top of the clear top were several bags of dressing. I took a chicken breast from the bucket and held it with the fingers of my left hand. With my right, I pulled a small folding knife out of my pocket. I had bought the knife at a local camping supply store for forty dollars. The designers were kind enough to install a button that opened the knife like an old-fashioned switchblade. I clicked the knife open and began carving pieces off the skin of the chicken breast. I sliced the naked chicken onto the salad and then began to eat. No one said a word while we ate, not to each other, and not to Andrew. Twice he thought about speaking. The first time I shhh'ed him without looking at him. The second time I just looked his way and he averted his eyes like a cowed dog.

We finished the chicken and Carl passed around wet wipes. Everyone cleaned up and tossed their trash into the empty bucket. I got up from my chair and turned to look at Andrew. He was staring at the table — at the men who had been eating while he sat bound in a chair. His skin was sallow and the hair on his head had wilted with sweat. One by one we all turned to look at Andrew Dickens. The bound man looked from one face to the next as though he were following the bouncing ball used to keep drunks singing along with a karaoke song. No one said a word to Dickens, not even when I slid the knife off the table and stabbed him.

CHAPTER THIRTY

I walked slowly across the room. I let Andrew get a look at me, then at the knife. By the time he understood what was about to happen, it was too late to struggle. I took his throat with my left hand and brought the knife down hard into his thigh.

The scream that came from Dickens' lips boiled up from somewhere deep inside like a kettle whistle. It was loud and shrill and went on and on. I wasn't worried about anyone hearing him; the only neighbour close enough to hear anything was an old woman who we had seen wearing two hearing aids.

I took a step back, leaving the knife buried to the hilt in his thigh, and waited for the sobbing to end. When Dickens finally managed to meet my eyes, I spoke. "You are going to do everything we tell you and tell us everything we want to know, or I am going to do that again."

Snot ran down the five o'clock shadow of the sobbing middle-aged man in front of me. Dickens blubbered and then cried when he looked down at the knife hilt trembling in his shaky leg. Slowly, a stain blossomed on his crotch until his pants were soaked from belt to knee with urine.

"Please, I'll do whatever you say. Please just don't hurt me anymore."

"Laptop password," I said.

Dickens gave it.

"Phone password."

Dickens gave it.

"Please," he said, looking at his leg and the blood creeping away from the puncture. "My leg. You have to do something about my leg."

"As long as the knife stays in and you stay still, everything will be fine." I wasn't lying; I had picked my spot before I stuck the man. It looked bad, but it was just a flesh wound.

"Please, I need to get to a hospital."

I ignored Dickens as I probed the laptop hard drive. The itinerary was in the same place it had been before. There had been changes since the attempt on the violin, but the changes weren't anything we hadn't expected. In fact, the alterations to the schedule didn't go as far as I thought they would have. I went through the document once, then another time. Beside me, Miles was rapidly moving his fingers along the surface of Dickens' cell phone.

"Who is directing everything tomorrow?"

"Tomorrow? You mean the concert. That's what this is about? I'm in charge."

"No," Miles said. "You'll be sitting in the office with a nice view from the hallway. Someone else will be down on the floor making sure everything is going according to plan. As far as I can tell from the contacts in your phone it will either be Jonathan or Adam."

"It's Jonathan," Dickens said.

Miles nodded and worked at the phone a little more. "It looks like the two of you communicate with texts and email mostly."

Dickens nodded.

"Guess you'd have to if you leave at half past three every day."

Dickens instinctively mustered up a bit of indignation at the dig about his work ethic, but it deflated before it made it past a narrowing of the eyes.

"Jonathan still at the concert hall?" Miles asked.

"What time is it?"

"Six," Carl said.

"Probably," Andrew said. "There was a lot to do before the show tomorrow."

"You probably pushed it until three forty-five today then."

I shook my head.

Miles laughed under his breath. "Didn't want to exert yourself. Alright," he said, looking up from the phone. "What do you want me to say to Jonathan?"

"Start with please tell my family that I am okay," Dickens said.

Miles kicked Dickens under the table. "Not you, Andrew."

I read through the file I had opened on the laptop once more. "They delayed the delivery of the violin until four. I'm guessing that they don't want it out of the vault any longer than it has to be."

"That means we have to do it the second way," said Miles.

"Fuck," Ilir said. "Seriously?"

I nodded. "Andrew, has any food been delivered for tomorrow yet?"

Andrew nodded slowly. "There were some cheeses and meats, some wine, smoked salmon the day before."

"Tell Jonathan that you ate some of the salmon and now you have food poisoning. Make him toss the food to be safe and tell him that he is running the show until at least the afternoon."

"Me?" Dickens said. "Okay, just put the phone to my ear."

Miles cuffed Dickens. "You really are an idiot, Andrew. He means me writing as you."

"What do I do, then?"

"Get some rest," I said. "Tomorrow, you're going in early."

CHAPTER THIRTY-ONE

SATURDAY

At three a.m., I shook Dickens' shoulder. He came to slowly and looked around the room as though he was hoping the nightmare he had been having was only in his head. He cried when he realized that it wasn't. All of the adrenalin that had been running through his body had eventually dissipated and Dickens had finally crashed around eleven thirty. At midnight, Miles took the BMW back to the parking garage where I had taken the concert hall director. Miles went up to Dickens' apartment and took everything the older man would need for the following day.

Miles got some takeout on the way back and Dickens ate the cold pizza with his two hands bound together. When he was done eating, I cut his wrists loose and gave him a packet of wet wipes to clean his hands and face with. While he was wiping down, I cut the ties on his legs and gave the knife wound a fast once-over. After we had gotten everything we needed from Dickens, I cleaned up the hole I put in his leg. The thigh was layered with gauze and wrapped tight with a bandage to prevent blood from seeping through his pants. The first aid had done its job; the wound had not bled through the layers.

"Walk around and get used to how the bandages feel."

Dickens looked at me like I had just asked him to do a handstand and walk around on his hands.

"You start seeming like you're more trouble than you're worth, and I might decide that I don't need you anymore."

That was enough to motivate the director. He used the chair to help himself to his feet and then he began dragging his injured leg around the floor. The right leg of his pants had been cut up to the mid-thigh, leaving Dickens with a dishevelled zombie vibe about him.

After a few laps around the dinner table, Dickens crossed paths with Carl. The driver shoved Dickens out of his way. "Walk it off, you pussy."

Dickens wanted to whimper, he wanted to complain, but he just kept shuffling on. Four Advil and a bottle of water improved the leg enough for Dickens to graduate from shuffling to walking without the support of whichever wall or furniture was nearby. After ten successful laps, I stopped him on his way past the card table and knelt to examine the dressing on his leg. The bandages had done their job; the wound was closed and all of the fluids were still inside. Satisfied the dressing would hold, I stood and went into the living room.

I came back into the kitchen a second later and handed

Dickens the suit he had picked up from the dry cleaners the other day; the suit was still in the thin plastic bag.

"Where did you get this?"

"That's your question?" Miles said. "You haven't said a word in like two hours and the first thing out of your mouth is about your suit?"

Dickens looked at the bag. "I was told not to talk."

"Just get dressed," Miles said.

Dickens opened the bag and ran his hand over the jacket. His eyes closed as he felt the smooth clean fabric. He was telling himself that it would be over soon, and that soon he would be back to wearing clean, tailored clothing and doing the kind of things people in fancy suits did.

"You want a minute there, Andrew?" Miles asked.

The words broke the spell and Dickens began putting the suit on. There were a lot of groans as the pants slid over his legs, but he managed to get them on without crying.

I finished putting on my own suit and grabbed the backpack. I nodded to Miles and he took a backpack of his own off the floor. "Three forty-five," I said to Carl and Ilir.

Carl nodded. Ilir was still sulking. "Whatever," he said.

I walked to the garage door. Miles followed. He stopped behind me and whistled three short sounds while he patted his thighs. "Here, boy, here. Who wants to go for a car ride?"

Dickens limped along behind us and into the garage.

CHAPTER THIRTY-TWO

At three o'clock in the afternoon, we had been in the office for almost eleven hours. We drove from the safe house to the concert hall and Dickens walked us in the front door, reset the alarm, and then walked us straight up to his office. Even on the day of the big event the concert hall didn't have twenty-four-hour security. The attempted robbery had put all attention on the violin, not on the venue, and as a result all of the thought and planning focused mainly on the instrument instead of on the concert. Even though security at the hall was lax, we took no chances. We kept the office door locked, the lights off, and sat on the floor when we weren't using Dickens' computer. The only time any of us ever walked more than five feet was when we had to urinate. In the almost twelve hours inside the office the small empty closet had been used as a toilet five times. Dickens, who was the first to christen the space, had fought it at first, but the water he kept nervously chugging eventually made a more compelling argument.

The insurance company and the security service reps

were not happy about their having to meet with Jonathan instead of Andrew, but the food poisoning excuse held. Jonathan, Dickens' number two, had been texting questions and updates to his boss all morning. He peppered the messages with diplomatically phrased questions about when Dickens would be getting there to help deal with all of the issues. It was clear he was treading water out there all by himself and starting to cramp. When I turned on the office lights and told Miles to text him and tell him to come up to Dickens' office, the reply was close to instantaneous. Jonathan was on his way.

"No," Dickens said. "You don't need him. You have me. Leave him out of this."

"Surprising amount of backbone for someone who just pissed in the closet fifteen minutes ago," Miles said.

Dickens shut his mouth and five minutes later an exasperated Jonathan entered the office. He was a handsome man in a blue suit who kept the currently fashionable amount of stubble on his face. I guessed it took him at least an hour a day to give himself the I-just-rolled-out-of-bed-and-don't-give-a-shit look. He walked with a graceful, confident stride that gave him the air of a dancer, but just the air — Jonathan had too much ass to be a dancer.

He stopped short of the desk when he saw the two of us with Andrew and said, "Oh, I'm sorry, Andrew, I didn't know you had guests in your office."

"Jonathan, I — I —"

I pointed a gun that Ilir's American Albanian connection had procured at Jonathan's centre mass. "Please step inside and shut the door behind you."

Jonathan cracked half a smile. "Is this some kind of joke? Because I don't get it."

"It's some kind of robbery," Miles said. "Now, be a good boy and do as you're told."

Around his neck, Jonathan wore a lanyard with a card that provided his credentials along with photo ID. Miles took the lanyard off Jonathan and lay it on the desk. On his way he picked up the backpack he had brought with him. Miles pulled a case out of the bag and set it on the desk along with the card.

"Can you make it work?" I asked.

"Shouldn't be an issue," Miles said as he opened the case. He looked back and forth from the case to the card. "Ah-ha. Lucky number two."

"Andrew, what is going on?"

"I'm sorry, Jonathan. I had no choice."

"No choice? What do these men want?"

Miles lifted his eyes from the contents of the case and I expected a comment. I was wrong. "I need three minutes."

"Three minutes for what?" Jonathan asked.

"Three minutes and quiet," Miles said.

There was something different in Miles' voice and Dickens heard it. "It will be okay, Jonathan. Please just do as they say."

"Empty your pockets," I said.

Jonathan didn't pose any more questions. He just stepped to the desk and began pulling items from his pants. When he was done, I pointed to a chair — Jonathan sat. I looked through the assortment of things on the desk. "This is all of it?"

Jonathan nodded vigorously.

"Who is in charge down there when you are up here?"

"No one really. Everyone is working in their sections. I just coordinate where needed."

"Nuh unh," I said. "There is always a pecking order."

"There really isn't."

I pulled back the hammer on the revolver and put the gun against the handsome man's temple. "Think harder."

"Tim! Tim does a lot down there."

The name was new to me. "Who is Tim?"

"He runs maintenance," Dickens said.

I picked up the cell phone that had just come from Jonathan's pocket. "Call him."

"I can't."

I put more pressure on his temple with the barrel of the gun. "Call him."

"He doesn't have a phone."

"He's right," Dickens said. "Tim is in his sixties. He thought pagers were too futuristic."

"What is your cell number?" Miles asked Jonathan.

Jonathan rattled off the digits so fast that we had to make him do it two more times before we were comfortable that we got it.

For a few moments Miles said nothing else as he hovered over the case on the desk. He finally lifted a card up to the light of the lamp on Dickens' desk and peered at it. He pulled the card away from the light and brought it close to his lips. He blew on the ID gently and nodded his head as though confirming something with himself. I held out my hand and Miles passed me the card. I had described the lanyard Dickens had worn when I first saw him and Miles had estimated the size of the picture on the card and made ten prints of varying sizes at a local photo shop. Up close to the lamplight, the surface of the new photo was a bit shinier than the rest of the card. Downstairs, in dimmer light, it would easily hold up to a casual inspection.

I passed the card back and Miles put the ID into the interior pocket of his suit jacket. He smoothed the lines of the suit and went over to the case one more time. He took another ID badge out. This one was attached to a clip instead of a lanyard. Miles attached the second ID to the front pocket of the jacket and stepped over to the door so that he could look at himself in the reflection of the glass. Satisfied, he went over to the desk, put the case back in the backpack, and zipped it closed.

"Well," he said. "Let me go introduce myself to Tim." The con man went out the door, leaving me with Dickens and Jonathan.

I took the cell phone from my pocket and called the first stored number. Carl picked up on the first ring.

"Yeah?"

"You ready?"

"Yeah." The driver was so cool he sounded bored.

"Five minutes," I said to Carl.

CHAPTER THIRTY-THREE

It was five minutes until the phone on the desk began to march like an army ant across the shiny oak surface. I picked up the phone and heard Miles speaking far from the receiver.

"Excuse me, miss, can you point me in Tim's direction?"

I couldn't hear the woman's reply, but Miles thanked her profusely.

Miles put the phone to his mouth and said, "Put the phone on speaker and have Jonathan ready to play ball."

I touched the button for speakerphone and put the phone down on the desk. Jonathan was watching me with his phone. I could read the look on his face; he wasn't cowed as easily as his boss had been. His mind was racing to find a way out of the situation. I motioned him over with the gun to remind him that there was only one way out of the office and it wasn't with Tim's help.

"Walk over to the desk on your knees."

Jonathan slid out of the chair to his knees and did as he was told. I moved behind him and put the revolver to the back of his head. I pushed against the handsome man's scalp until his chin was resting on the desk and his throat was against the edge.

"You give him whatever he wants and keep your words short and to the point. Answer when you're spoken to and don't even think about colouring outside the lines."

"A — Alright," he said.

A minute later, we heard Miles. "Tim? My name is William Bishop. I represent David Lind. He is playing the benefit tonight."

"I know who he is," a gruff voice answered.

"Of course. Of course. Anyway, I'm sure you heard about the little issue with the toilets."

"What issue with the toilets?"

"Seems they were overflowing onto the floor in the dressing room."

"No one told me a thing about that."

"Yes, well, nevertheless, it happened and Mr. Lind found the accommodations unacceptable. Not to worry, though, we have a plumber en route."

"Plumber? I'll have it taken care of right now."

Miles laughed. "I know you have people for that."

"It's not that —"

"I also know that there are union issues, but I am sorry, Mr. Lind is world renowned and his decision to play here was made because he was promised certain things. When they were not delivered, Mr. Lind made it clear that he was no longer obligated to play the benefit tonight. Mr. Dickens and myself have hashed it out and I am happy to say that we came to an understanding. If the toilets are fixed by a reputable company, the show can go on."

"We got maintenance people for this."

"I'm sorry to say, Mr. Lind doesn't trust your people, not after seeing the state of the bathrooms under your care."

"This is unacceptable."

"I have Jonathan Lamda on the phone here, and you can confirm this with him if you like."

There was a rustling as the phone was passed. "Jonathan?"

Jonathan squeaked a greeting. "Hey, Tim. Sorry about the bathroom issue. Andrew has been out all morning and it all fell on my plate. I need you to let the plumbers in the rear entrance. Mr. Bishop will take them over to the room. He needs to oversee the work." Jonathan was staying on script, but the words left his mouth without a trace of confidence. He didn't sound like he was behind what he was saying, but he didn't have to. He was just another guy who had to follow the orders that came down from above.

"You know the unions will have our asses if they find out about this, Jonathan."

"I know, Tim, I know. But you know," Jonathan looked at Andrew. "You know how it is. Andrew makes deals without telling the rest of us and then he leaves us holding the bag."

"Leaves us at three in the afternoon holding the bag," Tim said.

Jonathan forced himself to chuckle. "Sometimes it's two thirty." He found a patch of wall to stare at that was far away from Dickens' eyes.

"Can we keep this under wraps, Tim?"

"Fine, fine, but any other work goes through me, alright?"

I bent down and whispered in Jonathan's ear.

"Sure, sure, of course. Listen, while I have you, this Lind guy is a pain in the ass. Like that diva we had last month on steroids. His guy might be down there a lot today. Do me a favour and tell everyone to stay clear of him. I don't want him bitching at me any more than he has to."

"You got it."

"Thanks, Tim."

The phone was passed back and Miles said, "Thank you so much, Jonathan," before he hung up the phone.

CHAPTER THIRTY-FOUR

It was ten more minutes before Miles was back in the office. "We're good. How were the children?"

Jonathan, now bound with zip ties and gagged, moaned from his place on the floor. Dickens was in his office chair, both of his hands zip-tied together behind his back.

Miles looked at both men. "Never mind, I see they were naughty."

"The maintenance guy give you any trouble?"

"At first," Miles said. "But I took him along to supervise. He'll be tied up for a while. Get it? Tied up?"

I ignored the bad joke. "The violinist here yet?"

"Yeah," Miles said. "If you stick your head out the door, you can see him and his manager on the stage. He's warming up with his own instrument."

"He mind waiting on the stage instead of in a dressing room?"

"Not when I told him that maintenance reported the toilets overflowing sewage onto the floor. You'd be surprised," Miles said. "Classical musicians don't like shit a whole lot."

The clock on the computer screen across from Dickens told me that we had twenty minutes until the violin was scheduled to show up. I took out the burner and called the first saved number again.

Carl picked up on the first ring. "Yeah?"

"Problems?"

"None. We're good."

"There is nothing good about this," I heard Ilir say.

"Can it, kid." Carl was all business on the job. He was probably not much fun off the job, but he was absolutely zero on it.

"Be ready," I said.

I hung up the phone and walked around to Dickens' desk. He was sitting in the chair with his hands bound behind his back and his legs bound at the ankles. "Tell me how to bring up the surveillance footage."

"I don't — I can't do that here. We have a special office for that."

I rolled my eyes at Dickens and looked over at Miles. He was smiling widely from his perch on the edge of the desk.

"Remember a phone call a few days back, Andy? 'Sir, I know that you have an event coming up and we here at Safety First Surveillance specialize in securing events. How would you like to be able to view every camera in your venue from the comfort of your own office chair?'"

Dickens' mouth hung open a little bit.

"What was your answer?" Miles asked.

Dickens said nothing.

"Andy, what did you tell me?"

"That — That I could already do that."

Miles got off the side of the desk and tousled Dickens' hair. "You need to accept that you are not in control here. Just do what you're told and you'll walk out of this with everything you came in with still attached." Miles looked at me. "I'm going."

Dickens watched Miles leave. When the door closed, it took him a minute to look up at me.

"I'm sorry. I — I — I was just —"

"I know what you were doing," I said. "Just like I know what you're going to do next. You are going to tell me how to call up the camera feeds."

Dickens guided me through opening the program and I brought a grid of camera feeds up on the screen. Each square could be maximized for a better look with a click of the mouse. I found the camera watching the back door in the far left corner and maximized it. The loading bay was empty, but that would change any minute. Ten, to be precise.

CHAPTER THIRTY-FIVE

The armoured car was three minutes ahead of schedule. The driver pulled a sharp U-turn and backed it up to the rear entrance. The two rear doors opened and four men stepped out. One of the men was holding a case. The four men looked around the parking lot until they were satisfied. One man said something and then the four moved as a unit for the door. I minimized the window and found the one with Miles approaching the door. The footage was grainy, so I couldn't see what I knew was there. Miles had changed the clip-on badge for the lanyard that had Jonathan's name on it.

On the screen, Miles approached the four men with his right hand outstretched. The man who had spoken shook it and then moved his lips some more. Miles responded and lifted the card on the lanyard up so that the security guard could get a look at it. The look lasted five seconds — enough time for him to read the name. There was no scrutiny. The name on the card was what they expected to find, so it was enough. People are easy to con when they get what they expect to get.

Miles led the four men inside to an elevator and rode up three floors with them. I had already changed cameras when the doors opened and I tracked the men down the hallway. Miles led the security guards right to the dressing room that had been assigned to David Lind. I could see that Miles and the lead guard were conversing as they moved down the hall. The body language of both men told me that the conversation was a comfortable one. Miles stopped at a door and briskly knocked three times. He didn't wait for a response, he just opened the door and stepped inside. The four guards followed on his heels.

This was it. Nothing to do but wait and watch. Inside the room would be a show all its own. Miles' unannounced entry brought the whole group in on two men in the middle of a pre-concert warm-up. Both men would be naked, save for the pants around the ankles of the man thrusting against the ass of the other. The rest of the two men's clothes would be staged to look as though they had been part of a wardrobe bomb that just went off. There would be clothes on the floor, the couch, even on the blades of the ceiling fan.

Ilir had fought the idea, and then fought the position. He didn't want to be behind Carl and he didn't want Carl behind him. In the end, Ilir had no choice but to pretend to be the pitcher. Carl's moustache was something that would be remembered if it was seen, so it was best for him to be the farthest from the intrusive security detail. After letting everyone get an eyeful, Ilir would scream, "Leave the violin and get out!"

Miles would throw his hands in the air and feign concern for the privacy of his star; he would pull the violin away from the guard at all costs and leave it on the floor while the two men moved into the bathroom to cover up. If the guards didn't give up the case, Carl would take his face out of the pillow it was buried in and pull the two revolvers stashed underneath. Then it would be the security guards who would end up getting fucked. I stared at the small empty square on the screen for fifteen seconds waiting to see how things would go. Four men spilled out into the hall followed by Miles who backed away from the doorway holding two hands up in front of him in a gesture of apology. He pulled the dressing room door closed and then turned to speak with the four security guards. When the lead guard crossed his arms and shook his head, Miles threw up his arms and went back to the door. This time, he didn't just walk in. This time he knocked. He rapped on the door three times and then took a big step back as though a lion might burst through the door at any second. A small crack opened in the doorway. Miles tentatively leaned into the space and then the door abruptly closed. A second later the door opened again, this time wider, and a violin case was shoved through the door. The case was the same; the item inside was another story. The case was shoved against Miles' chest and he threw himself backwards like a silent-era slapstick star. The door slammed closed and Miles passed the case to the head of security. He said something to the group of men and then led them away from the door. They were on their way to the stage — the long way to the stage. Miles would make no secret that he was killing time while Lind and his manager got themselves decent. He would fill the vacant minutes by showing off the theatre to the four men and telling them all of the things he had learned on the internet the day before. When they got to the stage after the lengthy tour, they wouldn't be surprised to find violinist David Lind and his manager already there. They also would resist eye contact after seeing so much of everything else a few minutes before.

When Miles and the violin security-detail disappeared, I called Carl. He picked up right away.

"Hall is clear. Go," I said.

"Got it."

Carl hung up and a second later, two men in plumber's coveralls exited the dressing room. One of the men, the older of the pair, held a large toolbox. Three minutes later, I watched the two men leave the building. Two minutes after that, all hell broke loose.

CHAPTER THIRTY-SIX

I had no way to erase the surveillance footage, so I just closed the program and stepped away from the computer. I moved behind the chair and tipped it forward. Instinctively, Dickens pushed back to maintain his seat on the chair. His momentum sent him back into my arms, but I didn't catch him. I slipped my arm around his throat and looped my free hand around the back of his head. My right hand hooked my inner elbow, closing a tight knot around the man's throat. Jonathan could do nothing but watch as his boss lost consciousness. Dickens was out in ten seconds, I kept the choke on twenty-five. I lifted him out of the chair and dragged his unconscious body to the closet. It took a bit of juggling, but I got the door open without dropping the Symphony Orchestra director. I set Dickens down on his ass and then tipped his feet up towards his face. The dark closet swallowed him whole with a wet slurp from the urine-soaked carpet inside.

Jonathan had started to shimmy his body towards the door, as though he had a shot at opening it. He watched me come for him with wide, fearful eyes. I had planned to put him to sleep the same way I had just knocked out his boss, but Jonathan changed my plans when he tried to scream. His mouth opened wide, but the heel of my foot found his solar plexus before he could muster a noise. The air left the man's body in a whoosh and Jonathan's eyes suddenly opened wider as a new layer of panic settled in on him. I pulled the revolver, turned it in my hand, and brought the butt down across the handsome man's temple. The eyes fluttered and then closed. I dragged Jonathan to the closet by his belt and pitched him on top of his boss. I closed the door and had just started wiping down the room when I heard the pops. There were three of them in quick succession and then two more. It could have been lights breaking, or something falling to the stage from the rafters. It could have been any of those things, but it wasn't. The noises were gunshots.

I left the office and looked down onto the stage from the hallway window. Four men in yellow security T-shirts were on the ground; so was a man in a suit and another in a golf shirt. The seventh man on the ground was Miles. There was no sign of the shooter, and nothing to indicate that anyone had been actually shot. A second later, the security guards came up off the ground pulling at the weapons holstered on their hips. All four men moved off the stage and down into the orchestra pit. I put my face close to the glass and tried to see down into the pit, but there wasn't a good angle from the balcony.

I heard the office phone ring as I watched musicians and staff pour out of the orchestra section in all directions. I glanced back at the stage and saw two men still on the floor.

Neither was Miles. I gave up on the window, ignored the sound of the phone, and started moving. I went back into the office and wiped down the door, the desk, and the rest of the computer. Before I went back out the door, I ran the wipe over the closet doorknob.

I ran down the hallway to the stairwell door and used the wipe to open the latch. The stairwell echoed with the sounds of human panic and I forced myself to slow my pace and walk calmly down the stairs. I was halfway down when a small crowd burst through the second-floor door. There were six people in all, four women and two men, all of whom were holding cell phones. The bodies created a jam in the stairwell and the brief impediment gave a woman in her early forties a moment to glance to her left. She was short and wide and her dyed red hair was cut too short for her fat face. She locked eyes with me and squinted as she tried to place my face. I could read her thoughts like they were being broadcasted. If I was coming down the stairs from the boss's floor, she should know who I was, but she didn't.

The line started moving and the woman was forced to take her eyes off me. She was pushed forward by the surge of energy from the two women behind her and I followed in the wake. Three-quarters of the way down the stairs, the redhead risked a look over her shoulder at me. I saw her face turning in time to tilt my own and feign attention on navigating the steps.

The next look came in the lobby. The group of six, free from the confines of the hallway, expanded like Pillsbury dough from the canister. I went for the doors on the right, while the six employees angled left. The stragglers running out from the concert hall swept me up in their current and I picked up speed on my way to the door. All of the momentum dissipated on the other side of the glass doors. A throng of people, all of whom had been seeking the safety of somewhere else, had congealed in front of the concert hall.

I shouldered my way into the crowd in the direction of the parking lot and the van that Ilir had left for us. If I was lucky it was still there. Miles and I were supposed to meet up at the van and drive out together, but the gunshots had changed that, making it every man for himself now.

"There!"

The voice carried over the rapid conversations all around me. Everyone turned their head, everyone except me, towards the speaker.

"The man in the black suit. That's him." In my peripheral vision I saw a few heads swivel from the woman to my direction. I turned my head with them as though I were searching for the source of the commotion too and kept moving. The woman yelled some more, but without any reaction the crowd just wrote it off as a person in hysterics. I neared the outer edge of the crowd and found that I could go no further. People stood shoulder to shoulder in front of two police cruisers. The four patrolmen were out of the cars and asking everyone in polite, but firm tones, to stay where they were. There was no way I was getting past the cops without being noticed. I didn't waste time wondering how the police were on site so fast; I just turned and began threading my way back through the crowd. As I neared the front of the concert hall, I saw that two of the four security guards were out front. Next to one of the yellow shirts was the redheaded woman. She saw me on the edge of the crowd and began pulling on the security guard's shirt. I broke left at a leisurely pace and brought my phone from my pocket to my ear to obscure my face. I followed the concrete around the side of the building until I was out of sight and then I started running.

I made it to the other side of the building before anyone came around to follow me. I kept up my pace and sprinted across the rear of the building. I had covered about half of the distance when a police car rounded the corner. The driver saw me and immediately angled right and came to a quick stop. The cop riding up front was quick to get out of the vehicle and take a position behind the open door. I watched his hand go to his belt and start back up. Back wasn't an option — forward was all I had left. I pulled the revolver from behind my back and put three bullets into the squad car. My finger moved faster than the shooter in the concert hall and I didn't miss. The slugs punched through the driver side window and sent the cop down onto his knees under a shower of glass pebbles.

When the cop stuck his head up again, I had closed the gap.

"Drop the gun and put your hands in the air," I said.

The cop was scared and quick to obey. I heard the gun hit the pavement and then saw two empty hands come up into the empty window pane.

I moved around the door fast and kept my voice loud and aggressive. "Face down on the ground."

The cop did what he had been trained to make others

do without hesitation. I scooped the police issue pistol up, threw it into the cruiser, and took a step back over the prone body. My rear foot had just left the ground when I was spun hard into the passenger door. The bullet had entered high on my left shoulder and would have put me on my back if it wasn't for the second bullet. The shooter had overcorrected for the buck of the handgun and the second bullet came in lower and farther to the right than the first. The slug punched me in the side and ended my sloppy pirouette. My back collided with the side of the squad car and I slid down the cruiser door to the pavement.

The cop on the ground was quick to move for my gun. He sprang to his knees and grabbed the barrel with two hands. The cop wrenched at the gun and began twisting it away from me. My other hand wouldn't respond to what my brain was telling it to do. Luckily, my right hand picked up the slack. My finger tensed twice and the revolver bucked hard. After the second shot, the cop screamed and pulled two bloody hands away from the gun.

"Freeze!"

To my right was one of the yellow-shirted security guards. He had a black pistol trained on me — mine was still on the cop.

"Put the gun down, or I kill him," I said.

"Put your weapon down, or I will shoot," was the reply I received.

The bullet hadn't hurt when it hit me, but now my shoulder was starting to burn.

"No," I said. "Your gun. Now."

The security guard didn't move.

"Hey, cop, you got kids?" I asked.

The uniformed officer was cradling his hands. "Two," he said. "I got two kids."

"You want to see them again?"

"Yes."

"Then tell the rent-a-cop to put down his gun."

The cop wasted no time. "Put it down."

The security guard didn't move. I pushed myself up using the car at my back for support.

"Stay on the ground," the guard called.

I figured I had seconds, not minutes, before another cop or guard was on the scene.

"Tell him your kids' names," I said.

"Laura and Jenny. Their names are Laura and Jenny. Please, just put the gun down, man."

The security guard risked a look at the downed cop. He saw the tears, the pale face, and the blood. The security guard forced air out of his nose and then turned the muzzle of his pistol to the sky. He opened his other hand and showed me the palm. "Take it easy, pal. The gun is up. I'm going to put it on the ground now."

The job had been planned well. We had covered every angle, or so we thought, but change had a way of seeping in through the cracks and ruining everything in a flood. The only anchor keeping me from getting swept away were the constants I set for myself — limits that couldn't be crossed. The line was getting taken. No matter what — that was not going to happen. That one constant held me firm in the deep water rising around me. Everything was in flux. Everything, except me. I had not changed.

"It's going down," the security guard said as he slowly bent his knees to lower the gun the rest of the way to the pavement. "See?"

I swung the revolver right and covered the guard as his gun descended the last foot. The dark metal of the barrel clinked, like a dangerous cheers, when it made contact with the pavement. The guard, now unarmed, started to rise. I let him get to his feet before I put a bullet in his stomach.

CHAPTER THIRTY-SEVEN

There really had been no choice at all. There were too many pieces on the board. I needed to knock a few of the pawns over to stall the ones that were still in the game. Two targets, two choices — a cop and someone playing at being a cop. But when there is a real cop on one side and a pretend one on the other, there really is no choice. Both were white men of similar age, hair, and build. Both were from the same geographical area. Both shared the same physiology. Both were similar in almost every way. But shoot one instead of the other, and the response will be entirely different. The cop was hurt and that was bad enough — I didn't need the Buffalo police force to be any more motivated to come after me.

The security guard was on his side moaning. His yellow shirt was stained red and I could smell the shit spilling out of the hole in his gut. The wound was intentional — the bullet hole just above the beltline was deadly, but not immediately. With medical attention, the odds of him pulling through were good. It would take more than a doctor to save the guard's life though. It would also take someone putting pressure on the wound and someone else to call for help. One bullet took care of the guard, the cop, and whoever showed up next.

I angled my body and managed to get my good shoulder against the side of the police car. I dug my heels in and shimmied to my feet. I stepped sideways twice, my back still against the car, and fell into the driver seat. The engine of the patrol car was still running and the radio was squawking like an angry chicken. I ignored the radio, put the car into drive, and pulled a tight U-turn. I drove around the building, keeping the car at an acceptable parking lot speed. The crowd loomed ahead on my right and heads began to snap in the direction of the cruiser. The other cop had held his position, but that wasn't something that was going to last. At the edge of the crowd, I saw him squinting at the car. His eyes caught sight of me and his hand rose to his hip. I gave the cruiser a lot of gas and the bulky police issue engine responded by throwing me back against the seat. The gun the cop was going for hadn't even cleared the holster when I whipped past him and onto the street. A few seconds later, I heard the radio call.

"Dispatch, the suspect has Peterson's vehicle. I repeat. The suspect has Peterson's vehicle and he is driving south away from the scene on Erie."

Dispatch replied almost instantly and a call went out to several cars in the area. Cops began speaking over one another, creating a buzz like the angry soldiers of a damaged hive.

I followed the street as it veered to the right, quickly

made another right onto a street leading under the Buffalo Skyway, and closed in on the bumper of the first car I saw. My bloody palm slapped against the dash until the flashers came on overhead.

The Subaru hatchback responded by signalling and pulling off of the road onto a quiet gravel parking lot under the bridge. The driver stopped parallel to the road and began rummaging around inside the car, likely for license and registration. I pulled the squad car in behind the Subaru and scanned the lot. No one was around. I searched the front seat for the first aid kit, but came up empty. I grabbed the police pistol off the passenger seat, pulled out the keys, and went around to the back of the squad car. Inside the trunk, I found the first aid kit. I took the white box and put it down on the pavement. I went through what was left inside the trunk and stashed four road flares in my pockets. I needed a jerry can, but all I found was a half-empty bottle of Pennzoil. I grabbed the kit and, on my way back around the car, paused at the gas tank cover. I opened the flap and unscrewed the cap. The motor oil went in with an easy squeeze. I popped the top off the road flare and it hissed to life. I shoved the flaming end deep into the gas tank and ran to the Subaru. The woman had watched everything in her rear-view, but she had not yet decided to drive away. The flashers exuded authority and most people would do whatever they were told if they thought someone with authority ordered them to do it. The Germans had proved that fact to the world more than once. The obedient citizen still had her window down and her licence in her hand when I got to the open window.

"Was I speeding, officer?" She had trouble getting the words out because her eyes were on the rear-view. I turned my head and saw the smoke coming out of the cruiser's gas tank. There had not been much oil in the bottle, and it hadn't led the flames to the tank. Not yet anyway.

I reached into the car and unlocked the doors.

"What are you do —"

The woman, a petite Latina in her forties, didn't have enough time to finish the sentence before I got in the back seat.

I put the cop's pistol to the back of her head and said, "Drive."

The cars passing by rubbernecked the smoke, but not the Subaru.

"I don't understand. What is going on?"

I pushed the gun harder into her scalp, parting the nest of thick black hair. The barrel revealed a current of grey hair running under the surface. A siege was underway, and the woman needed chemical reinforcements if she was ever going to hold off the enemy.

"Signal, get into traffic, and start driving."

"Okay, okay, just please don't hurt me. Please." The second *please* was all fear.

"Just drive, lady."

The woman signalled and pulled onto the road. She didn't even attempt to reverse so that she could use the entrance to leave the lot. She just drove the Subaru over the sidewalk and onto the road. I turned my body and grunted down the stab of pain in my side. The cruiser hadn't exploded, but smoke had begun to pour out from underneath the vehicle. I didn't need fireworks, just enough heat to fuck up the forensics. I wiped my hand on my shirt and pulled out the cell phone I had bought a few days before. I was getting tired and shock was starting to creep up on me. I needed to be at the safe house fast. I dialled the third saved number and Miles picked up on the second ring.

"Where are you?" I said.

No jokes this time. "On my way to where I am supposed to be going. You?"

"Give me a street."

"Why? Where are you?"

I looked out the window. "Just passing Huron."

"Wrong direction," Miles said.

"No, it's not. The cops are behind me, so it's the perfect direction. I need you to meet up with me."

There was a short pause. "No."

I didn't say anything back. I understood. I wouldn't have gone back for him either. I ended the call and opened the first aid kit.

"Where am I going?" the woman behind the wheel asked.

"Just keep driving. There has been a change in plans. What's your name?"

"Monica."

"I'm sorry to put you out like this, Monica. Just keep driving and in a little while I will be gone."

"You're hurt," Monica said.

She was right. My side was bleeding badly. The shoulder hurt more, but it leaked less. I touched around my side and then around the shoulder and confirmed what I thought.

The bullet had gone through my side, but not the shoulder. The blood on my shirt was red, not black. Red was the best of a bad situation. I needed to stop the flow before I lost consciousness and then my ride. I shrugged out of the suit jacket and then the shirt. The movements were clumsy and the grunts loud. I ripped the undershirt off with my good arm and looked down at my stomach. An inch and a half to the right and the bullet would have missed me completely. The hole in the front was small — the one in back bigger. I opened the kit and saw a needle and thread, but it was missing another pair of hands. I shook the dizziness away and groped around the seat beside me. My hand closed around the cool cylinder of the flare and I brought the cap to my mouth. I closed my teeth around the plastic and pulled back on the end. The flare hissed to life and filled the car with light and smoke.

"Jesus!" Monica yelled. The car echoed her shock with a wild swerve.

"Roll down the windows," I said.

"What are you doing?"

"Just roll them down and keep the car moving. No matter what, you keep going."

All four windows receded into their housing and I felt air rush in to combat the sweat beaded on my forehead. I put my head against the door and let the air blow against me. I took two deep breaths and then I turned my head so that I could see the hole six inches above my back pocket. I kept my eyes off the flare — looking at it was like staring into a small sun. I took another look at the wound and watched it belch another splash of blood onto my skin;

then, I buried the flare into the hole.

I screamed out what was left in my lungs and then I passed out. When I woke a few seconds later, Monica was already pulling over. The gun came off my lap and sloppily parted the hair on the back of her head. "Keep driving."

She signalled and pulled back into traffic.

The flare was on the floor and still burning. The interior of the car smelled like burnt carpet and barbeque. I swore as I bent for the flare. I grabbed the rod and took in two huge gulps of air. I made more noise when the flare went in the entry wound than I had for the exit wound — I passed out for a longer time too. When I came to, Monica was already on the side of the road, her hand was on the door handle, and her seat belt was on its way to being retracted. I managed to get a fistful of hair before she slid out.

"Hands at ten and two on the wheel."

She sobbed, but did as she was told.

I reached over and took her purse off the passenger seat.

"Hey!"

"Drive," I said.

She wiped at her face and then put the car in gear again.

I took my ripped T-shirt and wadded it up one-handed. I pushed the rag to my shoulder and moved my torso around just enough to inspect the burns. There was still a bit of leakage, but nothing like before. I grabbed some gauze and tape from the first aid kit and began to work on dressing the cauterized wounds. I was able to get a patch made up using my right hand and my thigh as a worktable. I eased the dressing on both sides of my body and then made a third patch for the shoulder. For the last dressing, I used the rest of the gauze and almost all of the tape. I needed the bandage to stay on, so I wound the white medical tape around my arm over and over again, creating a mummified appearance from bicep to collarbone. I shouldered the shirt back on and did up the buttons. The jacket went on next. It was wet with blood, but the dark colour made it harder to notice than the stained white shirt underneath. From a distance, a really far distance, the buttoned jacket did a good job of concealing the wounds.

I leafed through Monica's purse and found a long pink leather wallet. Inside were pictures of two kids — boys, both of whom were high-school age. There was no evidence of a husband in the wallet, and no evidence of a wedding ring on the hand that was still at ten on the wheel. The two pictures had the same backdrop: a kitchen with windows showing a green backyard.

"Monica, I need you to take me to your house, and before you give me a reason why you can't, remember that I now know where you live. If you say no, I will kill you and go there anyway. Imagine your boys coming home to just me."

"Just let me call my kids and tell them to go to their dad's." There was less of a quaver in her voice when she spoke this time. The threat to her children had woken something inside, something primitive and maternal. The sound of her voice reminded me of a bear I had once seen at the zoo. The spectators crowded around her cub and the camera flashes invaded the space behind the bars. The old bear, rescued from a corrupt European circus, shook off years of abuse and injury and stood to her full height in front of her young. The people, all of whom were safe behind the bars, took steps back and groped for their young crying children. The woman driving the Subaru would do what she had to do. She would stand up for her cubs. No different than the bear.

"Fair enough," I said.

CHAPTER THIRTY-EIGHT

The kitchen table was scarred and battered. It was the kind of table that had seen thousands of dinners, hundreds of arguments, homework, birthdays, and holidays. I had never owned a table like that, not once in my life. I should have felt sad adding a foreign memory to the wood. My presence was something that would infect the cultured surface like a virus. The blood staining the tabletop would come off, but not really. It would stain deeper than the surface; it would stain the memories. Monica would scrub it clean again and again in the coming weeks, but it would be pointless — the virus was terminal. The table would be out on the curb before the end of the month.

Monica's hair was wet with sweat. I needed things from her medicine cabinet, and there was no way she was going up alone. I had made her shoulder me up the stairs and then down again. Beyond the sweat stains, Monica looked terrible. The adrenalin spike she had been riding from the carjacking was starting to ebb and exhaustion was settling in. But as bad as she looked, I looked worse. I caught a flash of my reflection in the bathroom mirror and saw a face that resembled mine, but could have easily belonged to someone else. My skin was pale and ashen like new concrete and I somehow looked ten pounds underweight. I thought I had done a good job keeping the blood in my body, but all of a sudden I started to wonder.

Downstairs, I sat at the head of the kitchen table with a feast of household wares stationed around me.

"Sit down, please," I said.

Monica laughed and pushed a wet strand of hair back on her head. "Men with guns don't say please."

"Have you been around many men with guns?"

She looked right at me without blinking. "Yes."

"Then you should know that pleases work better than threats."

"The men I knew didn't threaten."

"Maybe we knew some of the same people," I said. "Please, sit down."

Monica sat.

"Closer," I said.

She inched the chair closer.

"Closer."

She did it again.

"Closer."

Fed up with the word, Monica moved the chair forward with a hard shove. She was no longer shocked at her situation, and her hard disposition made me think that she wasn't lying about having been around men with guns. Her confession made what I had to do even more necessary. I opened my legs and inched closer until the wood of my chair touched her knees. Monica, obviously uncomfortable being so close to me, turned her face away to study the pictures on the fridge door. The gun was resting on my left thigh. I couldn't raise it high with my damaged arm, but I could hit the woman in front of me without even trying to aim. With my right hand, I began to wind the duct tape I had found in a drawer around the barrel of the revolver. After three rotations, I wound it around my hand several times. I let the roll of tape hang off my wrist and pushed the gun deep into Monica's side. She gasped at the invasion of her personal space, then recoiled. The gun stayed against her.

"Take the tape and wrap it around your waist."

She started to protest so I repeated myself and inserted the word "Please."

Monica did as she was told. The tape belched loudly as it came off the roll, wound around her body, hooked around my thumb, and started another rotation. After seven revolutions, I told Monica to stop. She ripped the tape from the roll and I smoothed the raised lip down.

"Good," I said. "Now take the scissors and cut my shirt off. Do I need to tell you what will happen if you get cute with the pointy ends?"

Monica looked down at her waist and squirmed a little in her chair. "You'll shoot me."

"I'll spasm involuntarily and the gun will go off. You'll be an active participant in your own murder. If I pass out, the same thing will happen if you try to get up from that chair."

"What happened to words working better than threats?"

"I'll still ask you nicely," I said. "The gun is just to make sure that you listen."

"You're insane."

"I'm out of options. Now, cut off the shirt, please."

Monica did as she was told. "Now what?"

"Hit the wound with the alcohol and then use the paring knife in the bowl to probe around for the bullet. There is going to be blood so have the paper towels ready to soak it up. When you find the bullet, take the needle-nose pliers out of the bowl and pull it out."

"Your hand will move. You'll shoot me."

"I won't," I said.

"Yes you will. Take your finger off the trigger."

I shook my head. "This is the way it is. Take the bullet out or I wait for your kids to come home and I make one of them do it while the other one sits in a chair taped to a gunman."

Monica's eyes welled up. "Goddamn you."

I picked up the belt I had taken off just before I sat and put the strap between my teeth. I spoke over the leather. "Do it."

The air went in through my nose and out around the belt. The breaths started smooth and even, but the first probe of the knife changed the rhythm. I focused on my breath — on getting it into my body and letting it out. I had come across books on meditation when I was a kid. I didn't view the texts as a means of finding myself, or God; it, like everything else, was for something more important than that. Everything I had ever learned about meditation I had bastardized for the job. The calm and focus that came from the practice of following the ebb and flow of my breaths became a tool for theft instead of a practice on a cushion. After a time, I could slow my breathing and wait for hours, even days, on a job. I was able to operate detached from everything and was undisturbed by the changes around me — a sort of Zen and the art of breaking the seventh commandment. But I had never come across a book about using deep breathing to handle battlefield-condition surgery.

The second probe of the knife was deeper and more painful than the first. I focused again on the air moving into my nose. The breath came and went, taking none of the pain with it. I bit the belt, tasted leather, and forced myself to take in another breath. The third invasive surgery attempt caused the pain to uncoil like a snake; the phantom serpent began to wrap itself in wider arcs around my body. The noise that left my lips interrupted the ebb and flow of air into my body. I let the guttural yell go until it bottomed out, and then I pulled another slow breath in and found the rhythm again. This time I didn't try to fight the pain — I felt every bit of it as I focused on staying conscious and alive. My heart rate slowed from a sprint to a run and my finger strained, but it didn't compress the trigger.

Monica operated without any consideration for me. Every deep probe that elicited a muffled scream brought her eyes to the gun at her side, not my face. I liked that — she wanted to live and that meant she would do what she had to, and that meant keeping me alive.

"How will I know when I find it?" she asked.

I spoke over the belt. "You will feel something before you

see it. You feel anything out of place, open the wound with the pliers and look."

Monica laughed a little, and then she imitated my voice through the belt. "Anything out of place. It's inside your shoulder, not under the couch." She kept working the knife and my teeth slowly worked their way through the thick leather belt.

After a minute, she said, "There."

I grunted, "Pliers."

Monica had no choice but to hold the wound open with her fingers while she went after the slug.

There was an agonizing pull before the pliers flew back with only a piece of tissue to show for all of the work.

"Fuck," she said.

Sweat burned my eyes. "Again," I said. The belt was still in my mouth, but my teeth were together in some places.

Monica tried four more times. It was during the fourth that I lost consciousness. I came to in the middle of a fight. I was losing. My head rocked left and I tasted blood. The next blow turned my face hard to the right. "Wake up! Wake up! Wake up!"

I opened my eyes and saw that Monica was crying.

"You were falling out of the chair."

I nodded and then swung my chin towards my shoulder. "You done?"

She shook her head and gave the gun another look. "Maybe you should take the gun away. I'll keep trying, I will, but if you pass out again, we're both going to die."

I shook my head. "Again." The belt tasted bitter in my mouth as I shifted it left and bit down into a fresh spot.

The fifth attempt was no better than the previous four, but the sixth was as textbook as home surgery with household items could be. The bullet came loose with a sound like a boot coming out of a deep mud puddle.

"Oh thank God," Monica said.

"Disinfect and then put a few layers of gauze on it," I said.

Monica did as she was told. Then, she went for a bandage.

"No," I said. "The first aid kit has a needle and thread. Stitch it up."

Monica pulled the kit closer and found the needle and thread without comment.

"Can you sew?"

"Better than I can dig a bullet out of a carjacker's shoulder," she said.

Monica threaded the needle and went to work closing the shoulder. Five minutes later, both of us were staring at each other. Blood covered everything on the table.

"What now?" Monica asked. "Are you going to kill me?"

"No," I said. "I don't want you dead. I want you to take your clothes off."

CHAPTER THIRTY-NINE

Everything we wore went into the garbage bag; so did everything we used in our DIY surgery.

Monica and I were both naked as she helped me up the stairs. From the hallway, I watched as she pulled clothes for me from her eldest son's room. I put on what I could and got help with the rest after Monica got dressed.

Back downstairs, I doused the table with bleach from the laundry room and then I made Monica take the garbage bag out into the backyard. The barbeque I had seen in the pictures in her wallet was exactly where it had been when the snapshots were taken. The grill was large and the tank was half-full. I had Monica turn on the gas before I turned all of the dials to high and clicked the starter. We waited, standing wordless, until the thermometer was redlining. I opened the lid with the tip of the revolver and then took a step back from the heat. I gestured at the bag with the gun and then swung the barrel in the direction of the grill. Monica understood and grumbled something under her breath while she stooped to pick up the bag. It was hard to get the lid down over the bag at first, but the heat had a way of sucking the life out of everything it touched and eventually the bag shrivelled enough for the lid to close.

Monica fanned the smoke away from her face while I chewed another painkiller I had found in the en-suite medicine cabinet. The bottle had expired, but the pain hadn't.

"You know I'm going to take your car, right?"

Monica didn't take her eyes off the barbeque. A change had occurred inside and now black smoke was marching like army ants from all of the spaces in the structure. "I know what you're going to do."

Tears welled up in Monica's eyes — she closed them, took in a long shaky breath, and held it.

"Take six of these," I said.

The breath came out and the eyelids raised. "What?"

"Take six of these."

Monica looked at the pill bottle in my hand. I had taken the sleeping pills along with the old bottle of painkillers when I had raided her medicine cabinet.

"I thought —"

"That I was going to kill you."

She nodded.

"No."

"Kindness works best," she said. The small smile on her face looked ridiculous.

"Nope. If your kids came home early and found your body, it would put the police on my trail faster than I am prepared for. But if they find you sleeping upstairs, they will at least give you the night before they worry about you. The night is more time than I'll need."

The colour drained from Monica's face as she realized that the only thing that was keeping her alive was convenience. It's hard the first time you realize your life really is cheap.

"Upstairs, please," I said.

It took twenty-five minutes for the pills to work. I tested the effects by putting the tip of a safety pin I found in the bedside drawer into the centre of the sole of Monica's foot. She let out a dreamy whimper and then rolled over and began to snore loudly.

The painkillers had started to kick in and I made it down the stairs without coming close to falling. I went through the first floor with a rag doused with the bleach and wiped every surface that even looked familiar. When I was done, I poured the rest of the bleach into a bucket I found under the sink. I dropped the pistol I took off the cop into the bucket and pushed it into the back of the cupboard with the toe of my shoe. The police issue gun was a better firearm than the revolver Ilir picked up, but it was a cop's gun and that made it stupid to carry. With a wounded cop in the hospital, the rest of the force would be in on the manhunt. Any ballistic evidence would just be a trail that could be followed. The gun had to go.

I was weak and tired — the last of the adrenalin in my system was waning. I opened the fridge with the rag and found what I expected a mother of two teenage boys to have — plenty of food. My stomach churned at the sight of the food, but I ignored it and reached for a two-litre bottle of Coke. I needed calories more than I needed nutrients and the sugary drink was an easy way to get them in. I put the bottle in the sink and used the cloth to open the cupboards. I found a bag of sugar in a lower cabinet and I put as much as I could into the three-quarter-full bottle. I took a deep breath and then brought the bottle up to my lips. The liquid was so sweet that it made me wince, but I took a deeper second gulp and then a bigger third.

The sun had begun to exit and the light outside was no longer as intense as it had once been. I slid behind the wheel of Monica's Subaru and took two more swigs from the bottle. I felt a sudden urge to retch, but I kept the contents of my stomach where they were. Behind the house, a dark column of smoke was still climbing like a vine. The neighbourhood smelled of charred plastic and I could see that every home around me had closed their windows. Soon, someone would bang on Monica's door. After that, they would call the police, or the fire department. Let them call whoever they wanted to; whoever showed up would just bang on the door, too. Monica wasn't going to answer, not tonight anyway. By the time she woke up to face the neighbours, I would be across the border.

CHAPTER FORTY

Keeping the Subaru at the speed limit, I drove north towards the safe house. The house was not the one we had brought Dickens to — this house was closer to the border. The safe house was another spot that Miles had visited with the real estate agent. It was as good as the first in every way, except for the fact that it lacked a garage. I parked the Subaru behind a rusted Geo Tracker two streets away from the house, wiped the wheel and doors with a rag I had taken from the house, and then stashed the keys in the driver side wheel well. The neighbourhood was near a community college and the realtor had told Miles that most of the homes were rentals. That fact, along with the poor condition of the house, scared off a lot of potential buyers. The place had been on the market for eight months and there had not even been an offer. Parking two streets over wasn't a necessity — there was plenty of parking closer to the safe house. I didn't even have to park right behind the Geo. On this particular street there were plenty of empty curbs. The summer month was a tranquilizer for the student housing market, making tenants sparse. But the Geo's presence on the side street gave me a way to obscure the front plate of the Subaru. The tight parking spot would slow down anyone looking for a particular arrangement of letters and numbers. The distance from the safe house was another layer that would bog down anyone on my trail even more. The numerous vacant rentals would all have to be searched before the police expanded their search to other streets. The layers of obfuscation and misdirection would buy me more than enough time to get to the border. I walked away from the car, pretending to belong on the street. I was glad no one was around; the only way I would blend in is if there was a zombie parade set to walk through the suburbs.

I crossed through two unfenced backyards and stepped onto a street running parallel to the one I had just been on. The homes in front of me had erected large wooden fences to keep animals in and people out. I went left until I saw a property without a fence that I could walk through to the street I wanted.

The safe house was dark from the street and the curtains on the windows were drawn. I crossed the street and went down the concrete path that ran along the side to the yard. The grass in the backyard was dead and yellow where it wasn't just dirt; the once-green stalks crunched like hay under my feet.

I approached the back door ready to knock; it opened before my knuckles even started their descent.

"I heard you weren't coming back," Carl said.

"I got held up," I said.

The driver backed up enough to let me in and I shut

the door behind me. On the kitchen table were open food containers and torn, grease-stained paper bags. Food was everywhere. We had stocked the house with food, water, and a laptop with a wireless card so that we could monitor the media. The curtains in the living room were drawn and the lights had been left off. None of the fading sunlight made it in from outside. Ilir sat on the floor; the laptop was on his knees. He only noticed me when the news went to commercial and he was able to tear his eyes away from the screen.

"Wilson! Holy shit. I heard you weren't coming back."

Same rumour; the two hearing it meant Miles was spreading it. "There was traffic," I said. "What has the news been saying?"

"Saying?" he said. "They're saying everything is fucked up. There's a manhunt going on for you right now. That guy you shot is in critical condition."

"Not dead, though," I said.

Ilir shook his head. "But there was something about injuries to an officer."

"Just his hands," I said. I looked around the room. "Where's Miles?"

"In the bathroom," Ilir said. "Guy's all cool and shit until the moment the job ends. Then he's got — what did he call it? A nervous bowel."

"Must have been something I ate," Miles said.

I turned and saw the con man coming down the stairs. The carpet had been torn up in some kind of first phase of renovation and no one had ever begun phase two. Miles was still in his suit. On the job, he had kept two buttons fastened. Off the job, the jacket was open, exposing the butt of the revolver tucked into his belt. He looked like he was one of Danny Ocean's guys. Sinatra, not Clooney. He stopped on the unfinished landing and looked me over.

"I thought you weren't going to make it back."

"So I heard."

"Hey," he said, holding his hands up. "You saw how bad it got out there. Going back was not in the game plan. Hell, a lot of stuff wasn't in the game plan."

"I understand," I said.

"So no hard feelings?"

I shook my head.

"You look like shit," Miles said with a shit-eating grin on his face. "Still no hard feelings?"

I ignored the joke and drank the rest of the soda from the bottle; the last mouthful was all settled sugar and it took a few seconds for it all to migrate from the bottle to my mouth. I set the empty container down on a plastic milk cart that was doubling as a coffee table. "Where is it?"

Everyone's eyes shifted in the same direction. Eight million dollars was leaning against the uncarpeted stairs. Ilir stayed on the floor with his laptop; it was Carl who moved for the case. He picked it up off the floor and held it out for me to take. I walked over and took the handle with my right hand and walked into the kitchen. I put the case down on the small section of counter space next to the vacant slot where a fridge belonged. The buckles shot back from the hinge like a rattlesnake lunging at easy prey. Inside the thinly lined case was a small musical instrument. The glossy surface of the dark wood had weathered over two centuries with grace. There were imperfections here and there from years of surely almost daily use, but they were the kinds of blemishes that made something more beautiful rather than less. I gave the violin a once-over and then took a step back to let the light from the exposed bulb bathe the surface. I tilted the instrument forward and the light stabbed into the openings that perforated the surface. Just inside one of the curved holes I saw the inscription.

Antonus Stradivarius Cremonensis Faciebat Anno 1837

I turned the violin in my hand and looked at the back of the instrument. The lines in the wood rose and fell in tight bunches like the sky in Van Gogh's *Starry Night*. The glossy varnish on the back of the instrument was thick enough to produce my reflection. My battered face reflected in the wood took something away from the calculated beauty of the violin. I moved away from the light and watched my face fade from the surface of the Stradivarius.

I took hold of the counter with my one good hand and placed the violin back into the case. Under my feet, the floor felt suddenly unsteady. I guided myself around the kitchen, using the counters for support, until I was close enough to cross to one of the folding chairs we had brought in. I groped through the wrappers and containers on the table until I found an unopened protein bar. I got it open with my teeth and took a huge bite of the bar. I was chewing loudly when Carl sat down.

"So what's the plan?"

"Same as it ever was. The police can have their manhunt, but the world will still march on. We just have to be sure to be in the crowd instead of on the parade route."

The protein bar went down my dry throat slowly, but the sustenance felt good. The painkiller I ate next felt better.

"They won't be watching the border," I said. "And if I'm wrong and they are — tonight there will be a hell of a lot to look at." There was a Bills pre-season game starting at seven and when it was over, the border would be swamped with people going back to their NFL-less cities in Canada. "Dressed in jerseys and hats, the four of us will blend in with every other car full of men."

"How bad are you hurt?" Carl asked. "Ilir said there were reports that one of the robbers was shot."

"Caught one in the shoulder," I said. "But the bullet is out and I'm stitched up." I saw no reason to mention the second bullet wound. "We're fine coming back from a football game. No one is going to look twice at a guy passed out in the back seat."

"Who took the bullet out?" Miles asked from the door.

"I found someone to do it for me."

"While being chased by the police?" Miles didn't try to hide his skepticism.

"Why were the police there?" I asked.

"Turns out," Miles said, "We weren't the only ones interested in the violin. There was a VIP scheduled to make an appearance. A senator who is a huge David Lind fan, and who also happens to be on the Homeland Security Committee, was scheduled to make an appearance. The cops were there setting up security for the event. The crowd ran right into them."

I thought back to the guest list we had stolen from Dickens. There had been two vacant spots that I had wrongly assumed were for the buyer and his representative. I cursed my stupidity and took another bite of the protein bar. "What happened on the floor?"

"I led the security detail up to the violinist and they were making the hand-off when someone in a mask came out of the wings. He threatened the guards with all kinds of violence unless they turned over the case. They handed it to him and he fired into the ceiling a few times. Everyone hit the deck and the masked man jumped into the orchestra pit. Everyone down there ran for the doors and the gunman disappeared in the commotion."

"Just like that," I said.

"Just like that," Miles said.

"The cops only reported one man getting away in the commotion. There was nothing about Dickens or his assistant," Carl said.

"Nothing yet, anyway," Ilir called from the living room.

"So what happened to the gunman?" I asked.

"A lot of questions today," Miles said.

I took another bite of the protein bar. "You have something to say, Miles?"

"I already said it. Who patched you up?"

"Your theory is the cops shot me, arrested me, patched me up, turned me, and sent me back here for you three in under four hours?"

"You said it, not me," Miles said.

From the uncomfortable looks on the faces of Carl and

Ilir, who had come in from the living room, I could see that this notion wasn't new to anyone. Miles had been spinning the same theory to the other men in my absence. I wasted no time pulling my shirt off. The gauze covering the wound was coloured red where the blood had wormed its way through. I pulled it off and turned my shoulder for the two men to see.

"If I got pinched, don't you think the medical care would have looked better than this?"

"Jesus," Carl said. "What the hell happened to you? It looks like a dog chewed on it." Then his eyes saw the burns. "Did you take another in the side, too?"

"It was a through-and-through, but it was a bleeder."

"Why is it all burned?" Ilir asked.

"Because," Carl said, "he burned it closed to stop the bleeding."

I pulled my shirt over my good shoulder. "The cops do a lot of that these days, Miles?"

The con man was uncharacteristically quiet.

It was my turn to ask a question. "Why aren't you already packed up? The game is starting in half an hour."

"With the news about the senator and the cop you shot, we figured there might be roadblocks set up. We thought it was best to sit things out here until the game ends."

I looked at Ilir, "The news mention roadblocks?"

He shook his head.

"Then we should go. We're more likely to get noticed squatting in a vacant property than at a game with tens of thousands of drunken, rowdy people."

"Makes sense," Ilir said.

Miles nodded.

"You sure you can travel?" Carl asked. "You took two bullets today. You can't see any light from the street, so we should be safe here for a few more hours."

I didn't answer Carl. I was preoccupied with the ceiling. Above the sink, the drywall had been opened up by the demo crew. Jutting out from the floorboards of the second floor was an open section of PVC pipe. Miles had been in the bathroom upstairs with nervous bowel since he got back. That was his story; the pipes told another. Their story said there was no water upstairs.

CHAPTER FORTY-ONE

"Get your stuff, we're going," I said. Miles and Ilir nodded and went through the doorway to get their things. I got a hand on Carl before he was out of reach.

"How many times has Miles been to the bathroom?"

"I don't know," Carl said. "A couple, I guess."

I nodded to the empty pipe in the ceiling. "You think after a few trips he might have noticed there was no water up there?"

Carl looked at the pipe. "Shit," he said.

"The opposite. Go up there and check it out. I'll keep an eye on Miles."

Carl nodded and walked out of the kitchen. I heard the stairs creak when he put weight on them and then Miles said, "Where are you going?"

"Gotta go before we leave," Carl said. The creaks told me that he hadn't stopped climbing as he said it.

I went into my pocket and pulled out my phone. Not the burner I got for the job — my phone. I hadn't thought about it after the bullets tore into me — another careless mistake. I powered up the phone and saw that there were two messages. One was from Ox, the other from a number I didn't recognize. I chose the latter and heard a voice with a British accent — Mr. Menace.

Mr. Wilson. Sorry about the delay, but the phones turned out to be trickier than I had thought they would be. I did as you told me and checked the black Samsung first. There were only a few calls made in the last couple of days and the numbers are all to phones across the border in Canada. I checked the other two cells and came up with something. The white cell has been active the last few days. Loads of calls. Several to a few Buffalo numbers. I tried tracing the numbers, but they belong to pre-paid cell phones. So I'm afraid it's a dead end. The other cell had only calls to one number. A residential address in Ontario. The package was mailed this afternoon. Cheers.

I swore under my breath. I had been wrong about Ilir and his phone like I had been wrong about the guest list. The white phone belonged to Miles. He had been calling local numbers and we had been hit by local Albanians.

I walked into the doorway. Miles was looking up the stairs while Ilir was busy putting the laptop and its cords into a backpack. When Ilir had the bag on his shoulders, I said, "Ilir, check out front."

"What? Why?" Miles said. "What is going on?"

I ignored Miles. Ilir didn't move; he stood in the middle of the living room looking with furrowed brows first at

Miles and then at me. He couldn't read anything on either of our faces.

I put some mean into my voice. "Check out front. Tell me if you see anything move. I mean anything."

The authoritative tone worked on the kid. "Okay, man. Okay."

"Wilson, what is going on?"

I turned my back on Miles and walked into the kitchen. Miles followed a few seconds behind.

"Nothing out front," Ilir called.

Miles was right behind me. "I asked you a question. What the hell is going on?"

Miles took a fistful of my shirt at the right shoulder and spun me towards him. Instinctively, both of my hands wanted to come up, but the bum shoulder made that impossible. Instead, I pivoted on my heels and turned with the momentum. I shot my right hand out and my hand extended like a snake bite. The webbed skin between my thumb and index finger jammed hard against the con man's throat. He staggered back a step and then brought his hands to his neck leaving the gun tucked into his belt unguarded.

I took the gun and stepped back. The sudden burst of speed had me light-headed and I groped for the top of a kitchen chair to keep me on my feet.

Ilir appeared in the doorway and echoed his last message. "You need to tell me what you think is out there because I can't see nothing out front." Ilir looked from me, leaning against the chair, to Miles, who was drowning on two legs. "You guys okay?"

CHAPTER FORTY-TWO

The loss of blood and painkillers had numbed the pain in my body, but they had done the same job to my mind. There was a heavy fog that had settled in slowly enough to go unnoticed — at least at first. The stabbing pain in my shoulder and side brought on by hitting Miles had cut through the fog like the beam from a lighthouse. For a few seconds, I had my bearings again. I was aware of a thought, or an absence of one. There was something that I had missed, and some part of my brain, the primordial part that was all survival instinct, was screaming a warning. The thought was buried deep, but it was surging against its confines. I rubbed at my eyes with my right hand hard enough to see spots behind my eyelids.

"Say that again, Ilir."

"What?"

"What you just said."

"There is nothing out front."

Out front. Out front. The words kept repeating in my mind. Miles gravitated towards the counter and I heard a squeak of breath make its way back into his lungs.

The thought crawled out of the shallow grave the medication had buried it in. There was nothing out front. I understood what the back of my mind had been furiously repeating. Out front was the logical place to watch, but when I showed up at the back door Carl opened the door and was surprised to see me. He had been told that I wasn't coming back. If it wasn't me he was expecting at the back door — who was he waiting for? A better question followed. How long had he been upstairs?

Miles was breathing shallowly now and he pushed off the counter and moved for the doorway. Ilir saw Miles' zombie shuffle and he took a step back, unsure about how to address what he was seeing. Finally, he found the words. "This is getting fucked, man. Someone needs to fill me in on what the hell is going on."

"I'll tell you," Carl said from the living room. "In the kitchen."

Ilir looked over his shoulder. "Just tell me now, Ca —" He stopped talking when he saw what must have been a gun in Carl's hand.

Being hurt changes things. You realize all at once the little things you used to be able to do effortlessly are now painstakingly difficult. For some, it might be bending over to tie a shoe or walking up a flight of stairs. For me, it was drawing a gun. Healthy, I could draw a gun as fast as any cowboy in a Sunday afternoon Western matinee. But with drugs in my system, blood loss, and tissue damage to my shoulder and torso, my movements were slow and clumsy. I was slow — not a cowboy anymore. Injuries change things.

They change you. You have to adapt, find new ways to do old things well.

Adrenalin was pumping again and the fog that had been so intellectually stifling had parted like the Red Sea in front of Moses. The police pistol came out from behind my back slow and steady.

Ilir was bringing his head back towards Miles and me with a look of confusion tinged with a blooming rage. It was the kind of look ordinary people got just after they realized that they've stepped in dog shit. The look on his face changed when I shot him in the chest.

CHAPTER FORTY-THREE

lir's body, propelled by a 9 mm slug moving just under the speed of sound, pitched back through the doorway and onto the floor. Above his body, two more bullets from my pistol screamed into the living room. Miles, who had moments ago been moving for the door, dove to his right for cover. He collided with what was left of the lower kitchen cabinets and scrambled left and then right looking for a place to hide. He came to a stop, two palms against the cabinet doors, and looked at me. If he had been carrying a gun, he would have gone for it already. I shot him a look that told him all he needed to know. Miles stayed where he was.

"Shit," Carl screamed. "Are you fucking nuts?"

"You thought I wasn't coming back, Carl. You said it yourself."

"What the hell are you talking about?"

"You opened the back door and were surprised when it was me on the other side."

"So?"

"No gun, just a look on your face. That's how I found you."

"Miles, he's lost it."

"If I wasn't coming back, who were you looking for out there?"

"Miles, are you hearing this?"

Miles looked at me and saw that the gun was on the doorway, not on him. "Yeah."

"Miles, he sent me upstairs a minute ago because he thought you turned on us. Then I come down the stairs and he shoots the kid in the chest. Now I'm the guy who's turned on us. Wilson's lost it."

"No argument," Miles said.

"He shot Ilir for no reason and he's going to shoot me for answering the back door. What do you think is going to happen to you when you're the only one left?"

I glanced at Miles. He had inched a bit towards the back door. He stopped when we made eye contact. "I was kind of wondering," he said.

Carl was good behind the wheel; he was better with his mouth. He knew I was beat up. I was slow and getting slower. The wheelman in the living room would be happy if Miles killed me; he'd be just as happy if I killed Miles. He would use the scuffle to flank me. Either outcome would have the same result — Carl alive with the violin and every- one else dead.

I ignored Miles and put two bullets into the wall at chest height. The slugs had more than enough juice to rip through the walls and streak through the living room. I didn't think I was lucky enough to hit Carl — luck was nowhere near me today — but they would shut the driver up for a few seconds.

I saw movement in the corner of my eye and I turned my head just enough to see Miles crab-walking towards the back door. There were windows along the back of the house; I figured he would attempt a dive through one of them if the opportunity presented itself.

"Calm down," I said. "You saw Ilir's face. Something was wrong with what he saw when he looked over his shoulder."

"But then you shot him," Carl called. "If I'm the bad guy here, why do that, Wilson? Why shoot the kid because he saw something?"

Fucking Carl and his mouth. There was no time to explain. Even if I could, my reason wouldn't absolve me, not in Miles' eyes. But I didn't need absolution; I didn't need to justify anything to the con man. Survival isn't a team sport.

"Go on. Tell him, Wilson. Why shoot the kid if I was just going to do it, too?"

Fucking Carl. I looked over at Miles. He wasn't going for a window anymore. He was watching me instead of the back door, and there was a gun in his hand.

CHAPTER FORTY-FOUR

I was slipping. The gunshots had done so much more than slow down my draw — they had slowed me down all over. I had missed the gun that had been on the table with the food containers and garbage. Miles had a revolver, one of the four that Ilir had got for the job, in his right hand. I had mine and the one I took off the conman. Carl had his. That meant the piece Miles pulled off the table had been Ilir's. The barrel wasn't aimed at my face though; it was aiming just low of centre mass. The height of the barrel told me that Miles wasn't totally convinced that I was the bad guy.

Having a gun pointed at you has a way of clearing things up. All of the unnecessary thoughts that usually cloud your conscious mind evaporate, leaving only the information that is necessary for making it through the next few important minutes. I had been slipping — now, I was rooted.

I had about thirty seconds to turn things around. The gun almost at centre mass meant Miles was almost convinced I was crazy. I glanced back at the doorway. It was strange that Carl hadn't made some kind of move. The job had left him with a fully loaded revolver; all it would have taken was four shots at chest height moving horizontally across the room at two-foot intervals. I would have to duck and cover at some point and, slow as I was, that would be more than enough time for Carl to come into the kitchen to use the last four shots up on my body. No bullets was a message in itself. Carl was clearly smart, so he obviously had a plan. He was clearly waiting for someone.

I had judged Carl wrong. He wasn't waiting for Miles to make a move or for him to occupy my attention. He was running out the clock. Someone was still coming to that back door and that someone would be the one to kill both me and Miles.

I lifted my index finger off the trigger and let Miles watch as I brought the finger to my mouth. I quietly shhh'ed him. He nodded, but the look on his face told me that he was skeptical. I pointed the gun at the floor five feet away from me and pulled the trigger.

The silence that followed was short.

"Miles," Carl called. "Tell me you took care of that psycho."

I lifted my finger to my mouth before Miles could blow it with some smart-ass comment.

"Nope," I said.

"Miles?"

"Even if his ears did still work, the brains on the floor don't anymore."

"You're insane."

"I'm a survivor, Carl. Now tell me who we're expecting."

Carl laughed. "Doesn't matter. They'll be here any minute."

Out of the corner of my eye, I saw Miles open his mouth. I shook my head.

"You sold us out?"

Carl laughed. "Hard to play the righteous crook when you just killed two of your partners. Hand over the violin and you can walk away."

I pointed at the back window and Miles crept over to check the yard. When Miles communicated the yard was still clear, I moved to the violin. The case was light enough that I could hold it up by wedging it under my injured arm. I nodded at the door and Miles turned the knob.

"Awful quiet, Wilson," Carl said. "Thinking about making a run for it? It's a good plan, but you really should have tried it a few minutes ago because the people I called. They're here."

CHAPTER FORTY-FIVE

Miles jutted his head out the door and quickly brought it back in. He slammed the door closed and backed away towards the wall I had already taken up position against. I slid down to the floor and Miles followed suit. He kept his gun on the back while I covered the living room.

"Send out the violin and you can walk," Carl called from somewhere in the front of the house.

I put my finger to my lips and waited for Miles to nod. The con man was my only advantage. The men outside had been in contact with Carl. Both they and he thought there was one wounded man in the kitchen. Having another man and another gun would give me a chance.

"Hard to believe you would be that generous, Carl."

I heard him laugh. "I know, but I guess a leopard can change his spots. Besides, what else do you have to go on right now? We aren't leaving without the violin."

Something else came out from the same mental graveyard I had dug up earlier. Something that Carl's choice of words had unearthed. Spots. Why spots? I stalled for time. "Who are 'we'?"

"I don't kiss and tell after I jump into bed with someone."

"You're asking me to trust them not to kill me. Hard to do if you don't know who *them* are."

"Funny thing, our business. It's all so secretive. No one really knows anyone. Hell, we only use first names. No one ever even asks about last names. Mine is Bogdani."

"I don't follow."

"It's the second most common Albanian surname."

"So when did you decide to switch sides on us, Carl Bogdani?" I didn't care because it didn't matter, but Carl talking to me meant he wasn't talking to the Albanians out back. It also gave me a general idea where he was. General meaning not near the doorway.

"It wasn't like I was a double agent or anything like that. A couple days ago was the first time I spoke Albanian in twenty years."

I pointed at the window and Miles looked out back again. He put his head up and gave the yard a quick look. When he sat back down, he shook his head. No way out — not yet anyway.

"Who did you speak to?"

"I called some relatives. Guys in our line of work. It was right after the attempted robbery on the house. I said to myself, 'Now these are some motivated countrymen. They want that violin fuckin' bad.' I figured anyone who would make a play that crazy had to be desperate, and desperate people pay. So, I put the call out and eventually ended up talking to someone who worked for Arben Malota."

I remembered the name of the Buffalo Pyrros Vogli.

"So, Malota's guys, they don't believe what I'm telling them at first. They've been feuding with Pyrros so long that they suspect everything to be a trap. But after the violin got stolen from the concert hall —"

"They had a sudden change of heart," I said.

"Bingo."

I heard the front door open followed by a hushed conversation. After a while, Carl said, "New deal, Wilson. The street isn't as empty as it used to be, and those bullets you fired seemed to have made the neighbours curious. Throw the violin out and you get to live."

I pointed my gun at the back door, and gestured for Miles to cover the back exit. "Curious neighbours means curious cops. How long before a car rolls up behind your backup?"

"I don't think you have any interest in cops, not after what you pulled today," Carl said.

"They want to arrest me, not kill me. I'll take my chances."

"I'm sorry you see it that way. You sure there's no way we can work this out?"

Carl was playing his own game now. There was nothing left for us to say, but he kept on talking. He wanted my attention forward rather than backward. It was a good plan, or at least it would have been if I didn't have an extra set of eyes trained on the sights of an extra gun.

"Just pass out the vio —"

A creak betrayed someone sneaking up to the doorway from the living room. I put a bullet through one of the kitchen cabinets in a spot that would let it out just beyond the doorway. Someone hit the floor just as the back door blew inward. Miles put three slugs into the man framed in the doorway while I shot at, and missed, another man trying to come into the kitchen from the living room. Miles fired again as I struggled to my feet. I moved closer to the doorway with the gun raised. I had missed from ten feet back — slipping. At five feet, aiming was no longer an issue — it was just point in the general direction and pull the trigger.

No one else tried to come in from the living room or the back door. The only visitor was silence until Carl's voice drifted in from somewhere in the living room. "You were telling me fibs, Wilson. Hello, Miles."

"Fuck you, traitor."

Carl spoke calmly. "We don't have any time left, so I'm going to tell you how this is going to play out. In a minute, one of my new associates is going to drive through the front door, through the living room, and into the kitchen. Those guns won't mean shit when the wall hits you."

While Carl was talking, I scavenged the two bullets from the revolver I had brought with me. I opened the cylinder on what used to be Miles' gun and flicked it out one-handed like Phillip Marlowe. The transition to my still working hand at the end of my dead arm was less smooth. I exchanged the spent brass with the two replacements and pocketed the shells.

"You'll smash the violin," I said as I transferred the gun back to my right hand. With a hard flick of the wrist, the chamber clicked back into place.

"Maybe, but we can't wait any longer for you to come to your senses, so it's a chance we'll have to take. Unless — you do the smart thing and slide the violin out into the living room. I'll give you ten seconds to think it over."

I looked at the violin and then at Miles. The con man shook his head. Miles was all in.

"Time's up. Are you going to pass it out, or do you really want to die over a two-hundred-year-old piece of wood?"

"We're going to pass —" Miles was already nodding as he raised the gun towards the back door and readied himself for another assault. "It out," I finished.

Miles stopped looking at the back door; he was looking at me instead, and he wasn't happy.

CHAPTER FORTY-SIX

"What the hell are you doing?"

"Getting us out of here alive," I said.

"You heard him, Wilson. The cops are on the way. We just need to wait out Carl and the Albanians."

"The cops aren't going to let you take the violin and walk, Miles."

"Don't act like you're worried about me. You're just worried about your own skin. You're on your way to being a cop killer and you're scared of what the boys in blue might do to you if they get you into the back of one of their squad cars."

"Clock is ticking," Carl called.

I moved for the violin and Miles did the same. I let him get a lead on the violin; I was going for my gun. Miles got a hand on the case when I whistled. He looked over his shoulder and saw the gun aimed at him.

"Fuck, again?"

I took the case out of Miles' hands and set it on the floor. I gave the case a shove with the ball of my foot and sent the leather box sliding across the floor. The neck of the case made it into the doorway; the rest of the violin was still on the kitchen floor.

"Kick it into the living room," Carl called.

"No," I said. "The case stays where it is until we're out the back door and still alive. If anyone moves on it, or us, I'll put a bullet in the middle of that case. You understand me?"

Carl spoke to someone in the living room for a few seconds. Then he said, "I got it."

I backed for the door and motioned for Miles to do the same. The con man was staring at the violin case. How he felt about the choice I had made was irrelevant. The case stopped being loot and became insurance the second it slid into the doorway. Now it was the only thing keeping Carl out of the kitchen and the Albanians out of the yard.

I stepped out back and checked the backyard — it was empty. The evening air was cool, and it felt good on my fever-damp head. In the distance, a lone siren called out; dogs answered from backyards. The sound was steadily gaining strength as the patrol car wound its way towards what used to be the safe house.

Behind the house was an old wooden fence that had been painted with a single coat of white. Even in the dim light, the more dominant blue underneath was still visible. I shuffled across the yard as fast as I could towards the barrier between properties. Up close, the fence looked in need of repairs; boards were cracked where they weren't missing and a wide section of the structure bowed inwards in the middle. There was no gate, and no way I would be able to climb it. I turned my back, lifted my right leg, and sent my heel back like a mule. Weakened boards broke under the stress and a small space was now visible in the fence. The space wasn't big enough for me to slide through, but two more kicks changed that.

I had started through the fence when another shot rang out from inside the house. The noise echoed in the neighbourhood and silenced the barking dogs for a second. More shots sounded as Miles ran, gun in hand, out the back door. He was careening around the side of the house when he noticed me, halfway between yards, looking at him. Miles stopped so quickly that his feet slid on the dead grass and he had to put a hand down on the ground to steady himself.

Miles sped across the lawn and followed me through the fence. We crossed through the yard and kept going across the street through two more yards to another street. We went right and saw a police car speed by the cross street ahead of us on its way to where we had come from.

"What happened in there?" I asked.

"I waited for one of them to reach for the case, then I shot him in the hand."

Miles thought it was pretty funny.

"Was it Carl?"

Miles shook his head. "I only saw the hand, but it didn't sound much like Carl.

"He say anything?"

Miles laughed. "Mostly fuck and shit."

I managed a smile. "We need a car."

"Why? We aren't getting over the border in a stolen car. We're all kinds of screwed. You shot a cop. A cop shot you. Your bullet holes smell terrible. We lost the violin. We almost got killed by another gang of Albanians. Who, by the way, before last week knew there was even one gang of Albanians?"

"Carl did," I said.

"Right," Miles said. "And if we manage to make it over the border, I'm guessing the first gang of Albanians we met will not be happy to see us. Not after you killed the boss's nephew and gave away the violin he needed to use as leverage in his trans-Atlantic Albanian gang war."

We met an intersection and turned away from the direction the police car had driven in. I scanned the road for something to drive. Another siren was approaching from somewhere. I was getting dizzy and it was hard to focus on abstract concepts. "I didn't give him the violin."

"Not technically, maybe. They had guns and more guys, but I don't think Pyrros is going to see it our way. Mob bosses are stereotypically unreasonable, and there's a reason for that. They usually have a habit of murdering people who underperform in the workplace."

I shook my head as I started across the street towards a Hyundai that was way too broken-down-looking to have a car alarm. Miles followed behind me. "I gave him a violin," I said. "I didn't give him *the* violin."

Miles hustled up beside me. "What are you saying?"

I tried the door and found it locked. I looked around the neighbourhood — it was all quiet. I wound up and sent my elbow into the passenger window. It bounced off.

I bent at the waist and breathed as deep as I could. Sweat dripped from my brow to the pavement. "Tell me you know how to steal a car."

Miles broke the window without a word, got in, and

leaned across the seat to open the other door. By the time I got in the car, Miles had it started. We drove out of the neighbourhood and onto a busier street that ran towards the city.

"What the hell do you mean it wasn't the violin? It was a Stradivarius. I saw the inscription inside the little hole."

I wiped my forehead. "Me too. I also saw the markings on the back. Something Carl said about a leopard not changing its spots made me think about the violin. The marks on the back looked like spots. Except the violin we had been paid to steal didn't have markings like that on the back. The Stradivarius we were after had longer waves like a zebra hide."

Miles clucked his tongue. "That's what you are basing this on? I'm sorry, Wilson, but you obviously have a fever and you're down a few pints of blood. You're not thinking clearly."

"You're right about that, but I can still subtract. Carl said the violin was two hundred years old. He asked us if we wanted to die for a two-hundred-year-old piece of wood."

"I remember," Miles said.

"You remember the date on the inside of the violin?"

Miles shook his head.

"1837. That is 176 years, not 288."

"So Pyrros was wrong about the violin's date?"

I shook my head. "No, someone beat us to it."

"What the hell are you talking about? We took that violin off the security guards. I was there when we did it, remember?"

I nodded as I rolled down the window. I stuck my head

out like a Labrador and let the moving air dry my head. "You were right," I said over the rushing air.

"About?"

"The fever, the blood loss, probably the smell. I can't think straight. Keep the car moving for an hour while I get some sleep."

"Are you serious? You want me to drive around in a stolen car taken three streets from a shooting?"

I think I nodded, but I couldn't be sure. I felt my chin touch my chest and then I was out.

CHAPTER FORTY-SEVEN

I woke to the sound of an invasion. The invasion was British and led by four men — John, Paul, George, and Ringo. I was on a couch in a dark room. Somewhere nearby a stereo was playing. I tried to sit up and ended up grunting before I fell back down against the cushions. Everything was stiff and all of my clothes were damp with sweat. I looked around the room and came up with nothing. I had no idea where I was, or how I got there. There weren't any windows, just old built-in shelves and an ancient RCA television on an equally old stand. Across my lap was a rainbow-coloured afghan blanket. I reached into some of the worn wide spaces in the weave and pulled the blanket off my legs. My second attempt to get off the couch was a roll instead of a sit. I fell onto hands and knees with another grunt, but this time I managed to stand using the arm of the sofa. I felt around for the gun I had been carrying and came up with nothing but the two phones that I had in my pockets. I checked the screen on my phone and saw that it was four in the morning.

Using the wall for balance, I walked to the door and pulled it open. The room was at the end of a hallway. I walked down the hall, as quietly as I could, towards the source of the music. I had heard the Beatles and I still sort of did, but it was background music to some kind of rap playing over the instrumentals.

At the end of the hallway was a cramped living room that contained a couch, a flat-screen TV, a coffee table, and two men. One of the men was Miles. The other was someone I had not met before. I stepped into the living room just as the man beside Miles bent to the table. I heard a loud snort just before his head jerked back up. Miles dove in next. When Miles came up for air, I was next to the couch.

"Look who's up," the stranger said. He was younger than Miles, which meant younger than me. His brown hair was shoulder-length and dreadlocked. The wispy moustache under his nose was all pushed to one side from being pressed hard against the plate in the centre of the coffee table. On the glossy black surface of the dinner plate were symmetrical lines of what looked to be coke.

"Hey, man," Miles said. "This is Tony."

"This your place?"

"Yeah, man. Mi casa. Bert didn't tell me your name."

"Ernie," I said.

Tony laughed. "Like the gay puppets."

"Sure," I said.

"You feel better? Bert said you were really sick."

"I need more than sleep for what I got," I said. I turned to Miles. "Why are we here?"

"Only place I knew that was off the street. Figured it was

better to turn up on Tony's doorstep unannounced than to drive around while you slept."

Tony took a deep inhale of a line and then pinched his nostrils closed. "Like I said, mi casa."

"How do you feel?" Miles asked.

"Like hell, Bert."

"You want something to eat? We got pizza," Tony said.

"No. No food."

"Ernie," Miles said. "You look like hell. Maybe food isn't such a bad idea."

I shook my head. "It won't stay down."

"Then at least take a seat," Tony said. "Get in on this if you want. Bert is buying."

"Who?"

"Me," Miles said.

"Jesus Christ," Tony said. "Your man, Ernie, is way out of it, Bert."

"I know," Miles said. "I need him in it."

"Take him to a doctor. They open in a couple of hours."

"I need him in it sooner than that."

"You thinkin' a prescription?"

Miles nodded. Both men looked at each other as they came to some kind of silent understanding. I looked from face to face completely in the dark about what was going on. For a second, I had forgotten where I was and who was sitting next to Miles.

"What do you have?"

"A lot of things. What do you want him to do?"

"I need him thinking clearly and able to move around."

Tony took a deep breath and let it out slow. "How bad

is Ernie? I know you said he was sick, but there is blood on his shirt."

I looked down at my shirt and saw that Tony was telling the truth. Blood had seeped through the gauze over the wound in my shoulder.

"He's bad," Miles said. "But he'll be worse if he doesn't start using his noggin again."

"Doctor Tony says laughter is the best medicine, but there is nothing funny about Ernie right now. So we move to the second best medicine and that, my friend Bert, is coke. Two lines stat."

"Sit down, Ernie."

Both men were looking at me.

"He means you," Miles said.

I shuffled to an armchair and fell into it.

"There's no way he's going to snort. Besides, he's too far gone for that. I say we mainline it."

"Inject it?"

"You got a better way to wake this dude up, Bert?"

There were no jokes this time. No smart-ass remark. Miles was uncharacteristically speechless. He just nodded — all the formal paperwork Doctor Tony needed.

"Give me a sec," Tony said.

The armchair was comfortable and I felt tired. I watched the stoner walk out of the room through slow blinks. First he was by the couch. Blink. He was on the other side of the room. Blink. He was gone. I blinked a few more times and then someone turned out the light.

CHAPTER FORTY-EIGHT

The lights came on all at once. My eyes fluttered and suddenly I was awake. Kneeling beside me were two men. Miles and someone else. They were holding my arm down and the new guy, some hippie, was injecting me with something. I put my foot against his head and pushed him away.

"Whoa," Miles said as I pushed at him with my arm. The needle dangled from a vein in my forearm and I wriggled my wrist until it fell out. Miles took a few steps back and raised his hands, palms out. "Calm down, Ernie. It's okay. It's okay. It's me, Bert."

The new guy was getting off the floor and rubbing at his face.

"I'd say it worked, Bert. Our patient is back in the land of the living."

"What the hell is he talking about?"

Miles patted the air again. "You were out of it. Delirious and not getting any better. You wouldn't eat and you kept passing out. I had to find a way to wake you up."

"What did you do to me?"

"Easy, Ernie, we just injected a bit of coke into you. No big deal."

I could hear my heart beating in my ears. Too bad for the kid with dreads that it wasn't loud enough to drown out what he had just said. I glanced around the room and my eye caught a beer bottle sitting next to the television. I picked the bottle up with my good arm and threw it across the four feet separating me from the guy with the dreads. The bottle hit the guy in the forehead and shattered. The dreads shook a little like vines in the wind as their owner's body caught up to the fact that the brain was no longer switched on. The guy fell back onto the coffee table, cleaving the surface in two on impact.

"Jesus Christ, Wilson. What the hell did you do that for? Tony was just trying to help."

"Help you, or help me?"

"Both of us. You were fading and there was no chance of getting you to a doctor at this hour, not one that would treat you without calling the cops about your shoulder. I brought you here so we could figure out where the hell our violin is."

I looked around at the shitty apartment. "To your dealer's place."

"I guess you could call Tony my dealer, sure."

I remembered the message from the Englishman about the cell phone. Miles had made plenty of local calls. I had thought the calls had been to Arben Malota's men, but the calls were not to any Albanians; they went instead to a white Rastafarian.

"So getting me loaded is your way of helping get the violin back?"

"I can't figure the angle out, Wilson. I tried. I tried again and again to figure out where we went wrong, but I kept coming up with nothing. I thought if you got some sleep you would wake up a little better, but you didn't. You were worse."

"So the next obvious choice is a boost from your fucking dealer?"

"You were shot by a cop, Wilson. If I try to get you to a hospital, or a doctor, you are definitely not going to get any better. We're going to need help from Pyrros to get you a doctor we can trust. That help will come with a price, and the only currency the Albanian accepts is old violin. We need to get it back. As for the coke, it was Tony's idea, but it wasn't a bad one. Sherlock Holmes used cocaine. It helped him think. At least that's what I heard."

"A seven-percent solution," I said. "Is that what your guy used?"

"What?"

"If you and Tony were following the Holmes example. That's what he used when he needed to keep his brain occupied."

Miles smiled. His handsome face was made even more handsome by the expression. I wanted another bottle. "A few minutes ago, you couldn't keep track of calling me Bert and yourself Ernie. Now, you're remembering minute details from books you read as a kid. I'd say it worked."

My heart was still racing. I swore I could feel the ball of muscle in the centre of my chest bumping against my rib cage. I touched my forehead and found it still wet. I forgot about Miles and did a quick inventory. My left arm hung limp at my side and any kind of movement was bad news. I probed at my side and winced at the response I got from the scorched nerve endings. As bad as the pain was, the fever had me worried most. The fever meant infection and that meant there was a ticking clock. Miles was right, Holmes had used cocaine, but it was to keep his depression at bay between cases. He never used it to help him solve cases. I had no choice but to go where Conan Doyle never did, because whatever time had been on the clock had to have been reduced by the addition of a chemical that was forcing my heart to run at a pace that would make a rabbit jealous.

"What time is it?"

Miles craned his neck so that he could see into the kitchen. "Four fifteen in the morning. What do you remember?"

"Carl crossed us and took the violin, but it wasn't *the* violin."

Miles nodded. "Anything else?"

"You brought me here and shot me up."

"Alright, so we're up to speed."

"Up on speed," I said.

"I do the jokes. You do the thinking," Miles said.

"Find me some clean clothes."

"And while I do, you find us that violin."

Miles walked out of the living room, down the hall, and into one of the adjoining rooms. He came back a couple minutes later with a pair of jeans, a black T-shirt, and a zip-up nylon jacket. "Good?"

I nodded and stripped.

"Any idea about the violin?"

"Some."

"Care to share with the group?"

"The violin in the case is the most curious thing."

"Why?"

"The guards lost possession of the case for a minute when they caught Ilir and Carl in action. What did we pack it with?"

"Something we bought second-hand."

"Right. We needed something that had the right feel to buy us a few minutes. Someone else had the same idea in mind, but they didn't go second-hand. Why would someone else swap the Randall violin with another Stradivarius? It was old, had to be less expensive than the one we were after, but it was still a Stradivarius. They don't grow on trees."

"They sort of used to," Miles said.

I was doing the thinking, so I guess he was doing his part.

"Think about it, Miles. When the cops opened that case we left behind, was there a chance they could have traced our violin to the seller?"

Miles shook his head. "There have to be a million just like it."

"Same question with the one we pulled."

"The odds would be better."

"Right, so why use it?"

Miles thought it over. "I don't know."

"Think about the method. The guy took the violin off the guards and then shot into the air. He didn't shoot first — he shot after he had the violin. He put the whole place into a panic. Everyone ran for the door."

"Us included."

I nodded. "Using the gun alerted everyone in Samuel

Hall. It gave security time to get in place at the exits. Our way, no one would have known there was a problem until the musician opened the case. When Lind saw the generic violin and sounded the alarm, the real Stradivarius would already have been on the street, and both you and me on our way out the door. There would be no chance for security to set up a perimeter."

Miles stared at me. "Agreed."

"So we have a rare decoy violin that the cops could surely track to an owner and a thief who purposely brings attention to the crime."

"This is all shit I knew, Wilson. I gave you the coke so you could tell me what I don't know."

"You know who owns Stradivarius violins?"

"Rich people and more recently Albanians from Buffalo."

"Musicians do. They are the best instruments, so the best players in the world use them."

"So?"

"So, one of the concert musicians stole the case and fired the gun."

"A classical musician?" Miles was skeptical.

I nodded. "He took it and walked out the door with it in his hands."

"Right into security."

"You said it yourself the instrument would be easy to trace back to the owner. The thief was counting on that. He stole his own violin."

"Why the hell would he do that?"

"Because the real Stradivarius never left the vault."

CHAPTER FORTY-NINE

"The widow?"

I nodded. "It's the only way it works. She and one of the violinists are in on it together. It adds up if you think it through. Two people are needed for the plan to work: someone to supply and steal a Stradivarius and someone to pass the fake off to the security guards. The widow and a musician are the only two who could make that work."

"So why are you so sure that the violin is still in the vault? It could be anywhere."

I shook my head. "No, the widow would leave it in the vault in case someone realized it was the wrong Stradivarius. That way she could just claim a mix-up. There would be no harm and no foul after that. And after the theft, no one would think to look in the vault again. If the cops believed the theft was real, they also had to believe the violin was the correct Stradivarius. The widow would be under scrutiny after that. Routine questions from police and insurance. She wouldn't have time to move the violin. Besides, why should she? It's in a safe that no one has a chance of getting into. Who's going to find it?"

"Us," Miles said. "But, maybe, just me."

Miles had a gun in his hand, and it was pointed at my head.

"Why did you kill the kid, Wilson?"

I didn't answer.

"You see why I have to ask. You and I are going to go and get that violin from the widow. If you're planning on killing me too, I think I have a right to know. So dish. Why kill the kid? He was a little obnoxious, but he wasn't that bad. Truth be told, he was growing on me."

"You think I'm bloodthirsty or psychotic?"

Miles shrugged. "I've met guys who are both."

"Replay the situation in your head. Carl was walking Ilir into the kitchen. Packing a nice tight enclosed space with another warm body. You and I were bunched together and Ilir obscured any view of Carl we were going to get. Tell me how it would have played out?"

It was Miles' turn to be quiet.

"He would have used Ilir's body as a shield while he shot you and then me," I said. "After that, Ilir would have gone next. I shot the kid because he gave Carl an advantage. It was an advantage I couldn't let him keep. The bullet wounds slowed me down, and I needed the extra seconds the confusion bought me to stay alive."

"So you shot him to save your own skin?"

"You wish it could have gone another way. Some outcome that would have made everyone happy?"

Miles was looking more at the gun in his hand than at me.

"Grow up, Miles. You might spend most of your time fleecing old women out of their pensions, but you're a criminal just like the rest of us, and this is not a business that makes people happy. It makes two things: money and dead people."

"It wasn't right. It wasn't what he deserved."

"Did you think about what I deserved when you said no to coming back for me?"

Miles didn't have an answer.

"No one gets what they deserve. If they did, there would be no one like us in the world."

I pulled my sweat-soaked clothes off the floor and transferred everything in the pockets to the new pants I was wearing. When I finished, I looked at Miles. He still had the gun in his hand. "You need to make a decision about that gun, Miles. In or out?"

Miles turned the pistol and looked at it in his hand. He tucked the gun behind his back. "How do we get at the widow?"

"What happened to all of the information we took off Dickens?" I asked.

"It was in the house. We were going to throw it all out on our way to the game."

I rubbed my chin. "Then we need to come at it another way." I looked at the unconscious body on the floor. "We're going to need him awake, and I'm going to need my gun."

CHAPTER FIFTY

"**W**ake up," I said.

Tony didn't stir, so I kicked him in the ribs. "Get up."

I got a moan, but that was it.

I took a half-empty bottle of beer off an end table and turned it enough to let a thick stream of beer fall onto the unconscious man's face. Alcohol soaked his dreadlocks and the neck of his shirt. Some of the liquid found its way up his nose and it started Tony coughing. He rolled onto his side and brought a hand up to his head.

"Oh, God."

"Get up," I said.

The dealer gave me a look that started with confusion, but quickly morphed into something darker.

"You hit me with a bottle, dude."

Suddenly he realized what he had said. He started probing his nose and teeth for damage.

"You shot me full of cocaine — I'd say we're even, but I'd be lying."

"Fuck, my head hurts."

"Physician, heal thyself," I said.

Tony ran his fingers over his teeth again. Satisfied they were all still there, he said, "Bert, grab me a bud off my night table, dude."

Miles nodded and left the room. I waited for the con man to come back and then for the dealer to light up.

"You got a computer?"

Tony nodded.

"Get it and log on."

"Why, man?"

"Because I asked you nicely," I said. I held out the Glock. "Want to see me ask mean?"

"What? No. I'll do it, man. I'll do it."

Tony reached under the sofa he was sitting on and slid out a thin, sleek laptop. He logged on and passed the unit to me. I walked into the kitchen and put the laptop on the counter. Both Miles and Tony followed me. While I went through the results of a Google search, I asked, "How long will whatever you dosed me with take to wear off?"

"You a user?"

"No," I said.

"Three hours, maybe. I dunno, you're pretty banged up, and you lost a lot of blood, so it's hard to say."

"You got more?"

Tony looked at me with a grin on his face. "You got money?"

"I have a gun."

"Store credit it is, then."

"You want to let me in on the plan?" Miles said.

I turned the laptop so that he could see the screen. It was the homepage for Samuel Hall. Miles followed the cursor as I dragged it to a link marked *Orchestra*. The link opened a new page. I scrolled down until I found the violin section, which included press photos of the musicians.

"The violin we took wasn't the one we were looking for, but it was still a Stradivarius. You don't find every Tom, Dick, and Harry carrying one of those around. Usually, it's just the premier players."

"So our thief must be pretty good."

I nodded. "This is a list of the people in the first chair position. Since it was a man in the mask, we can discount the female names right away. Now we're down to four possibilities. Our guy wasn't fat, so we can eliminate another name."

"That leaves three," Miles said.

There were three pictures on the screen. Two of the men were in their late forties. One was black, the other two were white. The black guy had a salt and pepper moustache and heavy bags under his eyes. The white guy in the next picture over had jowls and acne scars across both of his cheeks. The third man was in his early thirties and looked like something out of a Dockers commercial.

We both spoke at the same time. "That's our guy."

I clicked on Thomas Delgado's head shot and the site sent us to a brief bio page. There was nothing but information about the musician's education and experience.

I opened a new window in the browser and used the online phone book to find an address for Thomas Delgado in Buffalo, N.Y. There were four names.

"You really think he's in the phone book?" Miles asked.

"I doubt he has any reason not to be. Unlisted numbers cost extra and usually people don't spend extra unless they have to. He's handsome, but I doubt there are groupies calling his house at all hours."

"So do we call all of them and ask if they like to fuck hot trophy wives and play the violin?"

"I'm down for the first part," Tony said.

I ignored the dealer. "He's in his thirties. We find him on Facebook and check out his pictures. Most people put up personal images. There might be something there that we can use to pin down a location."

"If he's on Facebook," Miles said.

"Dude, everybody is on Facebook," Tony said. "Even me."

We both looked at the dealer.

"What? It's all about networking, dudes."

In the end it took five minutes to find Thomas Delgado on Facebook and another two minutes to use a picture taken in a coffee shop to identify a neighbourhood associated with one of the Delgados from the phone book.

"I'll be damned," Miles said. "He's local. Not even that far away. We can be there in ten minutes."

I had been awake on coke for half an hour. In that time, my heart hadn't slowed down one bit. The drugs in my system were running my damaged body at full throttle. Although I was standing and thinking more clearly, I could feel the speed ripping me apart like a meteor on re-entry. For a second, I wondered if there would be anything left by the time I hit the ground. The thought lasted only a second

— I was on a timer, and I didn't have time to waste. Miles had been right: I needed a doctor and that wasn't going to happen without the violin. The only conduits I had to a cross-border physician who would work on the likes of me were Ox and Pyrros. Contacting Pyrros now meant having to deal with the fallout over what happened to Ilir, or at least what we would tell him happened to Ilir. Pyrros would have questions and he would hold back doing me any favours until I provided answers he liked. That left Ox. The broker could find me a doctor, but he wouldn't keep the information to himself if push came to Albanian shove. Having the violin would keep Pyrros on hold, and away from Ox, long enough for me to get patched up.

"Tony," I said. "We're going to work. I need you to pack me a lunch."

CHAPTER FIFTY-ONE

"**D**udes, this isn't necessary. We're cool."

I was leaning against the door while Miles set everything up in front of Tony. While the dealer put together another loaded syringe for me, Miles concocted a sleeping potion out of Tony's cache of drugs.

"I'm serious. We're cool. I'm not even mad about you hitting me. I get it. And whatever you two are into —" He zipped his lips closed with his thumb and forefinger. "Your secret is safe with me."

"Tell him what will happen if he doesn't make the smart choice," I said.

Miles looked at Tony and there was no humour and no sarcasm. "He'll put a pillow over your face and put a bullet in your head."

Tony looked at me. "Dude?"

"Do people always have to argue this much to get you high?"

Tony laughed. "When you put it that way."

Tony injected what Miles had prepared. The junkie

alchemy was potent; Tony drifted farther and farther away from us without ever leaving our sight. After three minutes, he was talking to someone who wasn't us. We walked out of the room with the dealer's car keys and drove across the city to another suburb, this one closer to the water.

Thomas Delgado lived in a bungalow that looked to be something built just after World War Two. The landscaping out front showed a deft hand and a sense of style; so did the twenty-year-old Range Rover in the driveway. The car looked like the kind of thing photographers for *National Geographic* drove around the base of the Himalayas. Except this car had been repainted something metallic and the factory rims had been replaced with something contemporary.

Miles walked at a regular pace, which meant he was much faster than me. He stepped up onto the porch and waited for me to catch up. He raised his hand to the door, but before he knocked, he asked, "Are you okay?"

My heart had slowed in the car, but it was still beating twice as fast as it should have. I could feel my armpits getting damp and the nausea was waking up. I had just under two hours left on the dealer's cocaine estimate. "I'm fine."

"You don't look it," Miles said. "You look like shit."

"Do I look like a cop? Because that's what we need right now."

Miles took a step back from me to look at my clothes. He was still in the creased suit he had been wearing on the job — he fit the part. I didn't — I was in jeans and a blue unbuttoned Oxford. Both were tight on my frame.

"You look like the construction worker in the Village People."

I took a step back so that Miles' body would obscure me from the door. We didn't need Thomas Delgado to believe we were cops; we just needed him to think we were long enough to open the door.

"You knock," I said. "And remember everything we talked about in the car."

Miles nodded and said, "I got it." He then furrowed his brow. His handsome face was showing signs of being tired, but he made it even more apparent by subtly drooping his eyelids and letting his jaw sit crooked.

It was ten minutes to six in the morning. The neighbourhood was quiet, with only birds breaking the silence. Miles, now playing the part of the exhausted cop, hit the door with the side of his fist. The sound was a loud thump instead of a knock. I had to admit it was a smart choice. The sound would echo through the house more than through the neighbourhood.

We waited a long thirty seconds and then Miles pounded on the door again. Another thirty went by before we got a "Who is it?" through the door.

"Police, Mr. Delgado. We have some things we would like to discuss with you. Could you open the door, please?"

The door opened a crack and revealed a safety chain. From where I stood, I couldn't see Thomas' face.

"Sorry for the early hour, Mr. Delgado. We just have some routine questions to run by you."

The door closed and I heard the chain slip off. The door opened and I heard a familiar voice. "That's good, officer, because I have a question for you. Where the hell is my violin?"

CHAPTER FIFTY-TWO

Carl was standing back from the door with a gun in his hand.

"You're not going to shoot me, are you?"

"Not yet," Carl said.

"I meant him," Miles said gesturing over his shoulder. "He's got sort of a track record."

"I want both of you to step inside slowly. Anything stupid from either of you and I'll gutshot Miles here on the porch."

"Easy, easy, Carl," Miles said. "We're coming inside." He looked over his shoulder at me. "Right?"

I doubted I could have made a move if I wanted to. The cocaine was wearing off and I was starting to feel the effects of trauma and blood loss.

I made it into the house behind Miles and shut the door. Carl had us face the wall with our arms and legs spread. He did two quick and dirty searches and relieved us of our two guns. Had the search been more thorough, he would have found more, but he was probably worried about one of us making a move on him while his hands were busy. He pocketed my gun, put Miles' revolver into his belt, and then prodded the two of us down the hallway with his own weapon.

Thomas Delgado did well for himself. The house had old bones but they didn't show under the massive facelift performed on the interior. The floors were done in wide, dark hardwood and the ceilings all had crown moldings. When we stepped into the living room and onto the plush, expensive area rug, I had a moment of guilt about leaving my shoes on. Sitting on the couch was the man I had seen on the internet; only this man wasn't as handsome as the guy on the website. The cheekbone on the right side of Thomas Delgado's face looked like it had been caved in with something heavy and hard. I guessed the damage had been done by the butt of the revolver in Carl's hand. Thomas' head slowly swivelled to take the new intruders in. The vacant expression on his battered face made it impossible to read his thoughts.

"Sit down," Carl said.

I went for a chair, but Carl turned the revolver on me.

"Next to Tom on the sofa, please."

"Cozier that way," Miles said.

We walked across the area rug towards the couch. The coffee table that had, judging by the impressions in the rug, been centred in front of the couch had been roughly shoved aside. The table was sitting diagonally on the edge of the rug with one decorative wooden leg on the hardwood floor. On the table were two cell phones. One was in the far corner — close enough for Thomas to reach out and touch from his seat. The other phone at the far end of the table was Carl's, not the burner I had given him, but something sleeker and cooler. I remembered how easily he had handed over his phone in the diner. Of course it was easy; he had been carrying a throwaway for just such an occasion. He had been a step ahead of all of us from the start and I cursed inwardly for misjudging the driver's cunning. Miles took the centre spot on the sofa while I got the end. I eased onto the leather couch and heard the material groan as it ground against my damp shirt.

"I'm curious," Carl said. "How did you find your way here?"

"We figured out that playing the fiddle wasn't Tommy's only talent."

"That so? And how did you do that?"

"We found him because stealing is our line of work, not his. I'm guessing he's better at playing the violin," I said.

"I've never heard him play, but I bet you are right, Wilson. Tom is not as smart, or as smooth, as he thinks he is, not by a long shot."

He kept using our names. Carl had no intention of keeping us alive. That fact simplified things. There was no point in worrying about getting killed if it was a forgone conclusion.

"You here alone?" I asked.

Carl smiled. "My new associates cut me loose when they learned that the violin was not the one I led them to believe we were getting."

I pointed at the spots on Carl's shirt that looked like blood. "They cut you loose, or just cut you?"

Carl looked at his shirt. "Other way around."

"So you have two sets of Albanians angry with you now," Miles said.

"Nothing a violin won't fix, I'm sure."

"You lied to the Americans, probably killed one or two, and *you killed Ilir*. You're putting a lot of stock in one old fiddle," Miles said.

"So I killed Ilir, Miles?" Carl said. He didn't seem surprised.

"Word on the street," Miles said.

"Yours or his?" Carl said gesturing at me with the gun.

"Does it matter?"

"Sure, Miles. Sure it does. When we get the violin, we could take it back across the border to Pyrros. Just you and me. We'd split the take fifty-fifty."

Miles nodded his head slowly. "Why so generous? You have the gun; I'm guessing you're on your way to getting the violin. Why bring me in and split the profits?"

"I do have the gun, and I will have the violin, but you have something I need."

Miles shrugged. "Sounds kinky, Carl."

"You have your mouth."

"Real kinky."

"You tell Pyrros the truth, the real word on the street, and you walk away with half."

"Except it won't be the real word on the street," Miles said.

"The words don't have to be real. The money will be real enough."

Carl's cleverness kept surprising me. It had taken him

less than three minutes to start manipulating Miles.

"The knife in your back will be real, too, Miles," I said.

"The man has a point. You did try to kill us."

Carl snorted. "The man did more than try to kill Ilir."

"Why did you turn on us, Carl?" I asked.

"Why did you kill Ilir, Wilson?"

We both looked at Miles. Miles looked at Carl. "He asked first."

Carl narrowed his eyes at me. I could tell he wanted to kill me right then, but if he did, he would never be able to depend on Miles to cover for him. He needed Miles to sign on before he killed me.

"My kid," he said. "I wasn't lying when I said he was sick. He has a rare illness. It's genetic. Only one in every two hundred fifty thousand gets it. Rare illnesses don't get the same kind of research funding as common ones do. There's a doctor in Europe, but the fees — shit, they call us thieves. Anyway, I needed more than a third of the take for the next round of treatments, but I can make it work with a half." Carl nodded at me. "His turn."

"Miles knows why," I said.

"Care to show your cards to the rest of the table?" Carl said.

"It's not important anymore. The violin is the only thing that matters to all of us now. I'm guessing Alison has it." I leaned forward just enough to see past Miles to the violinist and fought back a grimace. "Judging from your face, Thomas, you fought giving her up, but you probably gave in about the time he caved in half of your face."

"Don't talk to him," Carl said.

I thought about the time and distance. Carl had been in the house long enough to get in, force answers out of Thomas, and get the drop on us. I gave Thomas' face another look and figured an hour was a conservative estimate. At this time of day, traffic was non-existent. An hour was more than enough time for someone to drive from the mansion to the violinist's house. It was more than enough time for someone to drive here and back. So why wasn't the widow beside Thomas? I thought about what the call must have sounded like. Had Thomas pleaded? Had he tried to be noble? No matter what he said, she must have heard the pain in his voice. A woman in love would have heard it, no matter what words he chose. She would have heard it and rushed to save him. Time and distance made a convincing case — something wasn't right. The widow should have been here by now.

"What did she say when you talked to her, Thomas?"

Carl looked at me, and then he looked at Thomas. Thomas didn't answer.

I took a harder look at the battered violinist. "Can he talk?"

Carl didn't answer; neither did Thomas.

"Can he?" Miles echoed.

Carl didn't have to answer my questions, but he wanted Miles on board and that meant he couldn't keep him in the dark.

"He didn't give her up. He won't call her," Carl said. "He won't even pick up the phone. After a while, he stopped talking altogether. But that ain't going to last."

"You going to do more than just mash up his face?"

Carl looked at Thomas, but the man wouldn't meet his eye. "Plenty more, Miles. Plenty."

I saw tears well in the corner of Thomas' swollen eye, but his mouth stayed shut.

"I don't get it," I said. I was speaking to Thomas, but he wasn't looking at me.

"Don't talk to him," Carl said. "In fact, just keep your mouth shut altogether."

I ignored Carl. "Why not pick up the phone? If you're trying to protect her, you're doing a shit job. If you die, she's the only one left. You think Carl won't go break her face, too?"

"That's enough," Carl said. He pointed the gun at me.

I sat back against the cushion and raised my palms to Carl. "One more question," I said.

Carl kept the gun on me.

"Thomas, what time is it?"

No one spoke. The question was a complete non sequitur for everyone; even Thomas was surprised enough to break his thousand-yard stare and twist his head enough to view me with his good eye.

Carl's eyes widened and then he let out a laugh. "How much blood did you lose, Wilson? That's the one question you need to know the answer to?"

Miles turned his head and met Thomas' eye. "Answer him."

Thomas broke his silence without any thought. "I dunno. Seven maybe."

"There," Carl said. "Are you happy?"

"You're way off, Thomas." I said. "Way off."

Thomas shrugged and went back to staring at the wall.

"Alright. Shut the fuck up, Wilson," Carl said.

I nodded and kept my mouth shut. The time for questions was over. Thomas wasn't a hard man; he was a professional violin player. The bones in the side of his face had been shattered. That kind of damage would have made any regular person spill their guts, but Thomas had taken it, and the threat of worse, without a word. Torture was a funny thing. People who grew up on a steady diet of Stallone movies thought the pain was what broke the person — it wasn't. It was the idea that the pain could go on forever that broke a person. Thomas had more in store; Carl had spelled it out for him, but he still kept his mouth shut. The idea of the pain going on didn't break him. I had thought that the pain going on might have been the point. I had asked about the time because if the violinist was bearing the pain for the minutes on the clock it bought the widow, it would have been all he could think about. But the question surprised Thomas. And when I told him that his guess wasn't even close, he just shrugged it off. Time wasn't a factor for him. He was holding out for a reason I couldn't comprehend. Maybe it was love. I didn't understand Thomas, but I understood Carl. The driver would keep beating the violinist until he got what he wanted. If he didn't get what he was after, it would only be because the violinist's heart finally decided to go silent too. We had all gone after Thomas because we knew the widow was safe as houses in her guarded mansion. The robbery and shootings had put her in the centre of a huge police and media investigation. There was no getting at her without Thomas' help, at least not right away. And with two sets of Albanians on his tail, Carl had no time to wait. He would keep pushing the beaten man.

Sitting on the couch in front of Carl was a bad spot to be in — one that was getting worse by the second. There were few moves left on the board and fewer that would get me off the sofa alive. I saw subtle weaknesses that I could exploit, but it would take time, and time was something I wasn't in control of. Our fate was tied to the fiddler. If Thomas died, Carl would pull the trigger two more times and then he would run.

CHAPTER FIFTY-THREE

Carl had been pacing back and forth for at least a minute before he stopped and said, "I don't get it."

We all said nothing.

Carl lifted the gun and pointed it at me. "Tell me what is going on. Why do you care so much about if he knows what time it is?"

Carl kept the gun aimed at my right eye. When I didn't say anything, he turned it on Miles. Miles smiled coolly, but the smile faded the longer the gun was in his face. He began to look uncomfortable. He flashed me a look and then gave the gun more consideration. I saw him begin to bite his cheek. A second later he talked.

"It's code," Miles said. "We didn't know what we'd find when we came through the door, so we came up with something in the car on the way over that we could use to communicate if we had to. Time means, 'It's time.'"

"Time for what?"

"He wanted me to come at you while you were focused on him."

Carl brought the gun back towards my head. "You always have a plan, don't you?"

"He's got a thing about being the smartest guy in the room," Miles said. "It's an annoying quality, really. It was cute when it was dangling Ilir out of the car, but now it's my life he's dangling. Sorry, Wilson, but you're fading. We can all see it. You aren't going to make it to the end of the race, but I am."

Miles got off the couch.

"I'm on the wrong side of the room."

The wheelman had a choice to make. If he needed Miles like he said he did, he had to let him off the couch — partners didn't point guns at each other. Carl watched Miles closely, but he didn't move the gun away from me. Miles walked to Carl and turned to face the couch. Miles had made his own play. He wasn't wrong about me fading. I was hot again and my heart was no longer beating strong. I had, at best, another couple of hours, and those were on-the-couch hours. If I got off the sofa, I figured my time would be cut in half.

"I'm going to shoot you in the head," Carl said. "Then we can really judge if you were the smartest guy in the room."

Carl thumbed the hammer and the cylinder clicked forward once. I waited for the gun to carry out my execution. I didn't plead, or put my hands up — Carl and Miles were already taking everything. I wasn't about to give them anything.

"Wait," Miles said. "We can't fire a gun in here. It's a residential neighbourhood at six in the morning. A gunshot is something people will notice."

"So what? You want me to let him live?" Carl sounded suspicious.

"No. If he keeps breathing, it's just a matter of time before he tries to prove he's the smartest guy in the room again. He needs to die. Just quietly. Use a knife."

"I don't have a knife."

"Thomas has to have something in the kitchen," Miles said. Without waiting, Miles went off in search of something sharp. From the couch, I heard drawers loudly opening and closing in the other room. A second later Miles was back holding the handle of a downward-turned chef's knife. "Use this," he said.

"Why don't you do it?" Carl said.

Miles looked at Carl. "You don't trust me?"

"I do, Miles, I do. I just need to see that you're all in. Just consider this sealing the deal."

"Handshake won't do?"

Carl shook his head.

Miles sighed and reversed the knife. Carl had the gun on me, but his eyes were on Miles. If he was worried about some kind of ruse, he didn't need to be. I had been watching Miles closely, looking for some sign that he was pulling a fast one. He was, after all, a professional grifter. But there was no sign that Miles was double-crossing Carl. He, and the knife, kept a wide berth of the wheelman the entire time.

"Alright," Miles said. "Alright."

Any hopes I had of Miles helping me out vanished when I saw the route he took. I had been hoping he would come straight at me. That direction would obscure Carl's view.

Miles could pass me something that way, or I could try to take the knife off him and use his body as a shield while I tried to find cover. Instead of straight on, Miles went around the couch. He was going to slit my throat.

I saw Carl's lips curl into a smile when he saw Miles' choice. The driver was pleased with what he saw. Miles stepped around Thomas, giving the violinist a wider berth than his still form seemed to require. I turned my body to watch Miles' approach. It also hid my hand moving into my pocket for the needle Tony had loaded for me. I was too weak to pull Miles over the back of the couch and too slow to spring at Carl. The best I could hope for was stabbing Miles in the eye with the syringe. The chaos that would ensue would be the only opportunity I had to move. I took a deep breath that was more of a shallow rasp and slid the syringe out of my pocket.

Miles stopped two feet back from the couch and shifted his weight back and forth over and over again. He reversed his grip on the knife and then switched back. He was stuck between slice and stab. He was used to ripping open pockets, not throats. He had no idea that both choices came with equal amounts of gore.

"Stop looking at me," Miles said.

"Just do it."

"Carl, he's fucking looking at me. I can see his eyes in the reflection of the picture on the wall."

"Kill him and he'll stop."

Miles sucked a breath in through his teeth and took a step forward. I tightened my fist on the concealed syringe in my hand and had a brief moment of worry about breaking it. I waited for the second step. When his foot moved, so would my arm.

No step came. Miles threw his hands up and said, "This is too fucked up."

"Do it, Miles," Carl said.

"Nope. Nope. This is not my thing. I can't just fucking kill him when he's looking at me."

"This is the deal."

"Carl, you need me as much as I need you, so stop trying to order me around. We can compromise. You shoot him. Just put a pillow over his head to muffle the shot."

Miles walked back around the couch and threw the knife through the doorway to the kitchen. "This is so screwed up. How did stealing a violin come to fucking stabbing someone in the head?"

I watched Miles shake his head as he worked through some kind of mental argument. Carl was watching, too. Thomas was looking at me. He had turned his head so that he could see me with the eye that wasn't completely swollen shut. I searched the eye and saw something there. It might have been pity, or it might have been hatred — it might have been both. The structure of his face was so warped that it made reading his expression impossible. Maybe he was just happy it wasn't his turn and the thought shocked him. It's not every day you're happy to see someone two feet away from you get shot. I looked into the one eye and felt a familiar tug. The side of my lip turned up and a small grin formed. The violinist had no idea what tune I was going to play. Thomas' one eye narrowed and then he turned away.

Miles threw himself into an armchair and ran his hands through his hair.

Carl gave Miles a few more seconds of his attention, but gave up on him when he realized the con man was no threat. "I guess I'm up."

"Just use a pillow," Miles said. "Jesus, listen to me. Use a pillow to muffle the sound of us murdering a guy. This is so screwed up."

Carl walked over to a loveseat and pulled a worn pillow off the sofa cushion. The corduroy fabric of the pillow was flattened from a head taking countless naps on it. The driver followed the same playbook as the con man and avoided coming at me head on. He held the gun at hip level as he started around the far side of the couch. I had lost the grin, but it wanted to come back out. Carl doing the killing meant Miles would be the only one left. Miles had no gun and he had ditched the knife. He would be empty-handed when I buried the syringe in Carl and took his gun. I took a breath and waited for the pillow. Needing to put the pillow over my head would mean that I would have to be within arm's reach. It meant the same for Carl, and at the end of my arm was a long needle.

Carl started around the couch and then Miles spoke. "No, wait. Make Thomas hold the pillow over his head."

Fuck.

Carl looked at Miles.

"Smart guy, remember."

Fuck.

Carl smiled and handed the pillow to Thomas. "You heard the man. Put it over his face." Carl threw the pillow to Thomas. The violinist made no move to catch it and the cushion bounced off his shoulder and fell to the floor.

"Pick it up," Carl said, jabbing the man's shoulder with the gun. "Or I rape your girlfriend on the floor in front of you."

Thomas bent for the cushion without argument. He stood with the pillow in two hands and looked at me. I didn't grin at him this time.

Thomas let the pillow fall as he turned on Carl. The cushion had been concealing a small paring knife with a hooked tip. Thomas buried the knife in Carl's neck. A second later, Miles was on the driver, wrenching the gun from his hand. The wrestling match was one-sided; Carl had no fight left in him after the knife entered his throat. Both men realized this at the same time and took a step back from the driver. Carl stayed on his feet while his hands probed the hilt protruding from his throat. Then the light faded in Carl's eyes and he fell to his knees.

CHAPTER FIFTY-FOUR

"**S**it back down," Miles said.

Thomas was looking at his bloody hands.

Miles had Carl's gun, but he didn't point it at Thomas. When he spoke again, his words were soothing. "You've had a rough couple of hours, Thomas. I know Carl did things to you, made you do things, and then I came along and put you in a terribly difficult position. It's a hard thing, killing a man. It's easier than something like that has any right to be. But this whole thing is almost over, Thomas. Almost, but not quite. I need you to sit down on the couch."

Thomas kept looking at his hands.

"Now, Thomas."

Miles put his hand on the man's shoulder and broke his trance. He sat back on the couch still staring at his hands. Through his broken face we heard him say, "I'm not sorry."

"That's good," Miles said. "We're not sorry either."

"Get up, Wilson." Miles still had the gun in his hand.

I nodded at the gun. "You going to make me?"

Miles looked down at the gun and chuckled. "No." He

put the gun in the back waistband of his pants. "Truth be told, I hate those things. I was always better at talking my way out of trouble than shooting my way out."

"Is that what you were doing there?"

"I didn't change teams, if that's what you're asking. We were in a bad situation and I got us out of it the only way I knew how. But don't trip all over yourself trying to thank me. I didn't stick with you out of loyalty, or because I think you're better than Carl. None of us have any white left on our hats. I backed you over Carl for one reason. You saw what he didn't. You knew Thomas wasn't ever going to talk. Carl would have figured it out eventually, but what then? I'm still with you because I didn't think Carl had a plan B, or C, or D, or whatever plan we're on now. It's that simple. Every original idea he had was violent, and that wasn't going to get us anywhere."

I slowly got off the couch and said, "Give me a minute." I walked to Carl's body and tried to bend over, but the pain was too great. I went down to a knee and relieved him of the gun he had taken from me. I took the gun Carl had taken from Miles out of his waistband and held it out for Miles.

The con man took the gun and said, "Great, now I have two."

I managed to stand without help and walked away from Miles towards the hallway. I walked towards the front door, one hand on the wall for support, until I came to a small bathroom we had passed on our way in. Thomas had put a lot of money into the updating the house — even the bathroom had been renovated. Everything was marble where it wasn't hardwood and stainless steel. I ran the faucet and splashed water on my face. My skin barely registered the cold water. I had sweated through the new clothes; even my socks felt wet. I checked my phone. The clock read 7:07. The coke had gotten me a good hour and a half followed by a lousy forty-five minutes. I opened the shirt and lifted the bandage on my shoulder. The stench was there — impossible to ignore, and impossible to rationalize away. There was an infection driving the fever, and that was just the symptom I could feel. Underneath it all, I knew the wound was poisoning me. I needed a doctor who could get a bag of antibiotics into me. Finding a doctor would require help. The States wasn't Ox's sandbox. He could get me a name of a doctor who did the kind of off-the-books treatment I needed, but it would take time. Time was in short supply. I would need help to get wherever I had to go, and someone to scout out whatever doctor Ox came up with.

I needed Miles. The con man owed me nothing. In truth, he had more reasons to kill me than to help me. But I wasn't dead yet. Miles had said the only reason he chose me over Carl was because I saw things the driver didn't, but there was more to it than that. Miles wasn't a killer. He hadn't shot me, not even when I shot Ilir and he thought I had turned on everyone. He hadn't raised a hand to Carl either; rather than get his own hands dirty, the con man had delegated the job of killing the driver to Thomas. Deep down, Miles was a thief, not a killer, and that was something I could exploit. I splashed another belt of water onto my face and felt a bit of the coolness seep into my skin. I knew what had to be done now, and it made the next decision easier. I pulled the syringe from my pocket and unhooked the belt

I had taken off Tony. I found a vein and yanked the cap off the needle with my teeth. The tip of the needle hovered over my arm while I tried to steady my shaking hand. The contents of the needle could kill me, but without the violin, I was a dead man anyway. I needed another couple of hours on my feet and there was only one way that might happen. I stabbed at my arm between tremors and pushed the plunger down fast.

I fell back, colliding with the toilet on my way to the floor, as a ball of flame sped up my arm towards my chest. I clawed at my shirt trying to tamp out the flames as a yell came from my mouth. Then everything went black.

CHAPTER FIFTY-FIVE

Someone was hitting me. That was my first thought. The second was out of left field. Someone was kissing me. I opened my eyes just as the hitting started again. Miles was straddling my chest; his two hands were together and pressing down on the centre of my chest.

"Get — Get off, me, Miles."

Miles took his eyes off my chest and looked at me. "Fucking idiot."

He took hold of the counter, climbed off me, and stepped backwards out of the cramped bathroom. I rolled to my side and tried to breathe deep, but it felt like Miles was still sitting on my chest.

"Another hit, are you out of your mind? It's only been a couple of hours."

"What happened?" I asked it already knowing the answer.

"You stopped your heart. Christ, if I hadn't heard you hit the ground you would have died in there."

"Where is Thomas?" I said.

Miles looked around. "Damn it!"

I rolled onto my stomach and got a knee under me. With the help of the counter, I got to my feet.

Miles called from the living room. "He's in here."

I stumbled out to the living room and found Thomas exactly where he had been sitting before.

"Didn't even get up," Miles said.

I looked at Thomas. He was a statue. He hadn't moved an inch. We were in a house. Houses had back doors, side doors, windows. He could have gotten out any number of ways, but he stayed right on the couch. "I don't get you," I said.

Thomas didn't say a word; he just kept staring.

"You know there is no point to all of this, right? We're just after the Stradivarius. Killing you, killing her, none of that gets us anything. It will just draw more attention to the case and make our jobs harder. We just want the violin."

"And it's not like you can turn us in," Miles said. "Hard to finger us for a crime you committed. So you have to ask yourself, what does sitting here really get you?"

"But you have to know all of that," I said. "You could have called the widow and had her leave the violin somewhere. That would have kept her out of it. But you wouldn't even pick up the phone."

Had I gotten it wrong? I thought it was about protecting the girl, but what if it was about the violin?

I pulled the coffee table back an inch and had to take a second to recover from the effort. I sat on the table directly in front of Thomas.

"Why steal the violin, Thomas? Tell me that at least.

Alison Randall stands to inherit a fortune. Why would she risk everything for a violin?"

Thomas' one good eye stared unblinking at me. "He didn't love her. He didn't love anything. He liked how she looked, he liked her at parties, and he liked her in bed, but he didn't love her. She was his pet. Something he kept caged up when company wasn't around. He told her what to wear, what to eat, what to say, and she had no choice but to do as she was told. He kept all of his money separate from her. She got an allowance from him like she was a child. But she put up with it. Put up with him. Deep down, she was afraid of him. Afraid of what he would do if she tried to leave. There were stories about his last wife, about what happened to her, but they were just that — stories. Everything got easier when he became sick because Alison saw a way out. She knew she would inherit everything he owned, not just money but her life too. But after he died, the lawyers told her that all of the money, everything, was going to charity. He made sure she would never really be free. She would get her car and her jewellery, but that was only a few hundred thousand. A few hundred thousand out of hundreds of millions. She was going to contest it, but that would take money. He knew that. I bet he wanted her to fight it. She would have to use up what little she had fighting for what was hers. In the end, she would leave with less than she came with. Less money, less happiness, less time. Stealing the violin was my idea. I've played all over the world for most of my life. I know of a few people who would buy something like that under the table."

"You already have a buyer lined up?" I asked.

Thomas shook his head. "I didn't think it was a good idea to try and sell it before I had it."

"So you came up with the idea. Did she fight you on it?"

Thomas shook his head. "She was on board right away. It was her idea to put my violin in the vault."

"You love her?" I asked.

Thomas nodded.

I didn't doubt him, or the story, but something was wrong. "Why didn't you leave?" I said.

Half of Thomas' face lifted into a sad smile. "She's free. Free of him. Free of blame for the crime. Free of everything. I'm not going to put her back in a cage. No matter what."

It was a good answer. A romantic-movie kind of answer. "But that doesn't answer my question. Why didn't you run? You could have called and warned her about us. Told her to leave town, hire security, anything. But you stayed on that couch. Why?"

Thomas said nothing.

I picked up the phone sitting next to me on the coffee table. I held it in front of the violinist's eye. "Why not take the phone and run?"

Then, I got it. In one split second, I suddenly understood. I grinned at the ruined face in front of me. "I get you," I said.

CHAPTER FIFTY-SIX

There were two phones in the living room — both on the coffee table. I had noticed both of them because I had been sitting on the couch and looking in that direction. But, standing opposite the couch, the phone was not in the line of sight. I had judged the second phone, the one closest to Carl, to be his spare — the one he had been hiding from me. But I had been wrong. The second phone was Thomas' phone. The one in my hand, the one that smelled like vanilla, was a woman's phone. The wheelman had been good, better at a lot of things than anyone realized, but he was still a little green. He had walked into the house sure that he would be able to force Thomas to give up everything. He had focused on the man; Carl hadn't learned that places can whisper all kinds of secrets if you just know how to listen.

I put my hand on the butt of the revolver in my pants. Thomas stopped looking at the wall; he was looking at my hand.

"Miles, go through Carl's pockets."

Miles got off the arm of the sofa and went to Carl's body.

"Don't get the wrong idea, Thomas. We're equal partners. He's not my boss or anything. He's just an asshole."

Miles started prying open pockets. He began doing a verbal inventory as he tossed items onto the askew coffee table. "Let's see. We got a money clip. Dibs on that. Cigarettes, a lighter, a cell phone, and some gum."

Miles wiped the blood he'd gotten on his hands onto Carl's pant leg and stood up.

"That makes three," I said.

"Three what?"

Miles saw the cell I was still holding in my hand. It didn't take him long to get caught up.

"So she's here?"

I nodded. "Upstairs, I'm guessing. That's why he didn't leave. We were by the only exit near the stairs. She couldn't get out without passing us, and he wouldn't leave without her, so he just stayed put."

"And he couldn't call her," Miles said, "because her phone was on the table the whole time."

Thomas had stopped looking at the gun. He was looking at me, and I was wishing I had already drawn the gun.

CHAPTER FIFTY-SEVEN

The violinist was on me like a predatory cat before I could even get the pistol all the way out of my waistband. The violinist was punching down with his right hand and groping for the gun with his left. Both the punching and the groping stopped when Miles kicked him in the damaged side of his face. Thomas howled and rolled off me. Both hands clutched at his face and muffled sobs of pure agony.

"You should really treat me better," Miles said to me.

"Just go upstairs and get the girl," I said.

"The violin, too," Miles said. He started for the hall but turned back to look at me before he left the room. "You okay?"

I pulled the revolver and slowly got to my feet. "Just go."

Thomas had gutted the whole house and replaced all of the old décor with new material, but he couldn't change the aged skeleton underneath. Every step Miles took up the stairs was announced with a creak. I leaned against a wall and listened to him climb. I kept an eye on Thomas; my other eye was on my phone. My chest hurt and it was hard to breathe, but my left hand worked just fine. Using my left hand I unlocked the cell and entered in the fewest letters necessary to communicate what I needed from Ox. I got a text back thirty seconds later. Ox would have what I needed within the hour.

Miles moved slowly from room to room upstairs. Every twenty or thirty seconds a creak from a different part of the ceiling told me where my partner was on the floor plan. He was almost directly above me when there was a noise much louder than a creak. It was a gunshot.

CHAPTER FIFTY-EIGHT

The sound of the gunshot ended the sobs coming from the man on the floor. Suddenly Thomas was on his knees, looking at the ceiling. Six more shots sounded above us. Each was paced a second apart. When I looked down from the ceiling, the swollen face was looking at me. The noise that came out of the man's mouth was guttural. He came off the floor and rushed to tackle me. This time, Thomas didn't have the advantage of being inches away from me. The violinist had to cover eight feet and the revolver wasn't holstered; it was in my hand. Before he had made it five feet, I had the gun up. I put a bullet into the top of his head. The bullet stalled the man's forward momentum and his body dropped straight to the floor like a foul ball.

I moved to the stairs and looked up. Fourteen in all. I had never counted stairs before, but now I looked at each one as a Herculean labor. I took hold of the banister with my left hand and took the first step using as many muscle groups as possible. The first six were slow; the second six were slower. I had to pause after thirteen and fourteen.

I ignored the first two doors — Miles' creaks had told me that he was past them. Ahead of the doors, the hallway went to the right. I stopped at the elbow and eased my head around the corner. Miles was on his side propped up on one elbow. He still had the gun in his right hand; his left was over his chest. In front of him was a door at the end of the hallway. The heavy wooden door looked like it was an original part of the house — something Thomas had decided to keep as a tribute to the past. The antique was no longer as pristine as the rest of the house. Seven bullet holes had perforated the wood.

Miles heard the creak as I came around the corner and lifted his gun over his shoulder.

When he saw it was me, he said, "Jesus, that took you a long time."

"Tell me that when you try and walk out of here," I said.

"The door was locked. I tried the handle and she shot me. Right through the door. Hit me in the goddamn chest."

I looked up at the door and saw the bullet hole five feet from the floorboards. It was the only one that high. The rest of the shots were lower in the door. The other six shots had come from Miles shooting up from the floor. The fact that he was talking meant the bullet wasn't in his lungs. I guessed the heavy wood of the door slowed the bullet down enough to make it only a flesh wound. I pulled off Miles' shoe and slipped off his sock.

"Put this over it," I said as I slid his shoe back on.

I moved against the wall and said, "Alison?"

I got no answer.

"Alison?"

I eased a hand onto the knob and used just enough force to twist it. It didn't move. I could see from the holes that the door was solid wood. Neither of us had a chance of kicking it down. Slowly, I eased my head towards the bullet hole made by the first shot. I glanced into the room and then pulled my head away before I got the same treatment as Miles. A second look told me that I didn't have to worry. There was a body on the floor.

I put the revolver to the knob and put a bullet through the brass. After that, the door opened. On her back, three feet from the door, was the beautiful woman I had seen walk into Samuel Hall. She was in a man's button-down and her underwear. The gun, probably the one used in the robbery, was on the ground next to her. There were two holes in the shirt surrounded by two large poppy-shaped stains. Two of the bullets Miles had fired at the door had caught her in the chest. I guessed she had been looking through the bullet hole like I had been when Miles began shooting.

In front of the bed was an antique chest. On top of the chest was a violin case.

CHAPTER FIFTY-NINE

Ox had lied. It took him an hour and a half to find me a doctor in Buffalo. He wasn't licensed to practise anywhere outside of Colombia, but that didn't seem to matter much given the circumstances. The man was a cab driver who lived, and worked, in the city. He had us meet him at his apartment where his nephew was waiting to help us inside. His niece moved the blood-soaked Volkswagen somewhere less conspicuous.

Luis was in his fifties and a drunk, judging from the hour and smell of his breath. I doubted he remembered anything he had learned in medical school, but there was no denying that the man knew gunshot wounds.

He went to work on Miles right away and directed his nephew on what to do with me. It was like watching someone play two games of chess at the same time. It took two hours to stabilize Miles and then the taxicab MD looked over his nephew's work on me.

"You need a hospital."

I shook my head. It was about the only movement I could manage.

"The infection is bad, and your heart is no sounding good."

"No hospital."

"If you make tomorrow, maybe you make the next day."

I made it to the next day. Miles was out of bed and eating when I came to. The niece was our nurse, but it didn't take long for me to see that she had designs on getting promoted to the role of Miles' girlfriend. I didn't have the strength to get off my back. I could only lie on the thin mattress Luis had placed on the floor and watch as the bag of black-market antibiotics hanging on a coat hanger attached to a battered hat stand slowly dripped life back into my arm.

I could sit up after two days. I could walk on the third. Miles had made contact with Pyrros and told him everything that had gone down. As expected, Ilir was a bitter pill to swallow, but the violin did what Carl had hoped it would. Pyrros understood the cost of doing business and he told us he bore no grudge. Neither of us believed him, but we believed he would pay for the violin and that was enough. There was another Bills game at the end of the week. Ox would cross the border for the game and cross back with two passengers and one item we weren't planning on paying duty for. Enough lives and enough blood had already been paid for one old musical instrument.